CINDY C BENNETT

SWEETWATER BOOKS
AN IMPRINT OF CEDAR FORT, INC.
SPRINGVILLE UTAH

© 2011 Cindy C Bennett

This is a work of fiction. The characters, names, incidents, places, and dialogue are products of the author's imagination, and are not to be construed as real.

ISBN 13: 978-1-59955-925-4

Published by Sweetwater Books, an imprint of Cedar Fort, Inc.
2373 W. 700 S., Springville, UT 84663
Distributed by Cedar Fort, Inc., www.cedarfort.com

LIBRARY OF CONGRESS CATALOGING-IN-PUBLICATION DATA

Bennett, Cindy C. (Cindy Carlsen), 1967- author.
  Geek girl / Cindy C. Bennett.
    pages cm
    Summary: Jen, a teenaged foster child and social outcast, makes a bet with her friends that she can turn Trevor, a straight-A student and self-avowed "geek", into a social outcast like herself, but quickly finds there is more to him than she expected.
    ISBN 978-1-59955-925-4
    1. High school students--Fiction. 2. High schools--Social aspects--Fiction. 3. Friendship--Fiction. 4. Marginality, Social--Fiction. 5. Foster children--Fiction. [1. Interpersonal relations--Fiction. 2. Wagers--Fiction. 3. Dating (Social customs)--Fiction. 4. High schools--Fiction. 5. Schools--Fiction. 6. Friendship--Fiction. 7. Foster home care--Fiction.] I. Title.

    PZ7.B43913Gee 2011
    [Fic]--dc23

    2011033130

Cover design by Angela D. Olsen
Cover design © 2011 by Lyle Mortimer
Edited and typeset by Melissa J. Caldwell

Printed in the United States of America
10 9 8 7 6 5 4 3 2 1
Printed on acid-free paper

For Lexcie, my amazing daughter, who forced me to finally finish Jen's story by insisting on new chapters to read daily, and whose enthusiasm for the story made the journey that much more pleasurable. You rock, chickadee.

CONTENTS

Contents

1

THE BET

THINK I could turn that boy bad?"

My two best friends—my *only* two friends, really—Ella and Beth, follow my gaze and laugh. We're sitting on the outskirts of the cafeteria, outcasts physically and socially. We're proud of this. We strive for this.

"*Trevor Hoffman?*" Beth scoffs. "No way, Jen."

"I bet I can," I say, chewing on one of my painted black nails as I gaze at my intended target.

"No way," they both agree.

I look at Trevor Hoffman and my grin widens. He is such a nerdy, Goody Two-shoes. Kinda cute actually. But he always has his shirt buttoned to the top and is a straight-A student who all of the teachers adore. He's the Junior Class something or other—not the president but one of the other officers. He's a little different than the other geeks in that he's sort of . . . cool-geek, I guess. No glasses, asthmatic wheezing, or too-short pants for him. But he's firmly entrenched with the geek-squad, a nerd to the core himself.

"I bet I could," I say, shrugging. "Might be fun."

Fun is something I desperately need. I can't tell Beth and Ella, but my life has become a dreary cycle of tedious monotony. I get up, go to school, go home, avoid the people

I

I live with as much as possible, and sneak out on weekends to party with my friends. There was a time when that was something to look forward to. I have to take it easy on that end now since this newest do-good family I've been foisted onto has a DEA agent for a father, who seems to be able to spot glassy eyes a mile away.

The first time I came home from a party, I'd been subjected to hours of maudlin lecturing from them on the dangers of drugs and drinking, with much crying by the mother and fact-giving by the father until I wanted to pull my hair out. They grounded me, which meant even more time spent in their charity-radiating presence. I'd have preferred they yell at or beat me—those things I can deal with. I'll do almost anything to avoid another lecture and grounding like that.

"Why him?" Beth asks. "Why not any of the other nerds sitting there with him?"

"Because," I say slowly, as if it should be obvious to them, "he isn't your typical run-of-the-mill geek. Any of those other dorks would flip immediately if a girl so much as touched them. But Trevor Hoffman is different. He's a geek, right? I mean, none of the cheerleaders would date him because he's not a jock, but they all know him, talk to him, use his help for their homework, whatever. And he *is* the Junior Class . . . Treasurer, or something like that. He would be a little more difficult to take down, more of a challenge—and more satisfying, you know?"

They laugh again. Looking at each other, they silently agree to the plan, an odd ability the two of them have, probably because they're identical twins, separated in looks only by Ella's small mole above her lip—amplified with an eyebrow pencil.

"If you can," Ella says thoughtfully, "we'll pay for your lip to be repierced."

That would be worth it. My current foster family has a no-piercing-on-the-face rule, which really cramps my style. At least so far they haven't banned my hair, makeup, or clothing choices because, as my newest do-gooder foster mother says, those things aren't permanent. Goes to show how much she knows.

I'll have to wait until the summertime to get the repiercing because that's when I'm due for my big blowup so that I can get kicked out and move on to the next unsuspecting do-gooders. It's been my MO for almost as long as I've been passed around, so I don't see any reason to stop now, even if the current ones aren't so bad. Though compared to what I've lived with, that isn't saying much.

"It's a deal," I tell her, hooking pinkie fingers with first Ella and then Beth in our traditional promise-making gesture. I attended this same school last year, though I lived with a different family then, so I've had the chance to get to know a few people pretty well. It was pure luck to be placed with a new family within the same school boundaries. Ella and Beth are my girls, having pulled me firmly into their circle when first they recognized my kindred spirit.

Beth pokes my lip where the scar from the last piercing shows faintly. "How you gonna explain that one to the Straw Hat?"

This is the nickname we call the foster mom, in reference to her penchant for wearing straw hats when working in her garden. The hats are utterly ridiculous.

"My time's up this summer, so it'll be a good catalyst."

Ella and Beth know my history; they understand without explanation.

"We'll miss you," they say at the same time.

"But you aren't going to win using this one as a bet," Ella says, indicating Trevor with a nod of her head. As if to confirm her words, Trevor makes a dorky face at his equally dorky friends, who all burst out in dorky laughter. And then he cuts his eyes toward Mary Ellen, a complete homebody girl who sits at the table.

Competition, huh? I muse.

I watch her for a minute. She's completely unaware that Trevor's display was for her. She sits quietly, shyly eating her lunch with her head down. She has long, straight, mousy brown hair, glasses, and shapeless nerd clothes covering her shapeless nerd body.

She's perfect for Trevor.

I smile. She's no competition for me. I am his complete opposite in every way, but when I'm finished with him, he'll recognize Mary Ellen for the mouse she is.

I stand up and turn toward where Beth and Ella still sit. A flyer hanging above their heads catches my eye. I pull it down with a grin and hand it to them.

"A school stomp?" they echo together, horrified.

"A stomp," I say firmly. "Tonight. We're going."

I look back toward where Trevor sits, straight and tall as befits a nerd of his station.

"Tonight, I begin," I tell them, walking away as they dissolve into laughter behind me.

***

We show up to the stomp. They have to admit us in spite of our heavy black eyeliner, cherry red lips, stark black hair with red streaks, and tight black shirts and miniskirts with thigh-high plaid stockings and black boots. They want to turn us away, these cheerleader-types, but they have to let us in: we have student ID cards.

We head over to the corner where a few of our "kind" stand, the few willing to brave something as mainstream as a school dance. Admittedly, it's mostly because it's a good place to gather while we figure out whose house we can go party at tonight. And tonight it probably has a little to do with the fact that they know my plan and are here to watch me begin my game.

I search Trevor out almost immediately—not hard to do with the nerd herd gathered all together. Varying degrees of nerd-dom huddle with one another, none dancing.

"There's your boyfriend," Ella says sarcastically, following my gaze.

"Watch," I say, beelining for him. The dance is in full swing, sweaty teenagers bouncing to the beat.

"Hey!" I call. He doesn't look. I tap his arm, and he turns, surprised when he sees me in front of him. He'd probably sooner expect to see a talking zebra in front of him.

"Wanna dance?" I ask with what I hope is a seductive look. Now, I think, is when his expression will turn to disgust and he'll turn away, making my goal harder—and giving my friends amusement.

But he doesn't.

"Sure," he agrees, ignoring his friends who *do* wear distasteful looks. I'm surprised he agrees, but I manage to hide it behind a smile meant to turn him to jelly. He doesn't turn to jelly, though he does have a look of vague puzzlement in his eyes. He follows me out to the dance floor, and we begin moving. He's not a bad dancer.

I decide to let him go after the first dance, the old

attack-and-retreat strategy, and back up a step, intent obvious. He's flustered, unsure what to do.

"Thanks," he says as I start to turn away.

He just thanked *me*, I think scathingly.

Dork.

But I refrain from rolling my eyes and smile again, reaching out to lightly squeeze his arm. He still doesn't turn to jelly, but something definitely changes in his eyes.

I keep an eye on him for a while, making sure he's aware of it. I'm always standing in his line of vision, always watching him, making sure he's aware of my attention. He turns away first every time, confused, and maybe a little nervous by my unexpected and unprecedented attention.

"How goes the plan?" Beth asks as she walks over to me, watching as Trevor once again glances my way to see if I'm still watching.

"I have him wondering," I tell her.

"You have him scared," she corrects.

"Maybe a little," I concede. "But mostly curious, I think. And you know what they say about curiosity."

"He's not a cat," she says.

"Sure he is. They all are."

She gives me an odd look. I'm about to explain that an *animal* by any other name . . . but then someone calls me.

"Hey, Jen."

I turn, annoyed at whoever is pulling my attention from my target, and see Seth. Seth is a bit of an enigma to me. I think he has a thing for me, but he refuses to act on it. He's definitely my type: long, stringy, black hair, tight black pants riding low, black eyeliner, and pierced ears, tongue, and lip. He is tall and skinny and weird. He's usually high. Seth is most definitely my type.

"What's up, Seth?" I ask dismissively, turning back to look at Trevor again—only to see he's looking my way, watching me. I give a slight smile; he flushes at being caught and turns back toward his own friends. I mentally compare him to Seth.

Night and day.

A slow song comes on, and I intensify my stare, moving toward him. One of his geek followers looks meaningfully in my direction. Compelled, curious, Trevor turns my way, and I lock gazes with him as I walk toward him, leaving Seth and Beth behind me, one corner of my mouth lifting at their rhyming names. Maybe they should hook up.

Trevor seems unsure as I continue my deliberate path toward him but stands as I come near. I tip my head toward the dance floor in invitation without speaking, and he follows me without answering. He places his arms lightly around my waist, holding me at a respectable distance. I'm surprised by the solidity of his shoulders beneath my hands—not soft at all.

I push closer. He backs up a little.

"Good song," I say quietly.

He shakes his head, indicating he can't hear me. I lean in toward him and, afraid of being rude, he leans down to hear what I'm saying.

"I like this song," I say, though I've never heard it before and have no idea who's singing.

"Yeah, me too," he says, and I hold on tightly, refusing to let him back away again. Once more afraid of being discourteous, he doesn't push me away, though he is stiff. Such a nerd.

He smells good, clean.

As soon as the song ends, his hands drop. I hold on a

little longer, then slowly draw my arms away, dragging them down his chest, which causes that change in his eyes again.

"Thanks," I say huskily, leaning in toward him again, beating him to the politeness, but my thanks is definitely not the same as his, and he knows it.

I turn and walk toward my friends, swaying the hips a little, and they grin at me.

"He still watching?" I ask.

"Oh yeah," Beth says.

"What did you do to him?" Ella asks. "He hasn't moved. He looks like—"

"—a lovesick puppy dog," they finish together, breaking down in giggles.

Seth doesn't look happy. Oh well . . . you snooze, you lose. Now he'll have to wait his turn because I'm going to have to focus all my attention on my new goal. And the prize, I add mentally, fingering my bare lip. I turn back to face Trevor, who's still watching me, looking a little shell-shocked. I'm still fingering my lip, and his eyes home in on this action. I grin at him, sweetly but with a little tramp thrown in for good measure.

This seems to unfreeze him, and he turns quickly away. I watch him as he goes to his friends and says something urgently. They are surprised and talk back a bit frantically. But he shakes his head firmly and walks away from them as they look after him in confusion. As he nears the door, he looks back at me. He doesn't look happy. Before I can smile, he turns away and is gone.

A slow grin crosses my face.

2

The Brady House + + +
Or Is It the Cleavers?

I TURN on the stalking at school, going out of my way to be in his path, watching him and smiling at him. He's unsure but courteous, so he smiles back, if a bit hesitantly. His smiles are always small and brief. If I'm with any of my friends, he seems intimidated and will avoid eye contact altogether, no matter how hard I try.

But if I'm alone, then he makes eye contact, and though his smiles aren't exactly what I might hope for, at least they're there. He's paying attention. His eyes reflect his confusion.

My friends are all amused—except for Seth, of course.

After a couple of weeks of this, I turn it up and begin saying hi. The first time I do this, he actually stops in his tracks, stunned. I keep walking. But the next time it isn't quite so shocking, and the geek says hi back—though he sounds unsure and only says it when I'm mostly past him. Wouldn't want to be impolite, I guess. That sensibility is something I can use in my quest, though.

On a Friday afternoon after I've gotten him used to saying hi as I walk past and smile at him, I walk right up to him while he stands at his open locker. His locker is, of course, neatly organized and clean, with his many books stacked tidily on the shelf. There are no pictures or anything that would make it personal. And definitely nothing like the chaos that is my locker.

"Hey," I say. He looks at me, stunned into stillness.

"Wanna go to a party on Saturday?" I ask quickly before he can morph into panic. "With me?"

He's speechless. Finally, after long seconds, he gives a little head shake, blinking slowly.

"Sorry, can't." He turns back to his locker, unfrozen by his words, pulling books down for his weekend of homework. "I'm having some friends over. Movies, snacks, that kind of thing," he says as if he can't stop the words. His brows pull together in a thinking kind of perplexity. *Good excuse*, I think, but then he surprises me.

"You can come if you want," he says nonchalantly, still not looking my way. But his baffled exhalation gives him away.

No, I don't want, absolutely not. Give me a break. Spend my only free weekend night hanging out with the Geek Bunch? However, I can't give him a reason to doubt my intentions toward him. He turns to look at me, about to retract his invitation if his drawn brows are any indication.

"Sure, why not?" I say quickly. I can tell he's astonished, but he won't retract now. He's way too well-mannered for that. Instead, he gives me his address, printing it neatly on a piece of paper, clearly doubting I'll show up.

"See you then." I flutter the paper, grin at him, and start to walk away.

"Uh, Jennifer?" He's clearly uncomfortable using my name.

"Jen," I say.

"What?"

"My name—I go by Jen."

"Oh, okay. Jen." He shrugs, discomfited, and clears his throat. "Did you want . . . I mean, don't you want to know what time to come?"

"Oh, yeah, of course."

"Um, about seven?"

"See you at seven then, Trev."

"Trevor," he says. "I go by Trevor."

I smile seductively, and he flushes, turning away.

***

Beth and Ella are laughing so hard tears roll down their cheeks when I tell them.

"I want to be a fly on the wall at *that* party," Beth says.

"If you can call it a party," Ella adds, which makes them laugh even harder.

"Have fun," they call sarcastically, wiping their eyes.

I finger my lip where they will soon be putting hardware and ignore them.

***

On Saturday I walk to Trevor's house, a perfect little family split-level with dormers, window boxes blooming with spring flowers, and a lawn mowed into perfect little stripes. I push the doorbell beneath a cutesy little plaque that reads: *Hoffman Family, Established 1980.*

Gag.

Mrs. Brady/Cleaver herself answers the door, freshly rolled out of an old sitcom. She has pants on instead of a dress, true, but she *is* wearing an apron, her hair and makeup perfectly in place, subdued, a string of pearls at her throat completing the picture-perfect image. She can't quite hide the flash of shock and disgust on her face when she sees the thing that's standing on her porch, but she recovers quickly.

"Can I help you?" she asks with a hesitant smile.

"Yeah. Trev here?"

"Who?" She looks genuinely confused.

"Trevor?"

"Oh." She's at a loss. "Um, well. Please come in."

She stands back and lets the wolf into the henhouse.

"Is he expecting you?" She sounds doubtful.

I shrug. "I guess so. He invited me."

"Oh." Pause. I try not to grin at her discomfort. "Wait here. I'll go get him."

She walks away, uncertain of leaving me unattended for even a few minutes. Good. A nervous mom becomes overprotective, sparking rebellion in a teen. I know this from experience and observation. This could definitely work in my favor.

I stand in the foyer, looking into the small living room next to me.

The room is neat and tidy, overpowered by the baby grand piano, which takes up most of the space. Besides the piano, there's a curio cabinet full of antique-looking garbage, a bookcase, and a small blue-flowered sofa with a doily—a *doily*—draped over the back of it.

The bookcase is filled with smart-people-type books from what I can see: Hemingway, Chaucer, Shakespeare, Steinbeck. Self-help, psychology, and philosophy books as well. This could be tougher than I thought. Or maybe not. I knew Trevor was smart when I chose him, so I suppose I shouldn't be surprised by his home reading material—and the décor seems just right for a nerd.

Trevor comes around the corner, an oddly welcome familiar face amid all this perfection. But then, I suppose he *is* part of the perfection. He only hesitates a second, so small it's *almost* unnoticeable, when he sees me.

"Hey," he says, his voice reflecting the fact that he didn't think I would really come.

"I didn't think you'd really come," he voices my thought. His honesty is too much, and I almost roll my eyes.

"You invited me." I put on a slightly hurt, chagrined look. "Should I go?"

"No . . . no, of course not. I'm glad you came." He recovers nicely, though he's not quite sincere in his words. "We're downstairs. Come on down."

"Okay." I act uncertain though I'm not. I knew he'd cave.

He reaches out to place his hand in the small of my back to guide me, unthinkingly, ever polite, but quickly retracts it as if burned when contact is made. I pretend not to notice, smiling inside. Keeping him off balance is a good thing—helps me keep the upper hand.

We walk through the perfect, clean kitchen where Mrs. Brady/Cleaver stands, wiping imaginary spots on the counter. She's actually spying on her baby—I know the type.

"Mom, this is Jen."

"We've met," she says with a fake smile, and I don't point out that I didn't ever tell her my name, nor did she tell me hers. We go down the narrow stairs tucked behind the wall with the stainless steel stove while Mrs. Brady/Cleaver watches me openly.

Downstairs are two of Trevor's dork friends.

"You know Jim and Brian, right?" he asks me. I know their faces but never had a reason to even want to know their names. I nod anyway. They both stare at me, Brian with a tortilla chip lifted halfway to his mouth, which is now dripping salsa on his shirt, as if a three-headed alien has just come into their midst. They're sitting on a big, overstuffed couch in front of an enormous flat-screen TV, watching some kind of robot cartoon.

I follow Trevor to the wet bar behind the couch. It's covered with boy snacks: chips and salsa, pizza, pretzels, and little hotdogs drenched in barbecue sauce.

"Go ahead and eat whatever you want," Trevor tells me. "There're drinks in the fridge. Can I get you something?"

He turns away to open the full-size fridge that stands in the corner. *He's obviously has never had a girl over before*, I think mockingly. Then again, that could be a good thing, helping me in my game.

"You have a diet Coke?"

"Uh, no. Not down here. But I'll bet my mom has one upstairs. I'll go grab one."

Before I can stop him, he turns and jogs back up the stairs, leaving me with the two geeks, who are still staring at me, jaws gaping.

"What's up?" I say, and they both look at each other as if I have spoken in another language and they're checking to see if the other can translate. Finally, Jim turns back to me.

"Not much." His answer sounds like a question.

They turn away, but I'm not going to let them go.

"Whatcha watching?" I call. In true dork fashion, they can't be rude, so they both turn back.

"Uh, it's called *Ghost Robot of the Twenty-Third Century.*" This time it's Brian who speaks, albeit somewhat reluctantly.

"Sounds cool," I say, and they look at each other again. Brian's eyes come back to me, and he finally places the dripping tortilla chip in his mouth, chewing very slowly, as if doing so will keep the noise from frightening the alien (me) and causing it to attack. I nearly laugh.

Two sets of footsteps come back down, and I turn to see Trevor, diet Coke in hand, trailed by yet another geek. He walks straight over to me.

He thumbs over his shoulder. "That's Mark."

"Thanks, Trev," I say, taking the drink. He narrows his eyes at me, and I correct myself. "I mean, Trevor."

Three others arrive shortly after, and we settle in for the geek-fest.

I sit among Trevor's dorky friends, eat pizza, and watch the science fiction crap movies they've rented. At first, they're uncomfortable with me there, no one talking much. But Trevor, ever the polite host, keeps talking to fill the awkward silences—making sure to look my way, so that I know I'm included in the conversation. I don't say much, but I watch Trevor, smiling a secret smile at him whenever he looks my way, which flusters him.

Eventually though, the nerd hormones take over and they can't temper their excitement over the movies, so they begin talking, having geek-debates over certain technical aspects of the movies and about the characters and their meanings and intentions. After a while, I forget my mission to keep Trevor off balance and begin to watch the spectacle that is this group, amused.

I also start to relax in spite of myself and actually laugh a few times at Trevor. The guy can actually be pretty funny. His mom comes down several times to replenish the snacks though they don't need to be. I can tell by the others' reactions that this is not normal. She glances my way each time she comes. I definitely have her on her toes.

I wait until everyone else has left before I go. Trevor walks me to the door, of course. I give his arm a squeeze again, à la the night of the dance.

"Thanks, Trev—or." He grimaces at the obvious add-on. "I had fun."

He glances out the door. "Did you walk?"

"Yeah."

"Want me to have my mom give you a ride home?" he asks.

"No." My answer is quick. "Definitely not."

"I can't give you a ride because my dad has my car tonight."

"That's okay. I survived the walk here, and I'm pretty sure I'll survive the walk home."

"It's dark," he states the obvious.

I look behind me in mock surprise.

"Wow, when did that happen? Hope it's not a full moon." This is in reference to the last movie we watched, which was about werewolves.

I look back at him, and he's smiling at my (very) little joke. He has dimples, which I haven't noticed before. Pretty cute—though they don't cover his dorkiness.

"Can I walk you home then?"

I shrug. "Sure. Why not?"

He nods and steps outside, closing the door behind him after telling his mom where he's going. I'm sure she's thrilled about that.

"Can I ask you something?" he says, hands in pockets as we walk. I look at him and think that dressed as he is in jeans and a T-shirt he could *almost* pass as a non-dork—except that his T-shirt depicts one of the comic-aliens from the first movie. "Why did you come tonight?"

"You invited me," I evade, surprised by his directness. I guess somewhat egotistically I expected him to be so overwhelmed by my attentions—or the attentions of any girl, really—that he would just be silently grateful.

"Yeah, I know. But you invited me to go somewhere with you first. Why did you do that?"

I shrug and fudge the truth. "I like you."

"You don't really know me."

"Well, you're kinda cute, I guess." I glance over and can swear he's blushing. "And I had fun dancing with you at the stomp. I thought you might be fun to hang out with."

He thinks about this for a few silent minutes.

"I'm not exactly your type," he finally says.

I stop and turn to face him.

"Trevor, do you think I'm looking to have you for a *boy-friend*?" My voice is flirty though chiding, a hint of southern belle thrown in for good measure.

He shuffles his feet, embarrassed.

"No, of course not, that's not what I meant. I just meant . . . well, I mean—"

"Relax," I say, cutting into his stumbling speech. "I'm teasing you."

"Oh." He smiles sheepishly, relieved. It does the trick, throwing him off the course of his questioning. I can see that now he's wondering what my last comment meant. Was I teasing about *not* wanting him as a boyfriend, or about *not-* not wanting him for a boyfriend? He isn't about to ask again.

He drops me off on my own doorstep, and just to keep him a little more off balance, I lean up and kiss him on the cheek.

"Thanks again. See you at school on Monday."

I walk in and close the door on his stunned face. All is going well, I think.

I'm also surprised. The night was actually not horrible.

3

THE WRINKLED PRUNES

D O YOU maybe wanna hang out tonight?" he asks me ten-
tatively on Friday after another week of my blatant flirting,
surprising me. I thought I would have to be the all-out pur-
suer. This might not take as long as I had originally thought.

"Can't. Family night and all that," I tell him.

It's the truth. This foster family insists on Friday nights
together, stupid family games or going to a brainless G-rated
movie or some other equally lame waste of my time. But I
have to go along because I'm not ready to be shuffled off just
yet. I would really miss Ella and Beth. Plus, I now have this
new project to keep me busy.

"Wanna go party on Saturday?" I ask.

"Can't, it's the third Saturday of the month." Like that
should mean something to me. At my confused look, he clarifies. "I have to be at the senior center that night. You could
come if you want."

"Okaaay." I'm fighting making the gagging motion—
seriously, the *senior center*? But I guess there are sacrifices to
be made if I'm to succeed. So I say, "Sure, why not?"

His eyebrows rise in astonishment, but he doesn't comment on my obviously unexpected answer.

"I'll come pick you up." At my look, he says, "It's too far to walk."

He has that look on his face, the one people get when they want to say something but also don't want to say it. My instinctive defenses come up.

"What?" I ask, a little defiantly.

"Nothing, it's just . . ."

"Just what?" I demand again, after a few moments of silence in which he appraises me, apparently trying to guess my reaction.

"Well, I used to be over in your neighborhood quite a bit, mowing lawns." *Well, of course,* I think. What a perfect geek summer job. He probably did it for free as some kind of charity work. "And I don't remember ever seeing you."

"Maybe because I've been there less than a year."

"Oh," he says, face clearing, mystery solved. "Did your family just move here?"

"No, as far as I know they've lived there for years."

"But . . ." Now Trevor looks really confused, brows pulled together, and I realize he doesn't know. I've just always assumed everyone knew I was a foster kid, as if it were tattooed on my forehead in bright, glowing neon.

"I live with a foster family, Trevor. Didn't you know that?"

"No, I guess I didn't." His forehead is still puckered.

"You can back out if you want." I try to sound flippant, uncaring, but truthfully it always hurts to be rejected because of this thing that is beyond my control, even if it is just a geek rejecting me. Reject me because of my looks or my attitude, my behavior or even my laugh—that's fine. But *this* I have no way to change.

His brows crash together more tightly.

"Why would I want to back out?" He sounds genuinely curious.

"Because I'm, you know, a . . . foster kid." I try, mostly unsuccessfully, to keep the hurt out of my voice.

"Is that contagious or something?" he asks, and it takes me a minute to realize he's *teasing* me.

"Could be," I finally say nonchalantly.

He shrugs and his face clears. "I'll take my chances."

***

"The *senior* center?" my friends choke out between laughs. "You are going above and beyond!"

"Never let it be said I don't commit," I tell them.

***

Saturday comes, and Trevor picks me up at six o'clock sharp. He comes to the door to get me. My foster mother is so overjoyed to see such a polite, clean-cut person here to pick me up—instead of the usual riffraff, as I've heard her call them when she thinks I'm not listening—that she is positively beaming. She doesn't even ask where I am going or give me a time to be home. I'm sure she knows she doesn't need to. Everything about Trevor cries out "rule-follower," so there isn't any doubt he will have me home long before curfew.

We walk outside and there in the driveway sits the coolest car ever.

"This is yours?" I ask, awed.

"Yeah. It's old, I know." He shrugs. "I'm restoring it, though it will probably be about as worthless restored as it is now."

"Are you kidding? A 1973 Chevy Nova four door, right?" I

don't wait for his answer. "No doubt it would be worth more if it were an SS Coupe, but seriously cool as is. V-8?" I ask.

"Yeahhh," he draws the word out slowly, looking from the faded orange car covered with spots of gray putty that look like oversized chicken pox, to me.

"You surprise me, Jennif—I mean, Jen." He smiles.

I just shrug, excited to ride in his car. I know cars from one of the foster families I lived with where both the father and the son were car fanatics. As usual, I feel a shard of regret when I think of them. They were my third foster family— and I had hoped they'd be my last.

The first two foster families came before I knew the game like I do now. I was still struggling with the circumstances that had put me in foster care to begin with, and neither family turned out to be fond of a paranoid, insecure girl who hoarded food and shoved a chair under her doorknob at night for security. Both had turned me back in, like a used car, or a broken toy, or unwanted wedding gift. I pretended it didn't matter, though it was heart-wrenching rejection.

The third family I came to was different. Consisting of a mother, father, and their only son, they took me in and treated me as if I'd always been a part of their family. Their son became an immediate brother, teasing and torturing me like a real little sister, but always with that underlying sense of love and security that came in true families. Not in *my* real family, of course, but in *normal* families.

That's where I learned about cars, spending hours in the garage with them, listening and learning. The TV was always on car shows or races. It was the first place I'd had a sense of security, of really belonging.

I thought I'd stay there forever.

Then the mother developed a fast-moving cancer. When

it became obvious she wouldn't live, the state removed me from their home, from *my* home. She died within six months of the diagnosis, and in spite of my pleading and my foster father's efforts, the state wasn't about to put a teenage girl back into a home with two males and no females.

That was when I decided to take control back. From that point on, it became *my* decision how long I would stay with any given family, and *I* would cause the circumstances that made the family turn me back in.

I've never made the mistake of loving a family again—no risk of heartache that way.

Now I sit with Trevor in this car that I see value in, that probably would have seemed a piece of junk otherwise, driving to the senior center. This time when he touches my back as we walk through the doors, his hand lingers just a little longer than necessary.

I'm pleasantly relieved that the place doesn't stink like stale urine as I had imagined it would. It's actually pretty nice, like a fancy hotel more than an assisted living center.

We walk into the cafeteria, and Trevor directs me into the kitchen. There are a few people standing here who just might have been born before the time of the dinosaurs. They—as well as those who are relatively younger—are all clearly shocked at my appearance and don't try to hide it.

Calls of "Trevor" in happy voices bound around the room. They might not be happy to see me, but they are clearly beyond delighted to see him.

"This is my friend Jen," he introduces me repeatedly, and apparently that's all the endorsement needed to get their approval. If Mr. Dork says I'm worthy of being accepted, then in their eyes it must be true. Soon they are chatting with me and asking me questions—where do you go to school, how do you know Trevor, what is your favorite movie—things that are thoroughly none of their business. But I'm working on my project, and so I smile sweetly and play the part, answering with things they want to hear rather than anything near the truth.

We serve the old wrinkled prunes the dinners that have been put together by the eclectic kitchen staff. The food looks nauseating. Trevor serves it as if it were a feast fit for a king— the do-gooder at his finest. Or so I think until we move into the common area as soon as they are finished eating. I'm just grateful that we don't have to do dishes until, to my horror and embarrassment, Trevor goes and sits at the piano and begins playing.

He plays old songs and *sings* along with them. Seems I'm the only one embarrassed, though; these centenarians love him. He knows almost every song requested of him even though they are songs from the beginning of time. He plays really well—not exactly surprising considering the mammoth piano sitting in his living room—and to my shock, he doesn't sing so badly either.

Those aren't the facts I'll share with my girls, however. I'll only tell them of his playing and singing old songs as the oldies sing and clap along. They will find that endlessly amusing.

By seven thirty, the biddies are exhausted, and aides come in to roll them back to their rooms. Trevor makes sure to tell them all good-bye, calling them by name. Or rather by *respectful* name, as befits the geek he is. *Mrs.* Jones, *Mr.* Anthon, *Mrs.* Green—never by their first names. A few of them wave to me, and I wave back because I have become acutely aware of the fact that Trevor's watching me discreetly. Most of them seem to have gotten over their initial shock by my appearance, though a few still look at me distastefully. Nothing I'm not used to.

"Are you hungry?" he asks me.

I look toward the kitchen and cringe at the thought of eating the same slop we served these people. Seems a little cruel to serve it to *anyone*.

"No," I say. My stomach rumbles loudly, giving me away. Trevor grins, and those dimples make an appearance again.

"Yeah, I can hear that you're not. Come on, let's get out of here and get some food."

"Oh, well in that case . . ."

He takes me to an Italian restaurant, where we're both out of place. I'm like a nightmare to the patrons as I walk in. The hostess at the front desk would turn me away if she weren't afraid I'd cause a scene (I would). And Trevor is way too buttoned up for the chic-type clientele.

I like it. Because he's now out of his comfort zone along with me.

They seat us at a table along the back wall in a cove, partially hidden from view by draping curtains held back by a hook sticking out of the dividing wall. I know this is on purpose to hide me from the rest of their guests, but Trevor acts as if it's an honor to be sitting here.

Our server comes over, definitely looking down her nose at me. Her eyes widen a little when she sees Trevor, and her eyes shift quickly back to me, and then to Trevor again in astonishment. We *are* an odd pair.

"Can I get you something to drink?" She directs her question to Trevor, not so desirous of looking at my offensive person again. I wonder how badly the hostess will have to pay when this particular server is finished with her shift for having seated us at one of her tables.

Trevor looks at me.

"Diet Coke?" he asks with a grin. "They have some really good Italian sodas too. I like the strawberry one."

I almost smack my head at my own stupidity. Of course he's been here before. He's not out of his comfort zone, he's just oblivious to how out of place he is.

"I'll have what you're having," I say.

"Two strawberry Italian sodas, please."

The waitress doesn't say anything, just writes the order on her pad and walks away, giving me another quick glance, sneer barely concealed.

"You've been here before?" I ask.

"Oh yeah, my family comes here all the time. It's pretty good. Haven't you ever been here?"

"Do I look like this is the kind of place I normally visit?"

He sits up even straighter, if possible.

"I'm sorry. Do you not like Italian?"

I roll my eyes at him.

"Italian is fine, Trev—Trevor. This is just a little . . . fancy, I guess."

He looks around at the other customers as if noticing them for the first time, then back at me, taking in my black and red hair, heavy makeup, tight black clothes.

"Oh. Sorry. I guess I've just gotten used to . . ." He trails off, flustered, looking away. "Do you want to leave? Go somewhere else?"

I have to admit I'm a little surprised. I've never been on a date where my discomfort was worth consideration.

"Nah, it's okay. It smells good. Besides, it'll give all these people something to go home and talk about. The freak they saw at dinner."

"You're not a freak." His denial is immediate, unexpected.

"What makes you think I'm referring to me?"

He freezes, cheeks darkening with embarrassment, and I smile at him to let him off the hook.

"Just kidding, Trev. You really need to relax a little." He forgets to correct my shortened version of his name. I lean forward. Subconsciously he does the same.

"So, really, Trevor? You don't think I'm a freak at all?"

"No." He sounds sincere anyway.

"And before you met me? Did you then?"

He shakes his head. At my lifted brow, he explains himself.

"No, not a freak. I mean, obviously I can't go to school and not notice you and your friends because you all dress a little differently."

"A *little* differently?"

He smiles with his killer dimples, and I find myself wondering why girls aren't all over those.

"Okay, a lot differently, especially with, you know, the makeup and all. And the piercings. But you don't have any of those."

"Not that you can see, anyway," I say lowly, seductively. The effect on him is immediate. His eyes drop a quick perusal over my body, and I can see his mind clicking, wondering just where those piercings might be. I decide to let him fantasize and not burst his fantasy by telling him the truth—currently I am pierce-free—or at least jewelry free. I suppose the holes are still there.

After a few minutes, he swallows the lump in his throat and squeaks out, "Oh."

I can't help it. I laugh. His eyes meet mine, and he smiles slightly.

"Are you teasing me?" I just shrug and leave him hanging,

counting on his ever-present courteousness to stop him from asking again.

The rude waitress comes back to take our order. I change my mind purposely three times so that she has to keep scratching it out on her pad, only to wind up back at the first thing I ordered. Trevor watches, eyes scrutinizing, recognizing that I'm doing this on purpose. Then, to my utter amazement, he follows suit and changes his *four* times. By the time he's finished, she is vibrant with irritation. As she walks away, Trevor looks at me and grins.

"She deserved that," he says.

"Yeah, but I can't believe you did it."

He shrugs, then looks at the table, chagrined, drawing an imaginary pattern with one long finger. "I'll leave her an extra tip to make up for it," he mumbles.

I laugh again, and he grins, peeking up at me from under what I notice are incredibly long lashes covering an amazing shade of green. *Huh,* I think. *I haven't noticed his eyes before. They're not bad. Kinda nice, actually. Almost killer.*

After dinner, which he insists on paying for—lucky for me since I'm short on cash—he drives me home, walking me to the door. It almost feels like a real date, which suits me just fine. It's important to my goal for him to start thinking of me as something other than a strange acquaintance.

"Did you have fun tonight at the senior center?"

"Oddly enough, I kind of did," I tell him. "The whole night was fun. Maybe next weekend we can—"

My words are cut off as my foster mother pulls the door open. She seems surprised to see us there.

"Oh, I'm sorry. I didn't know you two were out here. I was just going to go for a walk." Which I know is true because she goes almost every night—sans the straw hat—always trying to drag me along. Exercising is *not* the way I want to spend my evenings. Neither do I want to spend that much time hanging with her.

"Hi, Mrs. Grant. How are you?" Trevor asks.

"I'm fine, Trevor. Did you two have fun tonight?"

Trevor looks at me, as if expecting me to answer. I shrug.

"Yeah, we did," he says.

"Good, good," is her inane response. "Do you want me to wait for you, Jen? You can walk with me."

I give her my normal response, which is a look that says "You're kidding, right?" She translates correctly.

"All right, I'll be back soon, then. Bye."

"Bye, Mrs. Grant," Trevor says. I remain silent. She walks to the end of the driveway and starts stretching. Could she be any lamer? But Trevor either doesn't notice or doesn't care. He's watching me, a question in his eyes—one I don't want him to ask.

"I'll see you at school next week then," I say, turning to go into the house. He hesitates, but seeing that I'm not going to satisfy his curiosity, he sighs.

"Okay, see you later," he says. "And thanks for coming. I'm really glad you did."

I want to scream at his politeness, but instead I turn back, the little secretive smile that flusters him pasted firmly on my face.

"Me too," I say quietly, closing the door on his darkening eyes.

It's going well.

4

Bowling, of All Things

WANNA GO to a party *this* Saturday?"
Another week has passed, and though he hasn't quite worked up the nerve to approach me at school, he is many times the first one to say hi in the halls now.

"I've got a family party Saturday night. Sucks, but I gotta go."

"I'm starting to sound like a broken record here, Trev."
Again, he doesn't comment on my use of the shortened version of his name.

"It's okay," he says, closing his locker, arms loaded with books. "I'm just glad you still want to hang out with me. *Perplexed*, but glad."

Dangerous territory, that conversation, so I change the subject.

"How do you have time to do anything but study when you take so many books home every weekend?"

"I'm good at managing my time," he says with a shrug. "If you ever need help with studying, I could help you."

I eye his books skeptically. They're all AP and college credit courses.

"Somehow I don't think any of my books are the same as yours."

"Well, I've probably already taken some of your classes, so I could help." This nerd statement is given as fact, no conceit, just the truth. He'd probably laugh if he saw the kinds of grades I pull in my classes. Then again, his helping me with homework is another thing I can use in my quest. I tuck that thought away for now.

"I might take you up on that sometime," I say.

"Come with me," he says.

"Come with you where?" I ask in confusion, glancing behind him.

"Saturday. To my family thing."

"*Really*, Trevor? You want to show up to a family function with *me* in tow?"

He gives my outfit a once-over, taking in the shredded, tight black jeans; heavy black combat boots; and tight red sweater covered with a short black vest adorned with chains. It couldn't be more different from his pressed, dark blue jeans and long-sleeve shirt with not even the top button left open.

"Might make it fun for once," he says with a smile, and I laugh. I realize how very much I'm starting to like his big green eyes. I think about missing yet another party this weekend, what my friends will say, and all of that only to go to some stupid family function with the geek. He's coming around, though. I can feel it.

"Okay, sure. Why not?" I start to turn away, then add as an afterthought, "You want me to tone it down a little?" I run an indicative hand down my clothes with a questioning look.

"No," he says, surprising me yet again. "Just be you."

"More shocking that way?" I ask.

He looks about to argue, then grins.

"More interesting, anyway."

***

On Friday night, we're doing the family thing, me and the fosters. *Bowling*, of all the horrible things for them to choose from. Their two biologicals are free to come, so that means we're required to do something particularly boring.

Their oldest biological, Jeff, is married. He and his wife, Kari, are actually pretty tolerable. They don't look at me like I'm a piece of embarrassing trash their parents picked up like the younger one does, a college girl named Tamara, who was clearly a cheerleader. Her name is even pronounced in a definite cheerleader way—not like the spelling indicates it should be pronounced but like Tuh-mahr-uh.

I've heard her on the phone with her friends. She's horrified at her parents' "midlife crisis," which has caused them to take in a troublemaker like me, I'm their first foster. If I do my job correctly, I'll scare them off from the idea, making me also their last.

We show up at the white-trash-family-heaven, get our fashionable rental shoes, and pick out a pocked, dirty, greasy ball that carries who knows how many diseases from the previous users. I can only hope I don't see anyone from school, though I have no doubt about whether I will see any of my friends. They would sooner chew off their big toes than show up at Bowling Haven. Unless, of course, they knew I were here. Then they would come just to watch for their own amusement.

I'm changing from my boots to the *lovely* multicolored shoes, slowly and deliberately to annoy the cheerleader since the others are disgustingly, infinitely patient with me, when I hear a familiar voice.

"Hey, Jen, I didn't know you'd be here."

Trevor, his parents, and a brother I didn't know he had are pulling into the lane right next to ours. Trevor stands there holding his personalized bowling bag, smiling. Relief and something like happiness flood me as I stand up. *Happiness? Really?* I chide myself. *Get a grip, Jen.*

"Hey, Trevor. You guys are seriously here to bowl tonight?"

"Yeah. It was a last-minute thing. I thought about calling you but then remembered that Fridays are your family nights." He says this as if it's a desirable way to spend a Friday night and not the most torturous thing in the world. "What are the chances we'd come here and end up right next to you?" he asks as I slip the last boot off and slide my foot into the hideous bowling shoe.

"Pretty big co-ink-a-dink," I say, and he smiles at my lame word. Behind him I can see his mother's sour face at this turn of bad luck.

His father, who is a surprisingly masculine jock-type, and not bad-looking for an old guy, is watching us with interest.

"You wanna come meet my dad and brother?"

I shrug and start forward, only to nearly fall on my face when I trip on my untied shoelace, stopped from a full face-plant by Trevor's hands. I hear a guffaw of mocking laughter from the cheerleader.

"Whoa," Trevor says, steadying me. "Your lace is untied."

Thanks, Einstein, I think cynically, recognizing that my embarrassment is making me mean. So I keep my mouth shut, the whole if-you-can't-say-anything-nice thing. Then he bends down to tie it for me. I push back the little warm fuzzy that tries to surface at this completely humble gesture.

By now, though, Trevor's parents have wandered over

and are introducing themselves to my fosters. Then the fosters are introducing their biologicals, and everyone knows everyone and we're all a big happy family. Gag, choke, *and* retch.

Trevor's brother, Todd, turns out to be eight years older than Trevor—and has Down syndrome. He smiles happily and gives everyone a hug. I would be horrified if he was *my* brother hugging all in sight, but Trevor and his parents don't even seem to notice or think it odd. Apparently neither do any of my fosters, all of whom are happily returning his hugs. I've never been comfortable around anyone like him, so again I keep my thoughts to myself.

Though Trevor's mom is by no means happy with his friendship with me, she is apparently relieved that my "family" is normal. There is no mention of the fact that I'm a foster, so I'm sure she wonders how I came to be part of this group of bright, happy folks. Trevor's dad, Rob, seems genuinely pleased to meet me, no judgment in his eyes that I can see. I wonder idly if the Mom the Stiff had one night of letting her hair down and had a fling with some geeky nerd, or if Trevor was adopted since he doesn't resemble his mother physically much or his father *at all*. Then Rob smiles. He has the same killer dimples as his son, same green eyes as well, leaving no doubt as to Trevor's paternity, at least.

Trevor and his parents all put on their own personal shoes—by no means fashionable but definitely better than these three-toned clown shoes we have on—and pull out their bowling balls, custom-fitted to their hands and much better looking (and most definitely cleaner) than the bowling alley's house balls. For just one harebrained second I wonder what it's like belonging to a family where going bowling isn't embarrassing, so much so that you all have your own person-alized equipment.

I walk up to bowl. I'm always given top billing, I suspect as part of the do-good pact the fosters have made with one another. I would probably argue, but it annoys the cheer-leader that they let me go first, so I let it ride just for that fact.

I pick up the greasy ball, looking down the finger holes first to make sure they are at least clear, and huck it aimlessly down the alley. It barely snags the pin on the end. I turn around to find Trevor laughing at me.

"What? You think you can do better?" I ask cynically.

He shrugs and walks up to his own alley, picks up his Darth Vader ball, lines himself up, and throws a hard, fast, perfect curve ball, knocking all the pins down.

"Show-off," I mutter.

"Let me show you a trick," he says as I pick up my ball again. I don't really care to learn how to bowl, but I have his full attention, which is bothering both his mom and—for some reason—the cheerleader.

He stands behind me and wraps his arms around me, placing his hands on mine.

"Turn your hand like this," he says, manipulating my hand. "Stand here"—he walks me a little to the left—"and don't look at the pins."

"If I don't look at the pins, how am I going to hit them?" My tone indicates what I think of the lack of intelligence behind his words.

"See those arrows about halfway down the alley?" He reaches forward and points. I can feel the hard line of muscle in his arm pressing against my shoulder. This is another rev-elation, one that causes a little burn in the pit of my belly. *Get a grip, Jen*, I plead with myself more desperately.

"Aim for right between the middle arrow and the one to the right side of it. Take four steps, lean down on the last step and throw. But make sure you keep your thumb pointing forward."

He steps back and, oddly, I kind of miss the feel of him behind me. *Sheesh, cool it!*

"You know, Trev, you know way too much about this. Maybe you need to get a life."

He grins, bringing the dimples out, and suddenly I want to show him that I can do this, I can do what he taught me. I turn back toward the alley and do everything he said, to the best of my limited ability. I knock down most of the pins. I am stupidly happy, and I turn with a laugh.

"Good job," Trevor says, high-fiving me.

"Nothing to it," I throw over my shoulder as I strut off the alley.

Now it's the cheerleader's turn. She's actually a fairly good bowler, but she gets up there and throws a gutter ball, turning back with a pout on her face.

"I'm *terrible*," she moans dramatically.

"Don't worry, honey. You'll get it this time," her dad tells her.

She shakes her head mournfully and turns puppy-dog eyes on Trevor.

"Can you show me what you showed her?" she pleads.

"Sure," the nerd says, oblivious to her obvious game. He looks a little dazed, and I'm sure he's bedazzled by her. She is beautiful, I guess, if you like that blonde-haired, blue-eyed, all-American, wholesome girl-next-door look—which apparently Trevor does.

I glance at Trevor's mom, and she seems a little more relaxed at Trevor's attention on the cheerleader than on me.

Trevor follows her up, this girl who is far more his type than I am, but instead of putting his arms around her as he did me, he stands next to her and gives her the same instruction he did me. I know this is just because he's more comfortable around me, and she dazzles him, but it makes me happy nonetheless. It also makes her *un*happy—always a good thing.

Even better when Trevor asks if I want a diet Coke, showing the cheerleader that he knows me well enough to know what I like to drink. But then in true geek fashion, he also offers to get everyone else a drink.

I watch with dread as Todd has his turn, sure he will embarrass himself. He walks right up to the foul line, ball dangling by his side. He proceeds to swing his arm backward and forward, and I fear for those sitting behind him. He releases the ball on his forward swing, and it heads down the center, knocking all of the pins down.

He turns with a cheer and a laugh to be greeted by cheers from his own family—and by my fosters as well. Trevor looks at me and lifts his brows as if to say, "See, it's so easy, even he can bowl a strike." I stick my tongue out at him.

I bowl pretty good, wanting to show off a little, though I only manage one strike. Of course Trevor bowls far better, perfect in this as in everything else. He comes up with me most turns to give me pointers, always standing in close contact. The cheerleader tries to get him to do the same with her, but it's blatantly obvious what she's doing, to me at least.

Finally Jeff, the fosters' oldest biological, whispers something in her ear, which makes her give a true pout, and she stops trying to get to Trevor after that, proceeding to bowl almost as well as Trevor does.

Trevor doesn't notice her game.

By the end of the third game, my fosters and Trevor's parents are fast friends, and Todd is giving regular hugs to us all, his "new friends." This is a bad development. I can't exactly influence Trevor to the dark side if the families are going to exchange numbers and socialize.

Actually I *can*, I correct myself. It's just going to be more difficult, take a little longer. That doesn't exactly bum me. The fact that it *doesn't* bum me, bums me.

***

Saturday Trevor picks me up to go to his family party. My appearance definitely causes a stir. This horrifies Mrs. Brady/Cleaver but amuses Trevor's dad, oddly enough—and seems to have no effect on Trevor. He acts as if he shows up with a freak at every family function.

The funny thing is, because he acts that way, by the end of the night, most of them seem comfortable enough around me and treat me as if I weren't completely different from this upright clan. There are a few who try to keep me in my place as the visiting freak show, but overall, I find myself having an okay time.

"I don't see him turning," my friends say at school on Monday after they've reamed me about missing another party.

"It's a process," I explain. I tell them about bowling and about the dork-family party, turning their anger into amusement. I feel a little guilty at amplifying the truth to make it more outrageous and using Trevor's family to make them laugh, but sacrifices must be made on the way to success.

I've never been one to back down on a bet or a dare— even if it *is* starting to make me feel kind of like a jerk.

5

STARDATES AND THE SPOCK-GIRL

ANOTHER can't-party-with-you-cuz-I-have-plans Saturday night finds me with Trevor and the rest of the geek squad at his friend Brian's house. This time there are three girls besides me, all three confirmed geeks with absolutely nothing in common with me. They keep to themselves, flirting ineptly with the boys there. I guess I'm a little scary to them. They keep their distance from Trevor, though I can see the one girl watching him whenever she doesn't think anyone's looking. I'm just glad the little mouse Mary Ellen isn't here.

Brian's parents have made a rec room in the detached garage behind their house, with a flat-screen TV, pool table, fridge, and microwave. There are plenty of couches and bean bag chairs scattered around to accommodate large parties. His mom, who is one of the few adults who seems to take me in stride and isn't overly judgmental of me, has already filled the room with more food than a small army could eat and filled the fridge with sodas. She even put in a few healthy food items that a girl might like to eat instead of all the usual boy foods.

We've just finished the newest Star Trek movie, which I actually watched. It was pretty good—lots of action, hot leading actor. I had no preconceived notions though. I've never seen a single episode of the original on TV. Like anyone else on this planet, though, I'm aware of the basic premise and have a very rudimentary knowledge of it. So it has been with much amusement that I've observed Jim scribbling notes furiously throughout the movie, clucking his tongue and grunting as he wrote. That's more entertaining to me than the movie itself, especially as Trevor keeps glancing at Jim's writing with a grin, then rolling his eyes at me as if to indicate how ridiculous this is.

The reason for his concentrated note-taking soon becomes clear, however.

"Okay, here are the issues," he announces as soon as the final credit rolls—which we must watch every letter of until the very end of every single movie. Trevor groans, Brian grins, and the others all get a fanatical gleam in their eyes—except the girls. They wander off into a corner to talk, apparently having been witness to this before. "Let's start with the stardate used in the movie."

I jump a little as his comment incites a near riot, everyone talking over the others, even two of the girls. Trevor laughs at my reaction as they begin spouting numbers at one another, arguing about the possibility—and impossibility—of the dates. I am completely confused. Since when do dates have so many numbers and decimals in them? Where are the months? And, uh, it's just a movie. Fictional, right?

"It's incorrect," Jim is arguing, "unless we have some *unexplained* time warp here."

This comment sets off another explosion of insensible arguing.

"Wanna go for a walk?" Trevor asks me unexpectedly, speaking loudly to be heard over the commotion. I look at all the others, intent on their discussion. I feel pretty sure no one will even notice our absence.

"Sure, why not?" I say, getting up and following him out the door.

Once we're outside, I can still hear their arguments, and Trevor waves vaguely in that direction, looking a little mortified that I witnessed the weird scene.

"Sorry about that." He shrugs, shoving his hands into his pockets as we begin walking. "Once they get started, though, there's no telling how long they might go on like that. It can get pretty heated, a little loud and—"

"Boring?" I interject.

"Right." He smiles. Then he tips his head, looking at me oddly. "That's not really your kind of movie, though, is it?"

"Not normally, no," I dodge. "But it was okay. I kind of liked it."

"Really?" He sounds disbelieving.

"Well," I say, sensing that we're on the verge once again of dangerous explanation territory, "you know, the main guy . . ."

"Kirk," he supplies.

"Right, Kirk. He was pretty cute. The other guy—the one who doesn't smile . . . Spark?" I look at him, and he grins, shaking his head.

"Spock."

"Oh. Spock. Whatever. He was a little odd, but I could relate to him."

"*You* could relate to Spock?"

"Well, yeah. I mean, here's a guy who doesn't really have a place in the world where he fits. Not human, and not . . ."

I look at him to supply the word and find him looking at me with an unreadable expression.

"Vulcan," he says.

"Yeah, that. There isn't anyone who wants the guy. Not the humans and not his own people either. I mean, each tolerates him, right? But maybe doesn't fully accept him. Or that's how it seemed, anyway. Everyone considers him an oddity, right?" I indicate my own self—black skirt over blood-red tights, shiny black boots, striped corset over black mesh shirt, and pale face made more so by my heavily blackened eyes and reddened lips. "Kind of like me. Odd. But I guess I have one up on him; at least there are others like me. There aren't any others like him, though, are there?"

Trevor stops dead, and I stop with him.

"What?" I ask defensively, not liking the way he's looking at me. It's verging dangerously close to pity, and if there is one thing I don't tolerate, it's pity.

"You are odd, aren't you?" he murmurs, and I laugh. So much for thinking he pities me.

"You have no idea," I say as we begin moving again.

"So, what do your friends think of you hanging out with us instead of them on a Saturday night?"

I heave an internal sigh. Trevor is far too perceptive for my own good, for my game.

"They don't think anything. I live my own life, and they live theirs. They aren't my parents."

"Speaking of parents," he begins.

"Do we have to?" I groan, and he laughs. It is a deep, rich sound that brings out his dimples in full force and makes my insides heat up a little. Not exactly the kind of reaction I expect to have in regards to him.

"I guess not," he chuckles.

"Let's talk about Spock's parents instead. His mom was human, right?"

Trevor grins at me. I look away, not wanting to be unsettled by the dimples again.

"If you want, we could go back inside and they can probably give you Spock's entire lineage, both human and Vulcan," he teases.

"Uh, no thanks. I don't have that kind of time. Or patience," I add with a laugh.

"Yes, his mother is human."

"But how does that make any sense? If the Vulcans are emotionless, how does his Vulcan father fall so in love with a human woman?"

"They aren't emotionless, just really logical. I guess sometimes love isn't logical."

"Well, that's a pretty romantic observation there, Trev," I say sardonically. I glance up at him and see a slight flush in his cheeks at my words. I know when to push my advantage, so I step a little closer, hooking my arm through his. He stiffens at my touch. "But then, what is that thing people say? Opposites attract?" I stare at him until he feels compelled to look at me. "Guess there's something to that, huh?" I ask quietly, pressing closer still.

He continues to look at me silently, intensely, and something shifts inside of me. Somehow, in that moment, I lose the upper hand—and I don't even care. A warm breeze blows between us, causing goose bumps to break out across my arms, and I shiver. That breaks Trevor out of the spell, and he takes a step backward—small, almost unnoticeable, but I can feel it, feel the sudden space between us.

"Are you cold?" he asks politely, formally.

"No, I'm okay," I say, releasing my hold on his arm.

"Do you want to go back in?"

I look behind me and realize we've walked quite a ways from Brian's house.

"No, I don't think I have the strength to walk back into *that* discussion." I smile. He laughs lightly, shoulders relaxing.

"I'll walk you the rest of the way home."

"But you left your car back at Brian's," I protest.

"That's all right. We're closer to your house than his. I'll go back and get it after. That gives me an excuse to avoid a little more of their 'discussion.'" He makes little quotation marks in the air with his fingers—such a geek thing to do.

It doesn't take much longer to get to my house. Trevor picks up the pace a little and keeps the conversation on safe subjects such as my lack of mathematical prowess and repeating his willingness to help me with my homework. He stops at the end of my driveway.

"Well," he says, shoving his hands back into his jean pockets. "Thanks for coming over." As usual, he sounds questioning, wondering *why* I did.

"Thanks for inviting me. It was . . . interesting," I say, and he laughs.

"Guess I'll see you at school." He shrugs, still perplexed by my presence in his life.

"Bye, Trev," I purr, trailing my fingers across his shoulder, wanting to leave him a little off balance. I turn and walk up to my door. When I turn back, he's standing in the same place, watching me. I walk in, making the obligatory appearance with the fosters so that they can see I'm home in one piece. I walk up to my room, close the door without turning on the light, and cross to the window, lifting one slat of the wood blinds to look out—to see Trevor still standing there, watching my house, face shadowed but body language tense.

I know I should feel victorious, happy that I have him so flustered. Oddly, though, I want to open my window and call him over to talk some more, see if I can get him to bring the dimples out just one more time. He moves as if to turn away but catches sight of me watching him and freezes.

I pull back, letting the blind drop closed as I press my back against the wall next to the window, hiding. *Look who's flustered now*, I think. I laugh derisively at myself and turn back to the window, heart sinking just a little at the now empty space where he had stood.

"Get a grip, Jen," I mutter to myself, words that are fast becoming my motto. I sink to the bed, ignoring the funny twist in my stomach.

6

THE DANCE BEGINS IN EARNEST

YOU SHOULD go to Morp with me," he says off-handedly, as if my answer doesn't really matter. I know better.

We are sitting together at lunch as we have been almost every day since the stardate-incident weekend. We sit alone since I don't belong with his group and he definitely doesn't belong with mine. Each of those groups watches us intently, mine with humor and his with confusion.

"Is that your way of asking me?" I try—and fail—to sound hurt by the informal asking.

He glances at me and then quickly shifts his beautiful green eyes away. He's definitely nervous about my reaction to his asking. While in his eyes we have become something of friends—though odd ones at that—he is still unclear on the boundaries of said friendship.

Morp is the opposite of prom, casual but for couples, most couples coming either dressed the same or with some kind of "theme" to their outfits. I get an idea.

"I'll go if you dress like me."

"I'm *not* wearing a miniskirt," he teases, finally meeting my eyes, something like relief reflected in his own.

"Party pooper," I mutter. "How about just a little bit . . . rocker," I say.

"Okay," he agrees, leaning forward, grinning. "But then you come a little nerdy, like me."

"C'mon, Trev. You think you're nerdy?"

He rolls his eyes at me.

"Tell me *you* don't."

I shrug, then laugh.

"Well, let's recap, Trev. You get straight A's, you belong to all of the smart-kid clubs, and you always wear your shirts buttoned completely to the top." He reaches up and fingers his top button self-consciously. "I'll bet you know *Star Wars* inside out too." He drops his hand and shrugs, a grimace his affirmative answer. "Maybe just a *little* nerdy," I laugh.

"Which doesn't explain why you want to be seen with me."

"We're an odd couple," I agree lightly, treading carefully.

"Are we?" He's suddenly serious.

"What? Odd?"

"No, you know, the other . . ." He trails off, unsure.

I smile inside, well aware of his confusion regarding me. "Well, if single is one, and triple is three, then couple must be two. And we're two people sitting here. Even *I* know that, and you're the one who's supposed to be the math whiz here, Trev."

"Trevor," he counters automatically, quietly, unaware that he has even said the word. He watches me, seeming to decide whether to push me for a real answer for once, rather than my usual cryptic remarks meant to keep him guessing. He backs off, and I sigh inwardly in relief.

"So, what do you say? Do you want to go?"

"Isn't it girl's choice?"

"Is it?" I know he knows it is. He is an SBO (student

body officer), and they plan all of these useless activities. He looks at me slyly from under those long lashes, and I know he's teasing.

"Sure, why not?"

"Jen's famous last words," he mutters.

I lean forward and cover his hand with mine, tucking my fingers under his palm. His whole body stills. He looks at our hands, and then slowly his eyes rise to mine.

"Yes, Trevor, I would love to go to Morp with you," I say, throwing the husky-sexy tone in, now that he's off balance. I pull my hand away and lean back, biting into my apple, breaking the spell. He gives a little laugh. It sounds kind of like relief.

"Besides," I say, "if you think people are surprised by us now, imagine what they'll think if we show up as one another there."

Trevor smiles at this.

"Could be fun," he agrees.

"Definitely."

***

This agreement gives my friends no end of amusement. They want photos.

***

The dance falls on a Friday, which is totally awesome because it gets me out of stupid family night for once. When Trevor comes to pick me up, I find I'm not really fond of him in black leather pants and jacket, black leather half-gloves, spiked hair, chains dangling from his waist, black lips and eyeliner, though he did a good job and could easily fit in with my friends—excepting his perfect posture and clear eyes, of course. If it isn't necessarily my goal to get him to dress like this, it is still my goal to get him to turn bad—to be like me.

I'm wearing clothes borrowed from the cheerleader's closet. She wouldn't appreciate that I'm using her clothes to look nerdy. I wish she were here to know it instead of back at college. I'm wearing a letterman's sweater (really, you *letter* for standing in front of a crowd and acting like an idiot while leading them in cheers?) with a pink-and-yellow plaid tweed skirt, and shoes that look like they time-warped from the fifties. I have my hair twisted into two braids, though even that doesn't disguise its red and black coloring.

"Wow," he says, looking at me, though only at my face and not the usual up-and-down body perusal that I get from the boys I normally hang with. "You look really good without all that makeup on." Then realizing he might be coming across as impolite, he stammers, "I mean, you always look good, every day, but underneath all of that, you're really beautiful."

"I hope none of my friends see me," I say to cover the fact that his comment actually flatters me a little.

Pat and Sue (aka the fosters) are there with their camera. I smile and make nice because I don't want to offend Trevor—not because of anything noble like good manners, but because I need him malleable tonight.

Beth and Ella are at the dance—with their own cameras. I don't say anything to them, though I pass in front of them twice before they see me. It takes them a while to figure out which bland girl I am. It entertains Trevor that they don't recognize me.

Of course, his friends don't recognize him either, so he plays my game, lying low until someone notices. Beth and Ella have an upper hand in this since they are aware of our trick. They take some future blackmail pics of us before leaving. They have better parties to crash.

It's mousy Mary Ellen who recognizes Trevor.

"Trevor, is that you?" she asks while we're sitting on the sidelines drinking ultra-sweet punch, a perfect complement to my costume and a natural for who Trevor is.

"Hi, Mary Ellen." Do I hear a little longing in his voice, heightened attention in his eyes at her appearance? I scoot a little closer to him, pressing against his arm.

"Why are you dressed like that?" Her distaste is clear. She glances at me, no recognition in her eyes.

"Jen and I switched places," he tells her.

"Jen?"

Trevor indicates me.

"Jen Jones. You remember her from school, right?"

"Oh." It's clear she does not. "Yeah, right. Hi, Jen."

I slip my arm deliberately under Trevor's, lacing my fingers with his. She notices; so does he.

"Hey," my answer is flippant, a slight feline threat in there that she recognizes instinctively. The mice always do.

"Who are you here with?" Trevor is always polite, and only I notice the tremor in his voice. Is he nervous at my touch, or is it something else?

"Brian. He's getting us some punch." Brian of Trevor's sci-fi geek friends, the one whose house we were at for the big Star Trek argument. She waves vaguely behind her, eyes darting nervously between my face, Trevor's face, and our entwined hands. I keep my catlike smile in place, leaning closer to Trevor. Of all Trevor's friends, Brian seems the most normal, so I'm not at all surprised that the mouse would choose him as a date. She's geek-goddess personified, right?

"Have a seat." Trevor indicates the empty place next to him. The mouse slowly, uncertainly sits, graceful in a way I would never have suspected. I bristle that he is keeping her nearby, recalling his posturing for her on the day I decided to make him my pet project.

"You don't look so good dressed like that," she tells him without malice. Honesty and forthrightness are apparently inbred in geeks and dorks alike. Trevor looks down at himself and for the first time tonight seems embarrassed by his appearance. It bothers me that he's ashamed of looking how I normally look.

"It's just a costume," he says, shrugging.

"Yeah, but *I* look good, don't I?" I interrupt. I'm irritated and let it show. "I mean, *tonight* anyway, *tonight* I look good. What's your costume, Mare?"

"My name is Mary Ellen," she corrects. "I'm not wearing a costume."

"Huh." I manage to infuse the word with derision. Trevor is watching me and something flashes through his eyes that I haven't seen before—anger.

"Hey, guys."

Brian finds us and plops down next to the mouse. He's wearing a T-shirt bearing the movie poster from *Starman* that matches hers—I'm a little appalled that I know this— and hands her a cup of the punch that is bitter compared to her usual natural sweetness. This is way too much. I can't take it anymore.

"Let's dance, Trev," I command, not exactly nicely. He doesn't refuse me; his well-mannered upbringing won't let him.

"Trevor," he corrects harshly, standing and pulling me up with him, a little more roughly than I expect from him. I follow him to the dance floor; I don't really have a choice since my hand is still tangled with his. He's surprisingly strong.

I can feel the tension in his body as he wraps his arms around me. He still holds me at a respectable distance, though maybe not so distant as the first time we danced.

His body is rigid, and he keeps his gaze fixed over my head, not looking at me. He can't stay quiet for long—it's not Trevor's style to remain silent when something bothers him.

"What was that all about?" he demands.

"What?" I try to pretend innocence, but the look he gives me lets me know he sees right through it. "Fine. I mean, come on, Trev—*Trevor*. She was throwing herself at you. Bad form when you're with a date."

Suddenly he pulls me close, tight against him, suggestive, and I feel humiliated that he is giving me exactly what I have been shooting for.

"*She* was throwing herself at me?" His voice is low, his mouth next to my ear. "Was it Mary Ellen who was suddenly draped all over me, holding my hand, shooting daggers at you with her eyes? What is this game you're playing with me, Jen?"

A new sensation washes through me, one I am unfamiliar with—shame. I pull back and walk quickly away from him, out the doors into the cool night air. I'll just call Beth and have her come pick me up; I need a *real* party right now. I pull out my cell phone and angrily start punching buttons before slamming it shut. I can't call her when I have tears running down my face.

"Jen." He's behind me, close enough that I can feel the tension radiating from him.

"I'm sorry, Trevor. I don't know what's wrong with me." I sound pathetic to my own ears, and I hate it.

"Jen," he repeats softer, putting a hand on my shoulder. "Look at me."

I shake my head. I can't tell him the truth. I can't.

He steps in front of me, tipping my face up. I angrily wipe the tears away.

"Jen . . ." This time compassion fills my name, which

nearly undoes me, so I tell him part of the truth, breaking the mood.

"I'm sorry I was rude to your friend. But the truth is . . ." I take a deep breath and let it out. "Truth is, I'm jealous of her."

"Of Mary Ellen?" He looks skeptical.

"Yes. But I swear I won't admit it if you ask me again, even under threat of torture or death." I cross my arms sulkily.

Trevor laughs.

"Why?"

"Why am I jealous or why won't I admit it?" I stall. He just lifts his brows. I really do like his eyes.

"Because I'm not used to having my date's attention taken from me, especially by someone like her. Because she's obviously perfect for you, Trevor." I lift my hand toward the door we just exited. "*She's* who you should be with—she knows it and you know it."

"Someone like her? You mean someone like me."

I have no answer so I look away.

"I'm here with you."

An obvious, simple statement that doesn't really mean anything—so why does my heart lift at the words? Stupid.

"You like her," I accuse.

"Yeah, I guess I do." My heart plummets again. "Or I did. Maybe I still do. I don't know. But I didn't bring her to the dance. I brought you. It seems I spend all my time with you."

"Why is that?" I'm genuinely curious but aware that I could be opening a door I don't want opened. I quickly rephrase. "I mean, why do you *want* to?"

He looks thoughtful.

"You're funny," he finally says. "I laugh a lot when I'm

with you. I always have fun when I'm with you. And you try to hide it, but you're actually pretty sweet."

"That's a horrible thing to say," I say petulantly, crossing my arms tightly again. He chuckles.

"And you're really smart."

"Now I *know* you're lying."

"You are. But you try to hide that as well. And you're pretty."

"Worse and worse," I moan. He grins.

"And when I'm with you, I don't want to be anywhere else or with anyone else."

My heart leaps, and I groan. Guilt was never supposed to be a part of this. I should quit now, let him off the hook.

"I know I'm not exactly your kind of guy," he says. "But I like you. I'm not sure why you want to be around me at all, but I don't even care anymore, as long as I get to keep hanging out with you."

I moan again and lean forward, butting my head against his surprisingly solid chest. He puts his hands on my shoulders, rubbing his hands lightly over them.

"Why do you have to be so nice?" I moan, entwining my hands in the chains he shouldn't be wearing.

"I can be meaner if you want."

"No you can't. I mean, look at you now. I'm the one being a total jerk, and you come out here to make sure I'm okay."

I lean back and look up at him, yanking on the chains lightly.

"You wanna come back in and dance some more?" he asks.

"Are you going to make me hang out with *her*?"

He thinks about it for a minute. I grunt, pulling the chains again, and the dimples appear.

"Okay, no, not tonight."

"Thank you, my knight in shining armor."

He fingers the chains. "Well, maybe the shining part of that anyway."

"You're a funny guy, Trev . . . I mean, Trevor," I say as we walk back toward the school, Trevor holding my hand, which he squeezes at my comment.

"I really don't mind you calling me Trev." Before I can comment on this unexpected development, he changes into some weird mad scientist voice. "You should know I have talents I have not even begun to show you, my young apprentice."

"Can't wait to see those," I mutter as he laughs. "Just curious, though, Trev. Where did you get the clothes you're wearing?"

"Uh . . ." He trails off.

"Yeah? I haven't heard of a store called 'Uh.'" When he doesn't say anything, not even giving me a grin, I get suspicious. I stop, forcing him to stop with me.

"All right, Trev, 'fess up. It can't be that bad, can it? Who did you borrow them from?"

"I didn't borrow them."

"Did you steal them or something?" I laugh.

"No . . ." His answer is hesitant. Now I'm really curious. Finally, he mutters, "I rented them."

I'm stunned. "You can *rent* clothes?" He glances at me and something in his expression stops me cold. "Trev?"

"Fine. I got them at a costume shop, okay?"

"A *costume* shop?"

His jaw clenches, and I begin walking again, Trevor following slowly.

"I'm a *Halloween costume*?"

He's silent, waiting for my reaction.

"I don't know whether I should be amused or . . . or insulted!"

"Don't be insulted," he says quietly, "because what you're wearing could also come from a costume shop. *Everyone* wears some kind of costume, right?"

I grimace at his skewed logic, but he just grins and stops abruptly.

"I have an idea."

"Is it going to hurt?" I ask hesitantly.

"Maybe." He shrugs, turning and leading me out into the parking lot, toward his car. This has never been a good sign for me in the past. With the boys I've dated, leading me to their car was always a bad thing. It meant either they were sick of me and wanted to take me home, or they just wanted to make out—or more. My stomach clenches, but Trevor merely leans inside, turning his key until the radio comes on. He flips through a couple of stations until he finds a song, then turns back to me.

"There, now we can have our own dance, with no one to bother us or judge us," he says, taking my hand and pulling me to him. We begin slowly dancing, and my stomach finally realizes he means me no harm and relaxes. I smile at him.

"What?" he asks.

"You surprise me, Trev," I say, giving his own words back to him. He chuckles and pulls me just a little closer—still proper, but less than his usual formal stance.

Later at home, lying in bed and remembering the way he had held me a little closer during the slow dances after our fight, I realize I did not accomplish the goal I had set for the night: getting Trevor to go to the party with me following the dance. Somehow, I'm not really that upset.

7

OLD BIRDS AND SONGS

ON MONDAY, I still wear the black makeup, but I am maybe just a little less heavy with the eyeliner, and I don't line my ruby red lipstick with black. Not a drastic change, and so none of my friends comment, but Trevor notices, I can see by the look in his eyes. He also says nothing.

He doesn't need to.

The third Saturday of the month rolls around again, and I find myself back at the senior center, this time dressing a little more conservatively so as to not scare the old birds so much. Many of them seem genuinely pleased to see me again—equal only to the number who don't remember me from the last time through no fault of their own but only as a result of their age. Of course there are still a few who find me distasteful even in my toned-down state, but their numbers are comparatively small to the rest.

A few of them tell me their life stories, which are oddly interesting. Many of them have lived through the period of time when things advanced dramatically. Television and telephones were something they couldn't have dreamed of, let alone things like the Internet and cell phones. They lived through World War II—many of them serving there—sent their sons to Korea or later Vietnam, and now have grandkids and great-grandkids in the Middle East. They've lived through the Depression, and survived the loss of family members, spouses, and even children—many times due to tragic circumstances.

I think of my own piddly little life story, which seems unimportant in the face of their lives' challenges. My story is the thing that has helped me sustain my anger, helped me to justify so many things, and I'm a little upset that their stories have dimmed my excuses.

Trevor is goofing around on the piano, as usual, singing songs that make these oldies happy. Then he stops and begins playing a slow song while I'm helping an old lady to readjust her afghan—crocheted by her mother who is long since dead, she tells me. I'm surprised by the melody, slow and sappy. I glance up at Trevor, and he watches me while playing. The ballad is everything I profess to hate, with its flowing romanticism pouring out.

I kind of like it.

He only plays it for a minute or two and then pounds into a rousing "Great Balls of Fire" rendition with lots of over-the-top theatrics that please the prunes. I shake my head at his complete lack of inhibition.

We head to the Pizza Palace afterward, and I'm glad it's not another night of snobby Italian waitresses. *Everyone* goes to the Pizza Palace, so a geek and freak showing up together creates only a small stir.

A group of my friends sit in the back corner, waiting for a place to party. They wave me over, and I look at Trevor. He shakes his head.

"Go ahead," he says, ever polite. "I'll go sit over there."

He indicates the opposite corner, where a group of his friends sit, including the mouse Mary Ellen.

"We came together, right?" I ask. He nods. "Then we'll stay together. I'll just go say hi, and you can go say hi, and then we'll find our own corner to sit in."

"Okay . . ." He seems convinced I'll abandon him to eat the large pizza alone. "I'll go grab the pizza when they call our number."

"Trev, I promise, I'm only going to say hi. I'll be right back." He still looks skeptical. "But if you bring Mary to our table, I swear . . ." I let the growled threat hang, and he smiles.

He leans close. "It's Mary *Ellen*." I don't know whether to be amused or angry at his defense of her name, but he walks away before I have the chance to be either. I turn back toward my own friends.

"So, that him?" a girl named Gina asks. I don't know her well since she skips school most days. I'm not even sure why she stays enrolled. My only contact with her is usually at parties and is limited at best.

"Him, who?" I ask, shooting a look at Beth and Ella.

"The one you're fooling . . . you know, the *guy*—the bet you made."

"I'm not *fooling* him," I say, "just trying to bring him over to the dark side." This strikes them all as funny, and they laugh loudly.

"Maybe you should stop wasting your time and come sit with someone who is firmly on the dark side already." This is Kyle. He's no longer in high school, though that's more of an age thing and not so much a graduation thing. He waggles his eyebrows in comic suggestion.

"Where's the fun in that?" I laugh.

"Is that what this is all about? Fun?" Seth is the only one who's definitely *not* amused.

I finger my lip meaningfully while looking at Beth.

"Not *just* fun."

"Oh yeah," he sounds bitter, "I forgot. A lip piercing is involved. *That* makes it worth it."

I drop my hand. He stands up angrily and gets right up in my face, eyes glassy and livid. I can smell the pot on him and unconsciously mentally compare him to Trevor, who always smells so good, so clean.

"If I take you right now and get your lip pierced, will you drop this stupidity and start acting like yourself again?"

"She can't," Ella comes to my rescue. "It's not quite time for her to blow it with her fosters yet, right, Jen?"

"Besides that," Kyle interjects, "I'm interested to see how this plays out, see if she can do it. It's an intriguing game."

This is met by agreement from the others.

"Why are you doing this?" Seth asks, whining a little but still standing in his threatening pose.

"Jen?" I look over, and Trevor is standing there, watching me. For a second my heart drops. How much did he hear?

"Are you okay?" He cuts his eyes toward Seth meaningfully. Seth huffs out a sound that is both disgusted and amused that a *geek* would think to protect me from *him,* and then he stalks away.

"Introduce us," Kyle calls out, pretending there's nothing odd going on. Trevor and I both watch Seth slam out through the front door. I turn back to Kyle.

"This is Trevor," I say, residual guilt in my voice. "Trevor, this is everyone."

"I'm Kyle," Kyle says, sticking out his hand. Trevor the Polite doesn't even hesitate to shake it, and I'm miserable knowing they are mocking him while he is unaware. "You been hanging out with our girl for a while now. You should come hang out with us sometime."

"Sure, maybe some time." Trevor is stiff, sensing that something is wrong. He turns to me. "Our pizza is over there if you're ready."

"I am," I say, walking away without a backward glance. Trevor doesn't have it in him to do so, so he acknowledges them.

"Nice to meet you," he says, looking at me oddly when they all break out in laughter.

"Ignore them—they're jerks," I say as we sit at our own table.

"You think your friends are jerks?" He's perplexed.

"They can be."

"Was Seth bothering you?"

"You know who Seth is?"

"I do go to school every day, you know. I don't know him personally, but I know who he is."

"Oh."

"Is he, like, an old boyfriend or something?"

I laugh. "Hardly. He's sort of like your Mary. I might have wanted him at one time, but not so much anymore. He's pretty much a freak."

"Mary Ellen's not a freak," he denies automatically. Then, digesting the rest of my words, he leans forward. "You think I wanted Mary Ellen?"

"I'm not completely unobservant myself."

"Huh." He suddenly grins at me and leans closer. "What makes you think that maybe I don't want her anymore, then?"

His teasing doesn't work because I'm in misery at certain truths that are trying to surface in me.

"You *should* be with her. She'd be a perfect girlfriend for you."

"Not looking for a girlfriend."

"You're not?"

"Nope."

I narrow my eyes at him. Is he saying that because he doesn't want a girlfriend or because he thinks he has one? Then I grin. He's turned my little game of half answers back on me.

The boy is learning. I might just succeed yet.

***

Trevor takes me home and as usual walks me to the door. A new experience for me, having a guy do that every time he brings me home and not just the first time when he's trying to make an impression. I'm used to being dropped off at the curb.

"You wanna come in for a little bit?" I ask suddenly before I can chicken out.

"Sure." I have never asked him in before, and his voice carries his surprise.

We go in, and the fosters are sitting in the family room, curled up together watching some dumb old movie. They sit up when we come in, standing when they see Trevor behind me.

"Trevor! Nice to see you again." The mom sounds excited, as if he's a long lost relative that has suddenly appeared.

"Nice to see you as well, Mr. and Mrs. Grant."

"Did you kids have fun tonight?"

I really don't want to play this we're-a-real-family game, so I say, "We're going up to my room."

"Okay, sweetie," the mom says, failing her unspoken test. If it were any boy from my usual circle, there would not be an "okay" following my statement. I turn to head up the stairs, and Trevor follows.

"Leave your door open," the dad calls, and I smile, just a little. *He* knows—boys are boys.

We go into my room, and Trevor looks around with interest. The room is frilly and girly, all white lace and cutesy pictures of landscapes and butterflies hanging on the walls—a room from a magazine.

"This isn't what I imagined your room to look like at all."

"Yeah, well, this is how it was when I came here. Nothing here is mine, obviously."

He looks at me oddly.

"How long have you lived here?"

"Almost a year."

"And you haven't personalized it yet?"

"Why would I?" I ask curiously.

He lifts his hands as if it should be obvious.

"Because you live here."

"Temporarily." My answer shocks him, I can tell.

"How many places have you lived?" he asks.

"A lot."

"Why's that?"

"People can't really take me for too long at a time, Trev."

"I don't believe that. I don't get sick of being around you."

"Yeah, well, give it some time. You haven't been around that long."

"You don't give yourself enough credit."

"You give me too much. Can we talk about something different?" This particular conversation agitates me.

He looks at me for a minute, as if deciding something.

Then he sits on my bed, and I have to bite down to avoid bursting out laughing. His mom would choke if she knew where her baby was at this very moment.

"What should we talk about?" he asks.

I walk over and plop down on the bed next to him, flopping back so that I'm lying down, curious about what he'll do. He only turns a little so that I'm not talking to his back but makes no other move. *Huh.*

"Hey, what was the deal with that sappy song you were playing tonight?" I ask.

He turns away from me.

"You thought it was sappy?" He sounds a little upset. I sit up and scoot to the edge of the bed so I can see his face.

"Yeah, I guess I did. But good sappy."

He looks at me sardonically. "What, exactly, is good sappy?"

I shrug. "Well, you know, really romantic. That kind of thing."

"You don't like romantic?"

"Do I strike you as someone who likes romantic?"

Now he shrugs. "I think you have a lot of layers that you hide."

"Trev, you really have to stop thinking there's more to me than meets the eye."

"There is." I groan at his words, and he laughs. "To tell you the truth, that song was something I've been working on."

I reach out and grab his hand with a gasp.

"That's a song you're writing?" He nods. "And I bashed it." My tone indicates my distress.

"It's okay. Not a big deal."

"It *is* a big deal. I don't want to hurt you."

Even as I say the words that are the truth, I know they're

also a lie because everything I do now will eventually hurt him, or at least hurt who he is.

He gives me a wry smile and shrugs, self-conscious. "I wrote it for you."

"For me?" I refuse to acknowledge the feelings that try to push their way to the surface at this.

"Yeah, you know, inspired by you. Dumb, huh?"

I lean my head on his shoulder and place my hand over his, but instead of going stiff as I have come to expect whenever I touch him, he relaxes into me and leans his head against mine.

"Not dumb," I say. "Incredibly sweet. No one has ever done anything like that for me before."

He doesn't say anything, just turns his hand over and threads his fingers with mine.

"Will you finish it? For me?"

"Thought it was sappy," he says.

I lift my head and look into his great eyes.

"A little sap never hurt anyone."

So he's writing a song for me, I think later.

Geek.

I'm pretty happy about that.

8

MORE TIME

THE END of the year rolls around, and Beth and Ella corner me.

"You have summer school?" Beth asks.

"No, I barely squeaked by. You guys?"

"No, we're okay," Ella answers.

"So Trevor hasn't been to a party yet, and I'll bet he got a four point oh," Beth says.

"He's coming along," I tell them. "I just need a little more time. He's stronger than I thought. But I had him in my bed."

They both gasp in shock, and I laugh.

"Kidding! Relax. He was only sitting on the edge of my bed, but that's probably more than he's ever done before."

"You're on a schedule, you know," Beth says.

"Yeah, I know. Truth be told, these fosters aren't the worst yet, so I might take most of the summer with them."

"You're going soft!" Beth accuses.

"Bite your tongue, milady. I'm as hard as ever. Feel." I hold out my arm, tightening my biceps.

Ella steps forward and squeezes.

"Yep, definitely softer."

I drop my arm. "Maybe a little softer, but not what you're thinking." I point to my lip. "I'm not letting you off the hook that easily. All plans are still a go. Before the summer is done, you *will* see a new Trevor. And you'll probably have to take him over for me next year since chances of me getting another family in this school are nil."

"Which one of us?" they ask together.

"Maybe it'll require both of you," I say, my stomach clenching at the thought of Trevor at the mercy of either one of them, let alone both.

***

"Wanna go swimming?" Trevor asks about three weeks later, and I figure this is a good opportunity for me to really swing him my way. My body is one of my strong points.

He picks me up and lets me drive his cool car, which I'm revved about. I do like cars. I'm not wearing makeup because water on the kind of makeup I wear makes for some ridiculously large black streaks down the face. I have on a T-shirt and skirt over my swimsuit because I plan to make the most of the unveiling.

Trevor carries our stuff and finds us a spot on the grass in the sun.

"This okay?" he asks.

"Great."

Once he has the blanket spread out and sits down, I stand casually in front of him and slowly peel my T-shirt off. He is leaning back on his hands, sunglasses on, but he is very still. I have his full attention now, though he pretends otherwise. It's not good manners to stare, after all. I deliberately untie the wrap-around skirt and let it drop to the ground. He still hasn't moved. I bite back my smile.

"You gonna sit there all day or are we gonna swim?" I ask, hands on hips.

"Uh, sw . . . swim. I . . . I think swim."

I smile and hold out my hand. He looks at it for a minute, then places his hand in mine, and I pull him up. He throws his sunglasses back on the blanket, and I'm pleased to see his eyes are a little unfocused. Trevor takes his own T-shirt off; now it's my turn to be stunned.

Trevor actually has muscle, tight pecs and abs, and nicely rounded biceps—a pretty nice physique. Not at all the skinny, pale, shapeless wonder I expected him to be.

His bright yellow trunks are just what I would have expected. All they need is a Spiderman print to be complete.

We walk to the pool, and I slice in neatly with a dive. I come up and look back at Trevor, who then cannonballs next to me, dousing me.

"Nice," I tell him when he comes up for air.

"One of those talents I was telling you about," he says. "Race you to the other side."

He lets me win. He is a strong, clean swimmer. I tell him I'm on to him.

"Swimming lessons from age three to thirteen," he confesses.

"Self-taught." I'm smug. He looks impressed.

After swimming for a while and having a water fight that he easily wins, we climb out and walk back to our blanket. I'm unused to the lack of attention I'm getting from the other swimmers. Though my swimsuit is covered with black skulls, without my outrageous clothes and makeup, I don't particularly stand out. The anonymity is somewhat nice because I can relax and not worry about keeping the act up.

Trevor walks over to the snack bar and buys us water

bottles and Popsicles, the official foods for swimming geeks everywhere. When he comes back, he pulls the sunscreen from his pack and offers it to me.

I start rubbing it on my arms and legs, but when I get to my belly I happen to glance over and see that Trevor has put his sunglasses back on, frozen in the act of watching me, not even noticing his Popsicle melting in streaks down his arm. So I slow it down, make a show of it.

"Can you rub some on my back?" I ask. He doesn't answer, just throws his Popsicle onto the grass.

"Be right back," he says, then jumps up and runs into the locker room. He's back out almost immediately, and his arm is dripping, but with water now instead of Popsicle juice, though his arm is still streaked with red stains. He hurries over and sits behind me. He squeezes the lotion onto his hands, rubbing them together to warm the lotion up before putting it on me, taking longer than necessary to rub it around. He is most definitely affected by touching me.

So am I.

"There you go." His voice is unsteady.

"Okay. Here, I'll do you."

"Wha—?" his voice catches.

I lift up the lotion.

"Oh. Yeah. Okay." He turns around, and I squeeze the cold lotion directly onto his back. He jumps a little and breaks out in goose flesh. I rub it in, surprised again at the hard muscle beneath his warm flesh.

"You work out, Trev?"

"No. Isn't that apparent?"

"No, not really. I thought you'd be skinnier than you are."

He laughs. "I'm confused. Is that a compliment or an insult?"

"Yes," I say, and he's grinning as he turns back to face me.

"It's natural," he says in his Schwarzenegger voice, flexing his arms and chest, bigger muscles than I expected popping up.

"Nice," I say with a laugh, but my eyes tell him I'm serious. He drops his pose.

"I played basketball and soccer for a long time," he says with a shrug.

"Why don't you anymore?" I ask, trying to picture Trevor as a jock.

"My classes at school. I have a lot of homework. And since I'm pretty sure I'm not going to get into college on a sports scholarship . . . or on my looks," he adds facetiously. "I need to depend on my grades."

"Don't knock your looks, Arnold. The killer combination of your eyes and dimples could probably get you into a place or two."

"Two compliments in one day? That has to be a record."

"It's in my nature to be kind to the poor and downtrodden." I sigh dramatically.

"I'm neither, so you're going to need a new story," he says.

"I don't have one. That's the best I can come up with. So tell me, college boy, what do you want to be when you grow up?"

"A writer."

My eyebrows lift at this. "Of what? Comic books? Bad sci-fi movies?"

"Novels."

"I could tell you stories that would curl your toes," I mumble, but he hears me clearly.

"Tell me."

"No, I don't think so. I like you having this clean view of me."

"Clean?"

"Yeah. You don't know my dirt."

"You won't tell me?"

"Someday I might," I say, thinking of the day when he becomes like me and sees me in my real life. He'll know most of my dirt then, but not all. Some things I'll never tell him. I lay down on the blanket next to where he sits.

"Can I ask you something?" he says.

"I'm not telling you my dirt, Trev, dimples or no."

He leans back on his elbow, turning to face me.

"Not that. You'll tell me when you want. It's something else."

"Sounds serious," I tease.

"Kind of." He slips his hand under mine, lightly rubbing my knuckles. "You keep putting out all of these conflicting vibes."

I look up at him, then lean up on my own elbow so that we are eye to eye.

"What do you mean?"

"We're friends, right?" he questions. I nod. "And that's nice. Unexpected, but nice. But we spend a lot of time together. *A lot* of time. I'm with you more than I am with all of my other friends combined. And I'm guessing it's the same for you."

"I like hanging out with you, Trev," I say hesitantly, not sure where he's going with this. "But I don't mean to hog all your time. You don't have to be with me so much if you'd rather be with your friends."

"That's not what I'm saying. I'd *rather* be with you. I like hanging out with you also. I like it a lot. I like you a lot." He drops his eyes, watching our hands that are still held together.

"Ditto," I say, confused. He looks frustrated. I'm not sure what he wants.

"But then you do things that put out the vibe like you want to be more than friends." He's looking directly at me now, refusing to let me hide from him.

"Like what?" I ask flippantly. I'm trying to turn this conversation, put him ill at ease. It doesn't work.

"Like today. Your little undressing act for me."

I open my mouth to deny it, but in the end I don't. I can't when he's looking into my eyes like that, demanding honesty. I look down, chagrined.

"You noticed that, huh?"

"How could I not?" He laughs roughly. "And telling me you're jealous of Mary Ellen, touching me all of the time when you know what it does to me."

I want to be flippant and demand he tell me just what it does to him, but I'm afraid that he *will* tell me. After all, Trevor is nothing if not honest.

"What are you saying, Trevor?" I finally ask.

"I want to be with you."

"You are."

"You know what I mean. I want to know how you feel about me. Honestly."

I look at our hands folded together on the blanket. And just for now, I want to drop the game. For just a little while I want to be what he wants of me. Just for a little while.

"We're holding hands," I say, looking back into his gorgeous green eyes.

"Yeah, so?"

"I don't hold hands with my friends, Trev."

His eyes change, darkening a little at that. He kisses me then, leaning toward me as we lie on the blanket holding hands. A sweet kiss, asking nothing. It isn't anything like the demanding full-of-expectation kisses I'm used to. I can't help but smile at him when he pulls away. His answering smile is dazzling, taking my breath away.

"I need to tell you something, though . . ." I say. "Don't be offended, but, uh . . ."

He's patient, waiting for me to find the words. His thumb rubbing the back of my hand is such a pleasant sensation I almost don't want to say the words. But say them, I must.

"I really like you also, Trev. Completely unexpected, but there it is. I'm not quite ready to, you know, go *public*. Not with your friends and definitely not with mine, you know?"

I wait for the anger, but he goes against the usual grain again and smiles at me.

"Got a rep to protect, huh?"

"A *rep*?" I ask. "What, one night in leather and suddenly you're all hip and cool? You don't really use words like that, do you?"

"Of course not. It wouldn't fit in with my geekiness."

"Trev, that's not what I meant . . ."

"It's okay. I know what I am, and I'm okay with it. Maybe someday you will be too." He squeezes my hand. "I'm okay with not going public. I don't think my friends would be any more thrilled than yours. So until we see where this is going . . ."

"Kiss me again," I say softly.

"Isn't this public, though?"

"We don't know anyone here, not that I saw."

He obliges, ever courteous.

The freak and the geek.

What did I get myself into?

9

Tents and Blisters

"I'M GOING on a camping trip with my family."
We're lying side-by-side on the trampoline behind
Trevor's house, holding hands between our safely dis-
tanced bodies. His mom is still not thrilled about me
hanging out with Trevor, especially now that she's seen
him holding my hand and putting his arm around me.
That definitely makes her skittish. But after our bowling excursion, Trevor's parents and mine have become
quite social, and so she's marginally accepting. His dad *is*
accepting and always seems slightly amused by us. Todd,
of course, is always happy to see me, and I find that the
more time I spend with him, the less uncomfortable I am.
He's kind of growing on me.

"What? When?" I ask.

"In a couple of weeks."

"For, like, the weekend?"

"No, we're going for a week."

"A *week*?" I sit up, and he follows. "But . . ." I trail off and
look around his yard as if it might suddenly spring up with
little signs answering my questions. "What am I supposed to
do without you for a whole week?"

I feel a little panicky at the thought and tell myself it's only because I'm going to have a hard time continuing my campaign with him gone.

"I don't know. How did you survive before me?" I give him a dirty look and shove him in the chest. He dramatically rolls away from me, doing an entire backward flip over. I try not to laugh, but he's such a geek I can't help it.

"Ow," he moans. "Don't do that. You don't know your own *strength*."

"You're such a dork," I tell him, rolling my eyes.

"Yeah, that's why you love me."

"In your dreams, my little Goldum."

Now it's his turn to laugh.

"You mean *Gollum*."

"Whatever."

He's been trying to convert me into a sci-fi geek, but it seems I'm a hopeless case. His mother, Mrs. Brady/Cleaver comes walking out to the tramp, carrying two lemonades. I almost groan at the all-American-ness of it. She makes her presence *very* well known whenever I am over, always bringing us treats or suddenly having chores to do wherever we are. *You would suppose the woman didn't trust me*, I think wryly.

"How are your parents, Jennifer?" She always calls me by my full name even though Trevor has told her repeatedly I prefer Jen.

I almost think she does it to annoy me—and it does— which might explain my automatic flippant response that I have honed over the years for the amusement of my friends.

"Dead and in prison, thanks for asking."

Only as she freezes in the act of handing the lemonade over do I realize what I've said. I glance at Trevor and see a pained look on his face.

"Oh, sorry, you meant the *fosters*. I mean, the Grants." I laugh nervously. "I just realized I live with the Foster Grants," I babble uneasily. "You know, like the sunglasses?"

She's still staring at me, stricken, and Trevor's expression isn't far off. I decide it's a good time for retreat.

"I gotta go, Trev. Thanks for the drink, Mrs. Br—Hoffman."

I scramble off the tramp, shoving my feet into my flip-flops, and make a quick exit through the gate.

"Jen, wait."

Trevor catches up to me at the end of the driveway.

"Let me drive you home."

"That's okay. It's a nice day. I can walk."

"Can I walk with you then?"

"Free country," I say, walking away, leaving him to follow.

"You okay?" he asks a few silent minutes later. He has that concerned look again.

"Look, Trev, if you're gonna walk with me, then no heavy conversation, okay?"

"Okay," he agrees, but the mood has been dampened and it's a quiet walk home. He leaves me at my door with a quick kiss.

***

I'm lying on my bed, bummed about how bad this day has turned out when my foster Sue comes in, wearing the straw hat. She's obviously been out working in the yard. She's been trying to be a little more interactive lately but not overly intrusive, which makes it hard for me to be resentful about it.

"You don't look too happy," she states the obvious.

"Yeah, Trevor just told me he's going to be gone in a couple of weeks." I decide to skip the whole other issue that has depressed me. "I'm looking forward to a long, boring week hanging around here while he's gone."

"You've gotten to be pretty good friends with him, huh?"

"I guess."

"Carol called."

"Who?"

"Carol—Trevor's mom."

Funny, I haven't really ever thought of her as having a name. It's somewhat ironic that she shares a name with *the* Mrs. Brady. I speculate idly whether her middle name is June.

"What did she want?" I wonder if she called to tattle on my slip of the tongue.

"She called to invite our family to go camping with them."

I gasp, sitting up and turning to face her.

"What do you think?" she asks.

"You're asking me?"

"Well, Pat and I think it sounds like fun, but we decided it should be your decision. I don't know how you feel about camping but thought you might like to go if Trevor was going."

This is an amazing development—an adult who asks my opinion instead of telling me what I should want. I think about saying no just to see if I really can wield that kind of power, but I don't want to blow the chance to *not* have to spend a week waiting for Trevor to get home.

"Sure, why not?" I say, thinking that Trevor would appreciate that response.

***

"A *tent*?" I'm horrified.

"What did you expect? A wilderness hotel?" Pat holds

out his hand for one of the tent stakes I'm holding.

"No." I know I'm pouting, but I'm definitely not happy. "But at least maybe a *trailer* or something. *Anything* with a solid roof and walls."

Pat looks up at me and gives me a sardonic look.

"I feel certain that you'll survive this experience."

"Yeah, easy for you to say. It's not you sharing a tent with the cheerleader," I mumble.

"What was that?" he asks distractedly as he pounds the stake into the hard ground.

"I said it'll be on your head if I don't. They probably throw people in prison when they allow their foster kids to get eaten alive by a bear because they only have tents to camp in."

Pat laughs at that. I don't think he'll be laughing when they take his badge away for child endangerment.

"Okay, grab the other side of that pole and help me set this up."

Once we have the tents set up and all of our equipment stowed and organized, we gather at the Hoffmans' camp to cook dinner together. Trevor can see I'm in a bad mood and tries to tease me out of it. Not even an excited hug from my buddy Todd helps.

Trevor even does his Schwarzenegger impression because usually that makes me laugh. To be honest, even now I have to bite the inside of my cheek to hold back the smile trying to break out.

"Not gonna work today, Trev. I have to sleep in a *tent* with the *cheerleader*. Double whammy."

"You have to sleep with whom?"

"The cheerleader."

He looks blank.

"*Tamara.*"

"She's coming?" He perks up at the news, and I glare daggers at him. He laughs.

"I love your jealousy," he says.

"I'm *not* jealous of her."

"Riiight." The word is drawn out and cynical.

"Hey, Trevor, why don't you and Jennifer come and help us with these potatoes?" Mrs. Brady/Cleaver calls out chirpily, looking perfectly campy in her hiking boots and plaid vest.

"She likes to be called Jen," I hear Sue tell her from inside what they are all cheerfully calling "the supply tent," and my brows raise a little at her defense of me.

"Oh, right. Trevor told me that. I keep forgetting."

I'll bet you do.

We peel potatoes until I want to scream and then have to wait eons until we finally eat my first ever Dutch oven–cooked meal. It's the best thing I've ever tasted. The only thing that sours it is the arrival of the cheerleader just as we're finishing up. She should have been home from school sooner but was on some kind of mini-vacation with some friends. I wish she could have stayed just one week longer—or two months, two years, whatever.

Trevor ducks into the tent he's sharing with Todd and comes back out with a guitar. I'm shocked; I didn't know he played the guitar. He comes and sits near me, and I watch the cheerleader get up on pretense of stretching, only to reseat herself much closer to Trevor on the other side.

He starts messing around, jumping from song to song, not really playing, just goofing. Then with a slantwise grin at me, he starts jamming "Great Balls of Fire." I didn't even know it was possible to play that on guitar.

His father gets into it, and the two of them sing loudly with overdone twang in their voice, Todd joining in on the "Great Balls of Fire" words. They're kind of amusing. When they finish, everyone else claps, the cheerleader the loudest, but I only smile my secret smile for Trevor when he looks at me to gauge my reaction.

"Trevor will now be taking requests," his father announces in his best DJ imitation. Of course, the cheerleader is the first to jump on that.

"Oh, Trevor, do you know 'Father Abraham'?"

I roll my eyes at the geekiness of her request, but as Trevor is a true geek himself, he of course knows it, and everyone joins in—except for me. Then his father jumps into the bear song, which Trevor immediately picks up on.

"The other day," his father booms in his baritone and points at Mrs. Brady/Cleaver, who immediately echoes him.

"I saw a bear." Now he points at the cheerleader who happily echoes the words in pitch perfect tune.

"Out in the woods." He points at me, and suddenly everyone is quiet, even Trevor. I look at him, and he gives me a challenging look, brows raised, daring me.

I look over at the cheerleader, and she is triumphant in her certainty that I will make this miserable for everyone, so I look at Trevor's dad and echo him blandly. He laughs along with my fosters and moves on to the next person.

I don't sing along any more than that, but when I look over at Trevor, he smiles happily at me. The cheerleader is sullen—both good things.

***

The next morning when I crawl out of the cold, damp death trap, it's to see Trevor and his dad jogging past. Trevor sees me and stops. His dad slows a little, turning to jog backwards for a few steps.

"See you two at breakfast."

Trevor helps me up off the ground, and I feel self-conscious about my plain gray sweats and bed-head hair.

"Don't let me interrupt your run," I say.

"We're done. We were just headed back to camp."

"You jog a lot?"

"Almost every morning with my dad."

"Huh. That's something I didn't know about you."

"Just another of my secret talents." He grins, waggling his eyebrows comically.

I reach up to smooth my hair. "I look like crap," I complain.

Trevor pulls his ball cap off his head. He plops it on my head, smoothing my hair back behind my ears.

"I think you look cute," he says. I groan.

"Why do you say such mean things to me?" I ask.

"Come on, let's go get breakfast," he laughs.

Two hours later the cheerleader emerges, looking like she *is* staying in a wilderness hotel with all of the accompanying conveniences like mirrors and hair equipment, makeup perfectly in place. I am makeup free since I have no idea how to maintain my look while living primitively.

"Let me show you a camping trick I learned when I had longer hair," Sue tells me later. She pulls my hair back into two braids, then puts a triangled bandana over the top. She hands me a mirror, and I'm surprised. It's not really my kind of look, but definitely not bad—kind of biker-chick. I can deal with that.

After lunch, everyone decides to go for a hike. Even the cheerleader, though from the reaction of her parents, I can tell this is unusual. Sue took me a week ago to get hiking boots, showing me how to break them in. Apparently it didn't work so well; I end up with three blisters by the time we are at the peak.

"Here," Trevor says, kneeling down in front of me as I sit on a rock. He pulls my boots off, covering the blisters with some kind of cream and bandages.

"I thought you were supposed to pop blisters," I moan miserably.

"No, the skin forms a kind of natural protection. Can you make it back down?"

"Do I have a choice?"

His dad finds me a walking stick, and the cheerleader pouts about the attention I'm getting. She's in peak physical condition, so she doesn't have anything to complain about, as can be evidenced by the healthy glow emanating from her. Even Todd is doing better than me, not winded at all and chatting happily. He had worried over my blisters, patting my hand, until the blisters were covered with bandages. He then promptly forgot about them.

I'm slowing them down going back to camp, so I tell them to go ahead and I'll catch up. Trevor elects to stay with me, as I knew (hoped) he would. Unfortunately, so does the cheerleader. Because of the stick, Trevor can't really walk next to me, so she uses this opportunity to sidle up next to him, the narrowness of the trail forcing closeness. I seriously consider stabbing her with the walking stick.

"So, Trevor, have you played the guitar long?" she oozes.

"Only for about two years or so."

"Wow, you're really good for only playing that long."

"I've played the piano as long as I can remember. There's

not that much difference between the two, so it was pretty easy to pick up."

"I'd *love* to hear you play the piano."

Gag.

"Well, I didn't bring it up here with me, so . . ." He trails off, and she giggles like it's the funniest thing she's ever heard. I calculate the probability of causing her serious harm by tripping her with the stick. Unfortunately it's not that steep of a trail.

Then she tucks her arm through his, and my jaw clenches. Trevor glances back at me at the gesture and stops walking, turning back toward me, which effectively breaks her hold.

"You okay, Jen? Do you need to rest for a while?"

"I'm fine," I growl. "I don't want to stop. Let's just get back to camp." I don't want to spend one minute longer with the cheerleader than necessary.

"Okay, let me help you then." He takes the walking stick and hands it to Tamara. She isn't sure what he's up to and takes it without much thought. He walks in front of me, facing away, and pulls my arms around his shoulders.

"Jump up," he says.

"*What*?" Tamara says it at the same time I do.

"I'm going to carry you."

"No way, Trev. I'm too heavy."

"You don't weigh anything. It's pretty flat from here anyway."

"Trev, I don't think—"

He turns to face me, giving me a meaningful look.

"Here's the deal, Jen. You can get on my back, or I can throw you over my shoulder and carry you that way. You decide."

"It'll kill you."

"I've carried backpacks heavier than you on worse terrain than this. I'm not as weak as you think."

"I don't think you're weak."

The cheerleader sighs loudly, and I glance over his shoulder to see her watching this exchange unhappily. She definitely doesn't want Trevor to carry me.

"Okay. Let's ride," I tell him.

Trevor is a strong walker. He doesn't get winded or slow down, even with my weight on his back. Tamara walks just ahead of us, glancing back frequently. I decide to give her some misery. I cuddle closer to Trevor, keeping my face very close to his, whispering things into his ear to make him grin. She's angry by the time we reach camp.

I know Trevor guesses what I'm up to. I don't think he minds.

10

Marshmallows and Competition

I TASTE MY first roasted marshmallow, cooked by Trevor after I've burned five of them. It's delicious. The cheerleader asks him to cook her one, and because he is still Trevor the Polite, he does it. *I* don't have to ask. He makes me another, then as many as I want, without me ever asking. That burns her.

Lying in the tent with her that night, I'm looking out through the open screen roof at the amazing display of stars above us. I have never seen so many stars, but Trevor explained that they are always there; we just can't see them because of all the city lights. I try to find the constellations he pointed out to me.

"Jen?" My whispered name comes from the cheerleader's sleeping bag.

"What?" I hope my tone effectively conveys my irritation at the interruption of my contentment.

"So, are you, like, *after* Trevor?"

"After him how?"

"I mean, do you *like* him?"

"Of course I like him."

"No, do you *like* him like him?"

"He's my friend. Of course I like him."

"Are you being purposely dense?" She sounds frustrated, and I smile to myself because I am. Dropping the smile, I turn to face her, propping myself up on my elbow.

"What are you asking, Tamara? What do you want?"

"He's pretty cute," she says.

"I guess. If you're into nerds."

"He's really nice too. Strong. He carried you like you were nothing. And he's funny. *And* he has a great voice." There's a slow burn in my stomach at her words, so my own are harsh.

"Is there a point to this inane conversation about Trevor's superior character traits?"

"I think I kind of like him. So if you're not interested in him in that way, then I thought, you know, I could—"

"Aren't you a little old for him?" I cut her off.

"No, I'm only eighteen. And he's seventeen, right?"

"You're in college."

"I graduated early. I'm probably only a year older than him, if that."

I hadn't realized she's so close to my own age. She's two years ahead of me, school-wise, so I just figured she was at least that much older than me years-wise as well.

"If you don't have a problem with it, I think I might go for him."

Her words make me want to strangle her, but what can I say? *No, he's my pet project who I happen to like even though I didn't plan to and who thinks I'm something I'm not, so stay away until I've finished with him?*

"Knock yourself out," I say irritably, rolling back over to gaze out again. I don't think Trevor will stray. He's hooked pretty well in my snare. I think. I hope.

This could be fun to watch, anyway.

I pretend there aren't tears running down my cheeks.

***

She gets up early and makes herself into a cute jogger, hurrying to time her emergence from the tent just as Trevor and his father are warming up. She's obviously dressed for jogging, so what can the courteous pair of them do but invite her to join them?

To Trevor's credit, he sticks his head into my tent and asks if I want to come.

"Blisters," I say, pointing at my feet.

She follows him relentlessly all day, flirting shamelessly, laughing idiotically at everything he says. Later in the day, he manages to ditch her, no easy feat, and pulls me quickly away into the dense trees surrounding the campsite, walking quickly until we're out of earshot of everyone else.

"Can we slow it down, Jar Jar Blinky? The feet are protesting," I complain.

He turns to me with an apology.

"Sorry. And it's Jar Jar *Binks*."

"Yeah, right, I knew that. What's the hurry?"

"Escape."

"Escape?" I lower my voice conspiratorially. "From who? Or is it whom? I can never remember."

"From your sister." He sounds stalked.

"I don't have a sister," I say firmly, the teasing gone from my voice.

"Okay. Your *foster* sister. Whatever. She's driving me *crazy*."

This piece of news makes me happy.

"Yeah? What's she doing?"

"Everywhere I turn, there she is. She's constantly

underfoot, asking me all kinds of questions and laughing at everything I say, when it's not even funny. What's the *deal*?"

I nod seriously, considering his dilemma.

"I think I can help you, my young pad-a-man."

"Padawan," he corrects.

"Don't correct me," I continue, playing up my detective role, pacing and pulling on my chin, hand on hip. "I'm onto something."

I look at him silently until his patience ends—which is a total of about five seconds.

"*What*?" he explodes. I shrug and return to being just me.

"She likes you." He stares at me, stunned.

"*Likes* me? Isn't she a little old to like a high school kid?"

"No, she's only eighteen, graduated early. She should be a senior, going to school with us. Wouldn't that be a joy?"

"Why would she like *me*?"

I hold up a hand, ticking off her words on my fingers. "She says you're cute, funny, have a great voice, you're strong . . ." I trail off and drop my hands, shrugging. "Most likely because she can sense that I do, and she's nothing if not competitive."

He looks at me suspiciously.

"How do you know all of this?"

"She told me."

"She *what*?" He's incredulous.

"Last night she asked me if I thought she should go for you."

"And what did you say?"

"I told her to knock herself out."

"*What*?" His tone indicates his indecision over whether to be more angry or astonished by this.

"Never let it be said that I limited your options," I say, holding up one finger to punctuate my words.

He glares at me for a few minutes. Finally he walks toward me, deliberately, in a way that puts me on the defensive.

"You *are* going to pay for this," he says.

"Oh yeah? How?"

He doesn't answer, just pulls his lips back over his teeth in a menacing grin. I stand my ground.

"I'm not afraid of you."

"You should be," he says as he swoops down and throws me over his shoulder like a sack of potatoes.

"Put me down, you jerk," I yell, laughing, pounding his back.

He ignores me, striding with purpose. I can't see where we're going since I'm hanging behind his back, but it isn't long until I hear the rush of the river. I stiffen.

"Don't you dare, Trev."

"You have to learn a lesson, Cassandra."

"*Star Trek*! I know what that's from. That has to be my get out of jail free card!"

"Sorry, but not this time," he says, not sounding sorry at all.

He steps into the waist-deep river, dumping me in fully, freezing water submerging me. I come up sputtering and laughing, and he's standing, legs spread, head to profile, arms crossed over his chest in victory, looking fierce. I laugh because I know this stance.

"You're going down, Hercules," I say as I tackle him around the knees. He goes down easily, not even trying to stay up, coming up spluttering and splashing as if he's drowning. So I shove a handful of water at him, and the fight is on.

Finally, he catches me around the waist and pulls me close so that I can't splash him again.

"Your lips are blue," he tells me.

"Yours are too," I say, wrapping my arms around his shoulders.

"I know how to warm them up," he says.

In spite of the cold water surrounding us and permeating our bodies, this kiss has more heat in it than any he has given me before.

As we walk back to camp, clasped together and shivering, he asks, "Will you please call your sister off?"

I let his use of the term ride, knowing he's trying to rile me.

"Absolutely not. This is going to be way too much fun to watch."

"Just remember you said that," he threatens. "Because turnabout is fair play, right?"

"What does that mean?" I ask suspiciously. He only grins forebodingly in response.

Trevor turns it up with Tamara, being overly charming and courteous to a fault with her. Of course, this encourages her, and she presses her own suit harder, which only ends up annoying Trevor. *Very* amusing. After only one day he realizes he's only digging his own grave, so he goes back to ditching her whenever possible, pulling me along with him.

When she doesn't get the hint, he sings a sappy love song at the campfire, looking right at me, clearly singing it to me. She still doesn't catch on. He decides he has to be even more blatant.

I'm leaning against a tree, watching him try to maneuver away from her as she sits right next to him, helping him shuck corn. He had asked me to help them with a pleading look in his eyes, but she quickly negated that. So I'm simply watching, controlling the grin at his discomfiture. He finishes his pile in record time and comes over to me.

He puts one hand against the tree, leaning toward me.

"Please help me," he begs. His plea is genuine, and so I decide to show him some mercy.

"She's going into the tent," I tell him. "Kiss me."

"How's that going to help if she can't see?"

"You need a reason to kiss me?"

He thinks about this for all of half a second.

"Good point."

He leans in, lips on mine, placing his other hand against the tree on the opposite side of me, not touching me in any other way. A few seconds later, I hear the telltale gasp and know she has seen. He hears it too if his smile against my mouth is any indication. She loudly stomps away.

"Thank you," he says, leaning his forehead against mine. "She is *relentless*." A little worm of guilt wriggles through me. She isn't the only one who's relentless. My goal comes closer with every kiss.

"By the way, it's been nice seeing your face all week."

"You see my face every day," I say, confused.

He touches my cheek. "I mean your *real* face, not hidden behind all of that make-up. You're so beautiful."

"You're a dork, Trev," I say, looking away, embarrassed by the compliment.

"No, I'm not. I'm Hercules. You told me that yourself." I laugh and push him away.

That night he puts his arm around me when we sit around the fire, and I scoff at the silly gesture in my mind to reassure my friends that I did. Underneath I feel all warm and fuzzy.

He holds my hand, and I know I'm reeling him in, even if my heart pitter-patters a bit whenever he does.

He kisses me, and I pretend not to notice that my toes curl a little each time he does.

I decide I really like camping.

11

MR. GREEN IN THE STUDY WITH THE CANDLESTICK

LIFE BACK home with the cheerleader is not pleasant. She's pretty upset about the whole Trevor thing. I think she's under the impression that I made a move after she informed me of her intentions. I have no desire to enlighten her to the fact that Trevor and I had already a sort of arrangement.

Last year when I first came to stay with the Grants, the cheerleader had just left for college. She moved out the weekend before I moved in, so other than holidays, we haven't had to live under the same roof. Probably not a good plan to aggravate her as we're going to be spending the entire summer here, but then I've never been known to do what is best.

Third Saturdays have become a big part of the game. It makes Trevor happy that I willingly go with him each month to help. I would never admit it aloud, but I've come to realize that I really like the old geezers. Some I like better than others, mostly the ones who have been accepting of my presence all along, no matter how odd I look to them.

Mrs. Green has become one of my favorites, mainly because she steadfastly maintains that she was married to the infamous Mr. Green from the *Clue* game, and that he did it in the study with the candlestick. She can't usually remember what she had for lunch or what some of her grandkids' names are, but she always recalls her *Clue* story in perfect clarity with a glint in her eyes.

She and I are kindred spirits. She recognized it right away and has told me numerous stories of her wild teenage days. Funny because I just always imagined that when someone her age would've been my age, all teens would have been prim and proper. I don't tell her much about me because I don't want to dim our unlikely friendship even if she forgets things easily. She always remembers Trevor and me though, calling him my "young man."

I'm sitting with her, *crocheting* of all things. She had told me once that she wants to teach her granddaughter, but her granddaughter never comes to see her. No one ever comes to see her. I don't have a grandma, and since she seems to have been abandoned by her granddaughter, we have adopted one another. That's why I sit and crochet.

"Are you being nice to your foster family?" She always asks me this question, every week.

"It was easier before their daughter came home, you know? She really doesn't like me, and I don't like her, so I'm having a hard time being nice."

"She's jealous."

"What?" My hands still, and I look over at her.

"Well," she pauses, turning the afghan over on her lap as she begins a new row, "you've taken her place as the youngest daughter."

I shake my head. "I'm not a daughter. I'm just a foster kid."

"They don't treat you as part of the family?" She looks upset.

"Yeah, they do. I even have stupid chores. Doesn't make me a daughter."

"Ah, yes, chores. I complained about them to no end, resented having to do them, and resented my mother for giving them to me. That is, until I had my own home where *every* chore was mine. Then I wished I could go back to simply having the few chores my mother gave me. Did I ever tell you I was adopted?"

I look at her, surprised.

"No, you didn't." I look down at the lopsided mess that I'd imagined presenting to Trevor as a scarf when finished. I think I'll present it to the trash can instead.

"My own parents were killed in a car accident when I was only thirteen, such a critical age for a young girl." Her eyes never leave her gnarled hands, which keep gracefully twisting the yarn into an afghan.

"I was angry," she continues. "That's why I acted out so much. My adoptive mother and father had never had children, and I was not easy for them. But they always loved me, no matter what I did." Her faded blue eyes come up to mine. "My biggest regret in life is that I treated them so poorly when they were only trying to do right by me. Thank heavens they lived long enough for me to straighten up and thank them, to give them back some of the love they had so profusely given me."

She looks back down at the work she is performing.

"My other regret is that I didn't have a sister."

"She's not my sister." I know I sound petulant, but I can't imagine ever being grateful to have the cheerleader in my life.

"She's the closest thing you have," she says as she leans down to pull a new skein of yarn from her bag.

I'm silent, thinking about her words. I think of all the families I've been through and wonder how many of them had had sincerely good intentions that I've thrown away.

"Tell me about your parents," she says, and I know instinctively that she's speaking of my biological parents and not my foster parents. I have never told anyone the whole truth, only partial truths and only to serve my own purposes. I know that I can tell Mrs. Green and that she'll never breathe a word I say to anyone else, that there's a chance she won't remember most of what I say.

She patiently waits, and whether I tell her or not, she won't judge me. I set my crocheting down, look around to make sure no one is near and lean closer to her.

"I wish *my* parents had died in a car accident. That would have been so much better than the reality of them." She looks up at me, brows raised curiously. I shrug. "My dad had custody of me when he and my mother divorced because she didn't want me. I was really young, probably only two or three.

"Until I was six, my dad used me as his personal punching bag. He didn't ever enroll me in school, and so no one knew. When I was six, he got his gun out and commanded me to stand in the corner so that he could shoot me. I was afraid of him, and young enough to not know I could refuse, so I did it. It was a game to him. He was shooting all around me, wanting to scare me, which it did like you can't imagine. Someone heard and called the police. He died when the police came and shot him because he wouldn't put his gun down." I take a deep breath. Even after all these years, the memory terrifies me.

"So I went to live with my mom, who couldn't much be bothered with me since she was trying to survive her violently abusive new husband. I think she would have put up with him forever, because he mostly left me alone, only sometimes beating me. Until the day he came to visit me in the night." I stop, shuddering at the remembrance. I have to remind myself that he's gone now, that he'll never hurt me again.

"It was only once, but she heard my crying even though he had my mouth covered. She walked in, stopping him. The next day, she stabbed him until he died while he was passed out drunk." I shrug. "Now she's in prison."

I glance up, and Mrs. Green's eyes are on me, full of empathy.

"You've had a rough go of it, haven't you?"

I smile at her simple description of the hell that is my history.

"Could be worse, I guess."

"It always can, can't it? Though that seems to be bad enough," she says, clucking and patting me on the arm, as if she can sense that any more would undo me. That's why I like her so much, because she just *knows*.

I'm feeling a little watery inside, a little self-pity party going on, which wouldn't be the end of the world, except I hear a noise behind me and turn around to see Trevor standing there, watching me intently.

He heard—I can see it in his face. I read blatant sympathy there, which I know is genuine because it's how the geek works.

I run away from his sympathy, pushing past him and out the front doors of the Senior Center, looking for somewhere to hide. Then he is there. He pulls me into his arms and holds me, just holds me, nothing else, no false words of comfort, no groping, not asking anything of me, just giving me his strength.

And I'm undone.

12

NEW RESOLVE FROM THE LOST GIRL

TREVOR DOESN'T try to talk to me about what he overheard, and I'm grateful. There are a few social workers who know the whole story, but I don't think they've told any of my foster families. If they have, none of them have cared to mention it to me.

When I return home after we have a mostly silent dinner at the local diner—a happy medium between the Italian place and the pizza place, which is becoming a regular hangout for the two of us—it's to find the cheerleader sitting in my room. She's at the vanity looking at the picture of Trevor and I from the camping trip that's hanging on my mirror, right above the one snapped by Beth at Morp. I let out an unwelcoming grunt.

"What do you want? I'm not in the mood," I say, walking in and throwing my jacket across the bed. She doesn't say anything for a minute, just looks at the picture. Then she turns around and takes in the rest of the room slowly, eyes finally coming to rest on me where I'm sitting on the bed.

"Why don't you have any other pictures hanging in here, or anything at all that's yours?"

"What do you care?" I shoot back.

"Just seems odd to me," she murmurs.

"Well, if you have to know, I don't exactly have a lot of personal things."

She looks at me, a bit surprised that I'm so candid. I'm a bit stunned myself. I didn't mean to be, not with her.

"I don't think Mom or Dad would care if you wanted to get some things to put up. This room feels so . . . I don't know, like a showcase or something."

I shrug. "Doesn't matter; I'm not planning to be here all that long anyway."

She looks at me questioningly, but amazingly enough doesn't pursue that line of questioning. She has something else on her mind.

"Did you do it just to make a fool of me?" she asks, and I struggle to understand. What does moving out or hanging up a picture have to do with her? I guess I look confused because she clarifies.

"With Trevor, when we were camping? Did you steal him away just to make me look stupid? Or was it some kind of thing where you wanted to prove you were . . . I don't know, better, or sexier, or more appealing, or whatever, than I am?"

I think about telling her yes and letting her live with that. She doesn't seem angry or upset, though, just curious, and after the emotions of tonight, I find I don't care if she knows the truth. I'm not in the mood for games just now.

"No, I didn't. *We* didn't. Honestly. Trevor and I were already kinda . . . together, I guess. We were just trying to keep it on the down-low, you know? And when you asked me . . . I guess I just wanted to see what you could do, see if his head could be turned." I think about my words, what they are implying, and shy away from the thought.

"I'm sorry, it was a rotten thing to do to you," I say. Oddly enough, the words are the truth.

She nods, believing me.

"I guess he must really like you, huh?" Then she laughs. "I guess that sounds really conceited, like I'm so desirable that he must *really* like you to resist me. I didn't mean it like that."

I look at her, trying to figure out this weird absence of tension between us. "It's okay. You wouldn't be far wrong. If I'm being truthful, Trevor definitely belongs with someone like you and not me."

"Yeah? Why's that?" She seems truly interested.

"Come on," I say sarcastically. "I'm all dark and hard—trouble. You're light and bubbly, the . . . well, the cheerleader-type." I mentally cringe at the nickname I always call her.

"I've heard you call me that," she says. I look at the floor, not wanting to meet her eyes. "It's okay though."

I lift my brows at that, and she shrugs.

"I was a cheerleader in high school. I'd probably be one still at college if I had time."

"Why are you in here being nice to me?" I ask abruptly. "I haven't exactly done much to endear myself to you."

She shrugs and gets up, walking to the door.

"You should get some personal stuff in here," she says at the doorway. "I think my parents would really like it if you stayed."

She walks out the door but turns and sticks her head back into the room for a parting comment.

"I don't think you're as bad as you like to pretend you are. I wouldn't mind if you stayed either."

I flop back on the bed, feeling washed out. I roll onto my side, curling up in a ball, pressing my fists against my heart—too many roller-coaster emotions in one day for me.

"I'm *not* going soft, I'm *not* going soft," I repeat quietly, over and over, a litany. I reach behind me and pull the comforter over myself, too tired to get up and get ready for bed.

"*I am not going soft,*" I say again. Somehow, the words seem empty.

***

I wake up in the morning, weary. I look at myself in the mirror, surprised at the face looking back. *I* am lost somewhere under this face that shows an unfamiliar complacency.

This whole deal with Trevor is supposed to be me turning him, not the other way around. No real feelings involved. I strengthen my resolve, take a deep breath, and stiffen my spine. I'm not here to be friends with a cheerleader or to become anything resembling a real daughter, and I'm definitely not here to fall in love with some geek.

"Trev," I say later when we're in my room, me pacing the floor and Trevor sitting on the edge of the bed. He's a little disappointed in me today, I can tell. I'm back, the real me, the same one who first approached him so many months ago—a lifetime ago, it seems. He saw it right away by the full-force return of my look with severe makeup, wearing the tightest sweater and shortest skirt I own. I am dressed for success.

"Yeah?" he asks, clearly uncomfortable with my harsh tone.

"Look, we spend a lot of time doing what you want. I've watched more sci-fi movies than I even knew were available, spent time with your friends who are *definitely* not my type, gone with you to do charity, camped in a tent for you, went to your family reunion—"

"What is with you today?" he interrupts my tirade. "You've been on edge all day."

"What, you mean I'm not my usual cheery, sweet self?" I ask sardonically.

"Something like that," he murmurs. Then louder, "If this is because of what happened yesterday . . ." He trails off, and I know he's thinking about my unguarded confession to Mrs. Green. But I don't want to talk about that.

"Actually, *Trev*," he cringes at the way I spit his name, "this whole thing is feeling a little one-sided."

"*What*? What are you saying?" He's bewildered, palms up in supplication.

"How many times have I asked you to come with me, hang out with my friends?"

"You used to ask all the time, but you haven't asked for a long time."

His statement is true, but I'm not about to admit that.

"Well, I'm asking now. Or do I have to forsake my friends on top of everything else I've given up for you?"

"That's incredibly unfair, Jen. I haven't asked you to give up anything."

"Really? Is that what you think? Then why have you been looking at me like that all day?"

"Like what?"

"Disgusted because I look the same as I did when you first met me instead of like the watered-down version I've become lately."

He gets up, walking over to stand right in front of me, effectively cutting off my pacing. He's right in my face and though I can see the storm raging in his eyes, he doesn't yell or try to intimidate.

"I was attracted to you from the first minute you

walked up to me, and you know it. You made sure of it. I wouldn't care if you were now bald and covered in warts. Your *looks* aren't why I like you, why I want to be with you." His jaw clenches as he glares at me. "I'll talk to you later," he bites out.

I watch, stunned, as he walks out. Trevor has never walked away from me. My sails deflate, and I sink down on my bed. This isn't how I pictured it going. I wanted him to grovel, to do whatever I wanted to keep me happy.

Fifteen minutes later my phone rings. It's Trevor.

"Yeah?" I growl roughly, wanting him to know I'm still angry.

"When?" he asks. This throws me.

"When what?" It's hard to sound mad when you're confused.

"When do you want us to hang out with your friends?"

"Saturday," I shoot back, knowing there will be a party somewhere.

"Okay. I'll pick you up at seven."

"Fine."

"And Jen?"

"Yeah?"

"You're right—we have only done the things I've wanted. I'm sorry if I made you feel like what you want isn't important to me. It is."

I sigh. Why does he have to be such a dork, making my insides all gooey by saying such things?

"I'm sorry too. I don't want to fight with you."

"So, where are we going on Saturday?"

I hedge a little, afraid he'll back out if I tell him it's a party. "I don't know. I'll have to find out what's going on and let you know."

"Okay."

I feel that little worm of guilt trying to push its way up again at his easy acceptance and trust in me, so I push it down and offer a tiny olive branch.

"How about if you come over at six, and I'll make you something to eat first?"

"You cook?" he asks in disbelief.

"You're not the only one who has hidden talents, Scully."

"Scully's a woman. I think you mean Mulder."

"Maybe, maybe not," I say and hang up to the sound of his laughter.

13

Chicken, Flat Soda, and Vines

ON SATURDAY morning, my foster mother takes me shopping for food when I tell her my plan to make dinner for Trevor. I'm sure she has great hope that the nerd holds influence over me and will change me into the ideal foster child that she can show the world with pride.

One of the things I make is a killer chicken dish, although it's a talent I hoard. I let Sue give me advice on how to cook, since she's unaware of my ability. I tell her I want to do chicken and potatoes and let her chatter about preparation. After all, she's footing the bill.

I could get a job, but past experience has taught me that doing that only gives foster parents the idea of forcing me to purchase all of my personal necessities instead of getting them for me. I figure since they're getting money from the state for the dubious honor of having me live in their homes, they should pay for everything.

When we get back to the house, she hovers a little, but pretty soon I look over to see her smiling at me like the cat that ate the canary.

"What?" I ask.

"You've been keeping a secret, haven't you?"

My mind immediately races to discover which of my many secrets she might have discovered. I shake my head in denial, waiting for her to tell me which one she's discovered.

"I think you've been in a kitchen before. You almost look like a pro."

"Yeah, right." I shrug, relieved that this is her discovery.

"Seriously, you're cooking with a natural ease, and you look pretty happy doing it."

I hurry and put a scowl on my face, but this just makes her laugh.

"Ever thought of becoming a chef? Maybe opening your own restaurant someday?" she asks as I lean into the fridge to pull some items out.

I school my face before looking up at her—I don't want her to see on my face how close she has come to guessing my only dream, the one that crushes me with its impossibility.

"Maybe I can be a cook at the diner. Being a *chef* requires schooling. Somehow I don't see college in my future," I tell her.

"Why not? You're definitely smart enough."

"You've seen my grades, right?"

"I have, yes. I also know they aren't a true reflection of what you're capable of."

My anger sparks.

"And you know this after knowing me for less than a year?" I ask sharply.

"Yes." Her answer is simple, straightforward. I roll my eyes. She's almost as impossibly nice as Trevor is.

"Mind if I watch and learn?" Her question surprises me—and pleases me a little. I've never had *anyone* want to learn from me—if you discount some of the things I've taught my friends that were either illegal or at least not fit for polite company, as the saying goes.

When Trevor shows up—bringing me a big apology bouquet of wild flowers in true geek fashion—he makes my day with his genuine praise for my culinary skills. I'm also happy that he's come casual in a plain gray T-shirt and jeans, keeping the nerdiness to a minimum—and looking pretty hot in the process, I have to say.

"You look good, Trev," I tell him and get a kiss for my compliment.

***

The party is being held at a house I'm unfamiliar with. It belongs to a new kid who moved in after the end of the school year. Beth met him and found they had many of the same interests, those mainly being partying, skipping school, and adding piercings to their bodies—all things that had once been my center of interest as well.

"His parents named him Adama after some character in a movie, one I've never heard of. Some kind of battle movie or something," Beth had told me earlier when I called to tell her I was finally getting Trevor to a party.

"*Battlestar Galactica*," I said.

"What?" Her tone suggested I'd spoken in a foreign language, and I realized I knew this without even asking Trevor. *Wait till I tell him*, I thought.

"That's the name of the movie."

"And you know this because . . ."

"Long story." I changed the subject, not wanting her to know the extent of the geek knowledge I have absorbed. "Listen, Beth, this is Trevor's first party. Kind of spread the word to take it easy on him, will you? It won't help my case if we plunge him in full force."

"You abandon us all summer and you want our help?"

"I told you, it's a process. Tell Kyle. He'll take care of it."

She didn't make any promises, but as Trevor and I arrive at the party and walk in the front door, I can see she has talked to Kyle. The house is dim with music blaring, kids are drinking, and many of them are high, but there isn't any obvious drug usage going on; it's all being kept behind closed doors.

Beth and Ella meet us at the door, and Beth has in tow a tall, skinny kid with a flop of blond hair, bloodshot eyes lined with black, many facial piercings going on, dressed in solid black. He's exactly her type—and mine too. Then I look at clean-cut Trevor, compare him to Adama, and think maybe my type is changing a little, because Trevor looks so much better to me than Adama does.

Weird.

"Adama, this is Jen and Trevor."

Trevor glances at me with lifted brows, and I mouth, "*Battlestar Galactica*." He grins in response.

They lead us into the house, and even though Trevor and I still have something of an unspoken agreement about maintaining our "friends only" cover, he grabs my hand tightly. I look at him, wondering if it's making him nervous being here. Then he does an odd thing and pulls me closer and slightly behind him, and I understand that he's nervous about *me* being here, protecting me.

I laugh and pull away from him, stepping in front.

This is *my* turf.

Kyle comes out of a bedroom, followed by a billow of sweetly acrid smoke.

"Hey, hey, look who's decided to grace us once again with her presence," he speaks slowly, voice pitched too loud and too high. He leans in and plants a sloppy kiss on my cheek, then notices Trevor.

"Trevor, my main man," he calls, giving Trevor an uncoordinated high-five. "Long time no see."

"Yeah, how are you, uh . . ." Trevor looks to me for help.

"Kyle," I supply.

"Right, Kyle."

"I'm mellow and happy, man. Can I get you something to drink?" he slurs, leading Trevor stumblingly into the kitchen with an arm slung around his shoulder. I follow, wondering if I'm going to have to remind Kyle to take it easy.

"A Coke, I guess?" Trevor says.

"One Coke coming up."

Kyle pours a cup of flat Coke from a two-litre bottle. He gestures to an array of bottles behind him.

"Which additive, my friend?"

To his credit, Trevor keeps shock and disgust off his face as he surveys and sees that the bottles are all varieties of alcohol. He reaches out and grabs the cup from Kyle.

"Plain works for me," he says, and Kyle laughs, slapping him on the back, causing some of the Coke to spill out of the cup and over Trevor's hand.

"Someone has to be the designated driver, huh?"

Trevor just smiles humorlessly, but already Kyle is turning my way.

"And what can I get your royal cuteness?" I grimace at the unwelcome endearment.

Trevor looks at me, and I can see he's trying desperately to keep his look neutral even though he's curious about my answer.

"Diet Coke," I say, smiling at Trevor.

"Straight?" Kyle's tone indicates that this is an unusual request.

"Of course," I say firmly.

Kyle looks from Trevor to me and back again. The light bulb comes on. "Ahh, right."

I want to kick Kyle for being such a moron when I see the shadow that passes through Trevor's eyes. Kyle hands me the filled cup, and Ella comes to my rescue.

"Adama has a great patio out back. C'mon, I'll show you."

We follow her out of the hot, thick air inside the house to the clean, clear oxygen outside. There are some kids hanging out back here, talking or making out. Strangely the making-out kids make Trevor more uncomfortable than the kids drinking.

The patio is a complex pattern of bricks, with outdoor furniture around an unlit fire pit. This is hedged by wooden boxes of flowers, leading down to a carpet of dark green grass. It really is a nice yard.

"Your parents don't mind you having this many people over?" Trevor asks Adama casually, setting his cup of untouched flat pop down on the flower box ledge.

Adama smiles maliciously and gives a low laugh.

"Guess they probably would if they knew. But since they're in Paris, I doubt they'll suddenly show up."

"You don't worry they'll find something when they get home to indicate . . ." He waves his hand in the noisy direction of the house. "All of this?"

"Dude, I've got years of practice. They travel a lot." Adama laughs at his little joke, joined by Ella and Beth. Trevor looks at me like, *This is fun to you?*

"I'll be back," Trevor says to me.

"Bathroom's through the door and down the hall to your left," Adama tells him. Trevor nods as if that was his intention, but I know him. He's retreating—taking a break from what is completely different than anything he's done before.

As he goes in the house, Beth and Adama begin making out. Ella rolls her eyes and scoots over next to me.

"You got him here, but he still seems like the same old Trevor," she says. I shrug, and she looks thoughtfully toward the house where he disappeared. "Well, maybe not exactly the same. He dresses differently. Looks a little looser. Maybe your plan is working."

"Maybe," I say, not really wanting to discuss Trevor with her.

"He's actually kind of cute, don't you think?"

My camping tent conversation with the cheerleader pops into my head. This is sounding like a repeat.

"I guess," I shrug.

"You haven't hooked up with him, have you?" Her question, instead of horrified as it would have been a couple of months ago, comes out sounding hopeful. I don't want to play this game again, not with her.

"Not yet," I say and grin provocatively.

"Thinking about it then?" She's disappointed.

"Maybe," I say, knowing that will keep her away from him at least for a little while.

"Well, I guess there's always next year after you're gone." She laughs, and I smile through clenched teeth. She gets up as Trevor walks back outside, and as she passes him, she drags a hand across his chest.

"See ya later, Trev," she purrs.

"It's Trevor," he says, and my heart skips a little at his correction.

"Whatever," she says with an alluring smile.

Trevor sits next to me, stiff with tension. He looks at Beth and Adama, who are still going at it, and lets out a soft sigh that is full of distaste.

"Having fun?" I tease.

He gives me a slight smile.

"I'm sorry, Jen. I'm trying to. This just isn't my thing, you know?"

"Yeah, I do know."

He grabs my hand and threads his fingers through mine. I let him even though it sort of undoes the whole secrecy thing. I figure he needs it. Maybe I do also, a little.

"Guess this must be how you feel when we're with my friends, huh?"

"They're not so bad. I'm kinda getting used to them."

"Used to them," he repeats softly. He looks at me, eyes sad. "Guess this goes back to that odd couple thing, huh? There doesn't seem to be anywhere we're both comfortable."

"There are lots of places we're both comfortable," I argue. "We just have really different friends."

"And interests," he adds, looking back through the doorway into the house.

"Let's get out of here," I say.

"No, it's okay. These are your friends, and if you can get used to mine, I can get used to yours." His words are brave but laced with doubt.

"I *want* to go." I squeeze his hand, and he looks at me to see if I'm telling the truth or just trying to let him off the hook. Trevor doesn't belong here, not yet. I suddenly, urgently, want to get him out of here.

"You sure?"

"Yes, let's go." I lead him around the side of the house, not even stopping to tell Beth we're leaving.

"Don't you want to go in and say good-bye?"

I smile at him. Only a truly polite geek would think these kinds of kids would care about the niceties of society.

"No, I really don't."

We're around the side of the house, where vines drape both against the house and all along the fence above precisely trimmed bushes. The plants have the effect of silencing the din, giving the side yard the feeling of a private refuge. Trevor stops suddenly and pulls me into his arms, kissing me until my head is spinning.

"Thank you," he says, leaning back. "I know you're leaving just for me."

I pull him back in, and he capitulates easily, kissing me again.

"Thank *you*," I say, as he straightens up, "for coming with me in the first place."

He leans toward me again.

"It's okay," he says, grinning. "It's turning out to be pretty fun after all."

I didn't know it was possible to kiss while smiling, but I'm finding out it is.

14

KLAATU COMES IN PEACE

M Y PHONE buzzes at six in the morning, and I don't even bother to open my eyes to see who it is calling me so early.

"Yeah?" I grumble into the phone.

"So, thought you said you hadn't hooked up with him?"

"What?" I feel like I've stepped into the middle of a conversation. "Is that you, Ella?" I pull my alarm clock closer, squinting at it, as if that will change the time it reads. "Why are you up so early?"

"I'm not *up*. I haven't been to bed yet."

I think about how many times I had come home at about this same time in the past. I groan into the phone.

"Well, I have been. You woke me up."

"Sorry," she says, sounding anything but. "You told me you hadn't hooked up with your little pet yet. But that's not what I saw."

Her words bring me sharply awake, and I sit up.

"What are you talking about, Ella? It's too early for riddles."

"You and Trevor. I saw you last night. I was looking for you, and Ben told me you had left, leaving from the side yard, so I went to see if I could catch you. I saw you and Trevor there, going pretty hot and heavy."

She sounds angry, and I rub my face, trying to read into her deep silence.

"Well, El, you know how guys are," I stumble, trying to find footing in this strange conversation. "Sometimes you've gotta convince them in other ways."

"You haven't been with him that way before?" She still sounds put-out.

"No," I lie. "I mean, you gave me the idea last night."

"I did?" Now she sounds upset with herself, which is better.

"Yeah, I mean . . . he was a little upset by the party. Put yourself in his shoes. He's never been exposed to anything like that before."

"Yeah, I guess that's true."

"So if I don't want him to run away, tail tucked between his legs, I have to do something to keep him coming back, right?" I wince at talking about Trevor like this with Ella.

She laughs. "You know, Jen, you're a lot more devious than I suspected." I cringe at her assessment, mostly because it's true. "Well, keep it up, girl. I'm going to hit the sack. See you next Saturday?"

"We'll see," I say, hanging up. I lie back, but there won't be any more sleep for me now. Her words keep running through my head, and I sit straight up again. Somewhere in my game, I have come to respect Trevor, respect who he is and even his geeky values—my objective is to strip that respectability away from him, to make him more like me.

I should let him go, I think. He's not too far gone. I can stop now—step out of his life. That would be easy for me. A new foster family will most likely mean a new school, and he can move on, forget about me. I'm sure mousy

Mary Ellen will be glad to once again be the object of his affection. My stomach clenches at the thought of Trevor with her.

Even as I think of it, I know I'm too selfish to really follow through. I've been considering staying with the Grants, at least until I graduate at the end of next year. If I'm being honest, I have to admit I like them a little.

Then there's Trevor. I know there isn't any possibility of anything real between us, but I've had more fun with him over the past several months than at any other time in my life. I drop my head into my hands, scrubbing my face as if it will help solve this dilemma. I get up and walk over to the mirror, and I notice a third picture of Trevor and I stuck below the first. Where did that come from?

I pull the picture down and look at it. We're sitting on his trampoline, and I'm laughing into the camera, looking not at all like me, while Trevor's eyes are on me, lashes shadowing his eyes, dimples in evidence. I haven't seen this picture before, but I remember this day. Todd took it with his new camera, which explains why we're off-center and angled toward the corner of the photo. I press it against my chest.

There's one way for us to be together, I think. I can't ever be good enough for him, not the way he is now.

If I accomplish my original objective, though, if I bring him down, then he'll be on my level. Then Mary Ellen won't want him. *Then* we can truly be together.

***

I can hear Trevor in the backyard, cheering. I walk around with a smile and watch as Todd, jumping on the trampoline, drops to his bottom, bouncing a few times before climbing back up onto his feet. Trevor cheers as if he's done an amazing trick and leans over the edge to give Todd a high five. Todd is grinning ear to ear at his little brother. Then he catches sight of me over Trevor's shoulder and yells.

"Jen-Jen!" He always says my name twice.

"Hey, Todder," I call back, and he laughs at my name for him. He scrambles down to run over and give me a hug. I watch all of this from my peripheral vision since my eyes are on Trevor, who turned as soon as Todd called my name. He's smiling at me and doesn't look mad or disgusted with me like I thought he might.

"Todd!" Carol calls from the doorway. "Come on in now and get something to drink and get some sunscreen on." Todd easily dehydrates and burns in the sun and heat.

"Hi, Jen. How are you today?" she asks me. Ever since my foster mom defended my name, she has called me Jen, which is uncomfortably personal. I almost wish she would go back to calling me Jennifer.

I walk up to Trevor as Todd and Carol disappear into the house, holding a DVD in front of me like a shield.

"Klaatu comes in peace," I monotone.

"Is that—?"

"The 1951 version? Yep." I wobble the DVD from side to side. "I wouldn't bring you the—let's see, what did you call it?—the 'uninspired drivel that is the remake'? Did I get that right?"

"It wasn't all *that* bad, I guess. At least not when I watched it on DVD." He waggles his eyebrows at me in comic suggestion, and I laugh, remembering. When we watched it on DVD so that I could appreciate, as Trevor explained, the differences between the two versions, I seem to recall spending a good portion of the remake lip-locked with a certain sci-fi geek.

"Does this mean I'm forgiven?" I ask, smiling at him hesitantly.

"Do you need to be?" he asks.

"Well, you haven't called since Saturday night, so I thought maybe . . ."

"Oh, yeah, sorry about that. Todd was having an off day yesterday. By the time we were done with that, it was pretty late."

Todd sometimes has what Trevor and his parents refer to as "off days" when he spends the day with behavior issues ranging from crying to throwing tantrums to refusing to get out of bed.

"So you're not mad? You know, about the party."

Trevor walks over to me and wraps his arms around my waist, pulling me close.

"Why would I be mad? They're your friends, and if that's what you like to do, then . . ." He leans over and kisses me quickly. "I'm not interested in trying to change you, Jen. I like you just the way you are."

Guilt slices through me.

Mistaking the look that crosses my face, he asks, "Do you *want* me to be mad at you?"

I shrug and look away so he can't read the shame in my eyes.

"Might be kind of fun to make up," I say off-handedly.

He laughs at that.

"Okay, I'm really mad at you then." I look up into his guileless green eyes and sigh, giving myself over to his contagious calm.

"I'll let you forgive me if you kiss me again," I tease.

The dimples come out, and he sighs melodramatically, looking skyward as he pulls me closer with a smile.

"Man, the things I have to do . . ."

Then he's kissing me again—maybe not quite as sweetly as before but still by far nicer than anything I've experienced.

***

"Do you want to call the guys over to watch the movie tonight?" I ask.

My guilt is still driving my actions. We are standing by the tramp, and Trevor is reading the back blurb on the DVD case, as if he hasn't rented and watched it a million times.

"It's Monday, remember?"

Trevor has a mysterious Monday commitment every week and refuses to tell me what it is. In the beginning, it was a problem because my previous experience with secrets withheld by boyfriends usually ended up in my being hurt. But now I know that whatever it is, it's completely innocent, because that's how Trevor works.

"Oh yeah, I forgot how much I hated Mondays."

"When does it have to be back? We could do it tomorrow night."

"It doesn't have to be back. I bought it for you."

"You did?" He smiles like a kid on Christmas who got a Red Ryder, then gives me a thank-you kiss, which is worth *at least* ten DVDs.

"I knew you loved me," he says teasingly, then turns and jumps up on the tramp before I can say anything. He does an effortless back flip.

"Show-off," I mutter, and he laughs.

"Come try it," he says, pulling me up on the trampoline, setting the DVD on the padding along the edge.

"No way. I'll probably land on my head and break my neck."

"No you won't. I won't let you. I'll spot you."

Because I'm still riddled with guilt, I agree.

"Just get jumping really high, nice and smooth," he coaches. "When you're ready, just push backward, arms overhead, and I'll help you."

"Okay, but if I die, it's on your head," I grumble.

Trevor just laughs. I close my eyes and take a deep breath. On my upward jump, I lean back, feeling his hands on my back and my belly, pushing my feet overhead, and then suddenly I'm landing on my feet. My eyes fly open in surprise, and I laugh. Trevor just grins at me.

"See, I told you that you could do it. Wanna try again?"

"No." I drop to my butt. "Don't want to tempt the fates."

He drops next to me just as Todd comes rushing out the back door, followed closely by Carol.

"Sorry," she says. "He saw your flip, and I couldn't keep him inside."

"That's okay," Trevor and I call at the same time, looking at each other and laughing. Carol just waves and goes back inside. Todd scrambles up onto the tramp and bowls me over with a laughing hug.

"Jen-Jen, awesome," he cries.

"Okay, Todd," Trevor says, pulling him off me and back against his own chest, wrapping his arms tightly around his brother. "We don't want to squish Jen, do we, bro?"

"Can I ask her?" Todd is excited.

"Ask me what?" I say suspiciously, eyeing Trevor who still holds his brother in his arms.

"It's Todd's idea. He's been waiting to ask you, but if you don't want to, it's okay."

"Don't want to what?" I ask.

Todd looks at Trevor over his shoulder, waiting for permission. Trevor sighs.

"Go ahead and ask, Todd."

"Do you want to come bowl with us?" Todd is vibrating with anticipation.

"Bowl? As in, bowling?"

"It's okay," Trevor reassures me. "I told Todd you're not exactly fond of—"

"I'd love to come. When?" I cut him off, and his brows shoot up in astonishment.

"Monday. We always bowl on Mondays," Todd tells me, as if I should have known this.

"So, that's what you do on your mysterious Mondays?"

"Not so mysterious. Just, you know, what we do." Trevor shrugs. "We bowl on two different leagues, actually."

"*Leagues*?" I scoff.

Trevor smiles with chagrin, though Todd is nodding happily, wrapped in his brothers arms.

"It keeps him active," Trevor explains.

I look at him, trying to figure him out. "You were afraid I'd make fun of you—that's why you didn't tell me."

He smiles. "Well, you kind of just did."

Now it's my turn to be chagrined.

"You're right. I'm sorry. But if you're on a league, how can I . . . ?"

"We just finished with our last league a couple of weeks ago. We have a couple more weeks till we start again, so this is just practice."

"Practice makes perfect," Todd intones, obviously parroting a phrase he's been told.

"That's right." Trevor gives him a squeeze.

"Want to see my trick?" Todd asks me.

"Yes, I do," I say, cutting Trevor off before he can say no for me as he started to.

Trevor and I scoot over to the edge on the padded area, and Trevor glances at me, as if to say I don't need to do this.

"You're a really good brother," I tell him, kissing him lightly.

"Yucky! No kisses," Todd says, bounce-stepping over to pull us apart. "Watch me!"

Trevor grins apologetically, and I smile back, wondering how quickly I can bring him down to my level so that I can really belong to him.

***

We walk into the bowling alley, the same one we'd been to together before, Bowling Haven. Everyone here seems to know them, saying hello and getting hugs from Todd.

Trevor and Todd actually have a *locker* that they rent for their bowling balls. Trevor gets me some shoes while I try to find the least disgusting house ball that I can. Without the distraction of my fosters and being glared at by Trevor's mom and the cheerleader, I'm able to watch Trevor and Todd interact together. Whether Todd gets a strike or a gutter ball, he gets the same cheering and high-five from Trevor, and now from me since I'm on their team, as Todd says. He comes over, hand raised with every throw.

I would never admit it to anyone, even under torture, but I'm having fun. I admire the way Trevor is with his brother, younger in age but older in every other way.

I wish I had an older brother like Trevor. Maybe then I wouldn't be where I am, wouldn't need to bring Trevor down to my level because maybe I would be at his.

15

THE MONEY IS MINE

IT HAS been brought to my attention that this room doesn't particularly suit you."

I'm sitting in my room, looking at yet another picture that has been added to the mirror frame. This one is also from the camping trip, only it's me standing next to Sue, peeling potatoes, with the biker-chick look going, and looking oddly happy. I didn't think I ever looked happy.

"Are you doing this?" I turn to look at Sue.

"Doing what?" Her response is too casual to be forced, and she doesn't even glance at the pictures. I decide it's probably not her putting them up.

"Never mind. What were you saying?"

She sits on the edge of my bed and runs a hand across the white, frilly bedspread, almost longingly. Kind of strange, I think.

"I decorated this room to look how I'd always wanted my room to look when I was a girl. I suppose it never occurred to me that whoever lived here might want to decorate it in her own style." She looks at me. "It really doesn't suit you at all, does it?"

"It doesn't matter," I say, a little confused at this strange conversation.

"Of course it matters. This is your home. This is *your*

room. It should be a place that is welcoming to you, a place that's yours, filled with your own belongings."

"Well," I say, trying to ignore more of those stupid warm fuzzies that try to surface at her words, "you probably didn't expect someone like me to turn up on your doorstep."

"No, I guess I didn't," she admits, and I'm still trying to decide if her words should offend me when she adds, "but I'm sure glad you did."

I'm completely stunned by her words because she sounds so genuine.

"What if it had been a boy who'd come here?"

"It would probably have been as uncomfortable for him in here as it has been for you."

I laugh but look around the room.

"It's not so bad," I tell her.

"But not so good either." She smiles at me. "Don't you have things of your own that you'd like to have up in here? I don't know, posters or pictures or something?"

"I don't have too much," I admit. "When you move around as much as I do, you learn to travel light."

A pained look crosses her face at my words, and she reaches across the empty space to place her hand over mine.

"Then it's time to start accumulating. This weekend I want to take you shopping, let you pick out some things to put in here to make it your own."

I scrutinize her, wondering what game she's playing. I've learned that nothing is free; everything has a cost. What is her cost though?

"What if I don't stay here much longer?" I ask.

She blinks at this, looking a little hurt.

"You don't like it here?"

I sigh and roll my eyes.

"I didn't say I didn't like it. But . . . you know, a *foster* family isn't a real family. It's not permanent. I'll be eighteen in a few months. I guess the state will keep paying you as long as I'm still in high school, but graduation is less than a year away. If, you know . . . if you wanted to keep me that long, anyway."

She cocks her head and studies me silently. This makes me uncomfortable, and I squirm a little.

"Do you think we took you in for the money?"

"Well, what else is there? I mean, it's not like you knew me, right?"

"No, we didn't. But it was never about money. It was about giving someone a home and family."

Ah, of course. The do-good side of it all.

"I want to show you something," she says suddenly, standing up. "Come with me."

She doesn't wait but walks out of my room. I'm a little hesitant after the weird exchange we've just had, but curiosity gets the better of me, so I follow her.

She goes down the stairs and into the den. I've never really been in this room, other than poking my head in once out of curiosity. It seems like a pretty boring place to be, nothing for me here, so I've never had reason to wander in.

Sue walks over to the desk and pulls open a drawer. She pulls out a little blue book and hands it to me.

"What's this?" I ask, looking at it as if it might be poisonous.

"Open it," she says, crossing her arms and watching me.

I open the cover, and on the first page printed in neat block letters is

JENNIFER'S SAVINGS.

I look at Sue, and she makes a motion with her fingers to tell me to keep going. I turn to the next page and see what looks like a checkbook register, with dates and numbers, tallying up at the bottom of the page.

"I don't get it." I hold the thing toward her, waiting for an explanation.

"We should have told you about this before, I suppose. We wanted it to be a graduation gift. Each month we do receive a check from the state, and it gets deposited directly into this account. As well as money we ourselves put into it each month."

I stare at her blankly.

"It's yours," she says.

I pull the book back toward me and flip through some more of the pages. The sum continues to grow on each page, and my pulse picks up the pace a little. There has to be a *heavy* price for this, but I just can't figure out what it is.

"Why? What do you want from me?" My voice comes out slightly strangled sounding.

"Sweetie, we don't want anything. The money is yours. You can do anything with it you want. We've always had savings accounts for our kids for when they go to college. Of course, we'll pay for your college tuition and books, same as we did for Jeff and Tamara."

I raise a brow at the thought of *me* going to college but decide to skip that conversation just now. I hug the book to my chest as if Sue will suddenly snatch it away.

"It's mine?" I ask skeptically.

"Yes."

"I could go to the bank right now and take all of the money out?"

"Yes, of course. Look." She holds out her hand, and

reluctantly I hand it to her. She opens it to the first page again and points.

JENNIFER JONES *OR* SUE GRANT

"That means that money can be deposited *or* withdrawn by either of us," she explains, handing it back to me. "So, yes, you can go take it out, all of it. Today, if you wanted. The account number is listed right there."

"I could put this book in my room, then tomorrow go to the bank and take it all?" I question her again, still sure that there has to be a catch.

"Sure. If you want to keep the book, it's yours. I'll just let you know each time I make a deposit and you can keep track of it yourself."

"Why would you do this?"

"Because we think of you as our daughter now."

Her statement is simple, to the point—it cuts me to the core.

"I have a mom," I say defiantly. A flash of pain crosses her eyes.

"I know that. I'm not trying to replace her."

"But you're giving me all of this money, and you want me to change my room." I hear the suspicion in my voice, but I can't help it.

Sue heaves a sigh, and it's the same sound I've heard other mothers make when they're dealing with their own teens, exasperated but not angry.

"There are no strings here, Jen. No one is trying to . . . I don't know, hurt you or make a fool of you, or whatever it is that you suspect. We're just trying to be—"

"*Nice?*" My word slices into her, full of derision. She doesn't say anything, just watches me. I suddenly feel overwhelmed, and I turn from her steady gaze and flee back to the frilly room that has never really bothered me before. Now it feels alien, strange.

I slam the door and collapse on the bed.

I open the little book again, looking at the final tally, which is more money than I've ever even seen in my life. *Of course*, I think, *if I can go to the bank at any time and withdraw all of the money, then so can* she. After my strange little performance she's probably already regretting having told me and is deciding I'm not really worth it after all. I decide there's no time like the present to test her words.

I jump back off the bed and race down the stairs, grateful to see that she's still here. She calls my name as I run past her and out the front door. She has the advantage of a car, so I have to be quick.

The bank isn't very far from the house. Nervously, I walk up to the counter and shove the book across to the teller, who looks at me oddly.

"I want to withdraw this money," I tell her, trying to sound convincing but mostly sounding nervous.

"Do you have your ID?" she asks, bored.

I pull my rarely used driver's license out, and she looks at it carefully, glancing up at me as if to see that my face and the face on the license are one and the same, comparing the name on it to my name in the book.

"How much do you want?"

"All of it."

She looks at me more closely, the narrowing of her eyes very minute—I probably would have missed it if I hadn't seen the same expression on so many other faces throughout my life.

"Did you want to close the account then?"

"Uh, no." I don't *think* I want to close it, not sure I even have that authority.

"There's a twenty-five dollar minimum that needs to be kept in the account to keep it open," she says, and I can practically hear her roll her eyes.

"Okay, that's fine," I try not to feel like the thief that I'm sure I am. Sue said it was mine.

"How do you want it?" the teller asks.

I'm not sure what she means, so I shrug. She sighs and begins counting the money out, laying it across the counter as she goes so I can see that she isn't ripping me off. Then she slides it into a big stack and places it in an envelope.

"Thanks," I say uncertainly. This has been too easy. Something isn't right.

"Have a nice day," she intones.

As I walk out of the bank, I eye the security guard warily, certain that he's going to tackle me and force me to give the money back. He doesn't even look my way, and suddenly I'm out in the open, with an envelope stuffed full of more money than I could have ever imagined in my hands.

I return home, sneaking up to my room. I bury the envelope in my sock drawer, quietly closing it as if someone might hear and come storming in to steal it away. Then I realize that's the first place they will look, and I quickly retrieve it.

I open my closet and pull out my little box. This is where I keep everything that's important to me—it's the one thing I do take from house to house. I place the envelope in the box and then shove it back into the closet, burying it beneath a pile of dirty clothes. I hope no one gets curious enough to search it. With a guilty heart, I climb under my covers.

16

A Thief Confesses

WHAT'S WITH you this week?" Trevor asks. We're in my room, me lying across the bed and Trevor sitting on the floor near me.

"What do you mean?"

"You've been kind of . . . snippy," he says.

"*Snippy*?" I mock. "What are you, my grandma?"

"See what I mean?" He looks up at me. "Is something wrong?"

I glance guiltily at my closet. Neither Sue nor Pat has said anything about the pilfered money. Tomorrow I'm supposed to go shopping with Sue to "remodel" my room, as she says. I wonder if that is when she'll bring the money up, telling me to pay for the purchases myself.

"Okay, I'm going to let you in on a secret," I tell him. "But only because I feel really guilty, and if I don't tell someone, I'm going to explode."

I pull the box from my closet and open it. I can see Trevor glance curiously at the contents, but in his everpolite way, he doesn't ask. He just waits. I pull the envelope out and hand it to him, dropping down to the floor next to him. When he looks inside, his eyes go so wide I worry that they might pop out of his head.

"That's a lot of money," he says, just in case I didn't already know. Then he looks at me suspiciously. "Where did you get it?"

"It's mine," I tell him defiantly. Typically trusting, he relaxes.

"Then why are you feeling guilty? You should put that in the bank so you don't lose it or have it stolen. I could take you down and you can open an account."

I roll my eyes at him.

"I don't need to *open* an account. The money came *from* my account."

Trevor looks confused, so I tell him the story, glossing over certain parts—those parts mainly being my own thoughts.

"Wait, you think Sue would tell you about this, tell you it's yours, then take it away?"

"Well, when you put it *that* way, it sounds silly to think that," I say defensively.

"That's because it is silly. Sue and Pat seem like good people. I'm pretty sure she's not trying to pull some cruel prank on you."

I rip the envelope out of his hands.

"I know that!"

"Then what's going on, Jen? What's *really* going on? Because I don't think this is about the money."

His words bring repressed feelings boiling to the surface, and I look away as tears brim, trying to flow. I brush them angrily away.

"You don't know," I say irritably. "You don't know anything. Your world is all about happiness and sunshine and security. I don't have that luxury. I never have."

He doesn't say anything, just pulls me tightly against him so that I'm sitting with my back against his chest. He wraps his arms around me, and in that silent show of support, I find my safety.

"Tell me," he says softly, giving me the chance to pretend I didn't hear if I don't want to tell him.

"You know about my . . . real parents," I stutter over the words, and he gives me a soft squeeze. "But after them, there have been a lot of foster families. There aren't that many people out there like Pat and Sue.

"A lot of foster parents are in it for the money and for the free labor they get from foster kids—or at least the ones I've had experience with. What can you do, right? I mean, they have you by the throat. You have to do what they say, try to stick around as long as possible because it's better than the shelter. You might be surprised to find that there aren't a lot of families looking for a black-haired, pierced, rebellious teen to take into their homes." I try to sound flippant, but it doesn't quite flow.

"Yeah, I know, woe is me," I say disdainfully as if he'd contradicted me. "I'm not complaining, because I haven't had to spend much time at the shelter. But I've learned a few things. And one of the biggest is that nothing is free, Trev. There's always a cost. I just don't see what Sue's price is. This is a new game for me."

Trevor is silent for so long that I finally look up at him. He's looking at my mirror, which seems to spout a new photo every couple of days (and which Trevor claims is not him). It's nearly covered all the way around the edges now. Finally, he glances down at me, and I'm grateful that his eyes aren't filled with sympathy—*that* I couldn't take.

"Did it ever occur to you that she isn't trying to play a game with you?"

I stare at him. No game? There's always a game. Even as I think this, I realize that it has never been a game for Trevor. I can't say the same for myself, but for him it has always been genuine, no expectations, no payment expected. If he can be this way, I suppose it's possible that maybe others can as well. Sue and Pat seem to be cut from the same cloth as Trevor.

As my mind empties of suspicion and fills with something like hope, I smile at him.

"What?" He sounds suspicious, but he's smiling and his eyes are clear.

"Wanna give me a ride to the bank?"

**

I confess my thievery to Sue, who laughs at me. I wasn't expecting that reaction, for sure. Disappointment at the least, a call to have me immediately removed from her home at most. I hand her the book meekly. She hands it back.

"Why don't you keep it in your room? You can add as well as I can." I look at the proffered book, but my new resolve to trust my fosters—I mean, the Grants—causes me to shake my head.

"No, I trust you. You keep it for me until I need it."

She shrugs, not realizing how momentous my decision is, and casually tucks it into her rear pocket.

"You ready to shop tomorrow?" she asks.

"You still want to take me, after I stole that money?"

"You can't steal what is yours," she laughs.

Just like that, my week of stressing and worrying over the savings account is made null and void. It's weird, this feeling of trust, this sense of almost belonging.

**

One thing I will say about Sue is that she sure knows how to shop. I'm exhausted long before she is. She lets me choose everything, subtly guiding me to accents and colors that end up looking great together. I don't know how she does it, but once we return home and fix my room up, it's exactly the room I've always wanted but haven't dared hope for.

My room transforms to red and black, a complete opposite from its bright white. It's darker now, like me. Unlike me it is also elegant and welcoming, not something I would have expected from these colors. The frill is gone, and it's plain and simple under the elegance.

She even bought frames for my multiplying photos, and now they hang in a cool collage above my bed, replacing the bland, hopeful landscape that had hung there. On the other walls hang a couple of prints of paintings by Dali. The surreal, dark paintings appeal to something in me, though I suspect Sue isn't as impressed by them. She bought them for me, anyway.

Just like that, it feels like home.

17

OFFERS AND ISSUES

I'M SPENDING most of my time with Trevor now. Other than Beth and Ella, I haven't taken the time to make any real friends. Making friends is a lot of effort to put forth when your stay is a temporary one. I might have made more of an effort originally if I'd known I would have the good fortune to end up with two separate families in the same school zone. By the time I came to stay with the Grants, I was back to having less than a year to stay—or so I'd thought. Now that I'm planning to make it a little more permanent, I feel a little sorry that I didn't make the effort. Mainly because Beth and Ella are pretty angry with me about the whole Trevor deal and aren't speaking to me much.

I was as honest with them as I could be, leaving out my feelings for him. I told them that I decided I like hanging with him, so they're off the hook with the bet. They completely don't get it. They think I've sold out, which I guess is true to some degree. I'm okay with that because I'm liking both myself and my life better these days.

Then two things happened to upset my new balance. First, a conversation with Pat and Sue, and second, an offhand comment made by Trevor on the heels of that conversation, which solidified an idea in my mind.

Pat and Sue had sat me down and asked what I thought of the idea of adoption. At my stricken look, they had assured me that they weren't trying to take the place of my natural parents, that they just wanted me as part of their family. They had even told me that I could keep my own last name—as if that name means anything to me.

I couldn't tell them that my hesitation wasn't due to either of those reasons. My hesitation stemmed from that raw wound called hope. I've been looking at it from every angle since they told me, and I can't figure out what possible ulterior motive they might have. That's making me think maybe there isn't another motive. Maybe they really like me enough to just want me as part of their family as they said.

Then I think about the commitment involved in saying yes. It's a lifetime commitment, no going back.

It also means getting permission from my imprisoned biological mother—my mother, who has written to me only once, soon after she was convicted, and who has not contacted me again in spite of the hundreds of letters I've written to her. I haven't written to her for over three years now.

It's while all of this swirls around, clouding my head, that Trevor makes his comment. We're in my room listening to some music on the new stereo that Pat brought home for me the day after Sue and I remodeled my room. My mystery box happens to be sitting on my vanity because I cleaned out my closet earlier and just haven't put it away yet. Trevor occasionally glances at it, and I'm aware of his intense curiosity. I'm also counting on his good manners for him to not ask about it.

"You don't talk about your parents much," he says without warning.

"You're here almost every day, Trev. You know as much about them as I do."

He peeks up at me from underneath those beautiful long lashes, effective since he's sitting on the floor next to the bed, and I'm lying on it, head propped up on my hand, my other hand hanging over the edge, fingers entwined with his. I try not to melt at the glance. He has no idea how appealing his eyes are.

"I'm not talking about Pat and Sue," he says quietly, and because I'm a little lost in the sea green of his eyes, it takes a minute for the words to penetrate. He senses when my gaze changes, his hand tightening instinctively over mine to keep me from pulling away.

"I'm not trying to pry," he begins, his ultra-politeness battling with his curiosity. "It's just that . . ."

He turns, not relinquishing his grip on my hand, sitting up on his knees so that he's eye level with me.

"We've been . . . together . . . for a while now. You pretty much know everything about me. But there's a whole chunk of your life that's a big blank to me." He shrugs, looking down at our tangled hands. He brings his free hand up, tucking my hair behind my ear, then caressing my jaw with his thumb, sending goose bumps skittering across my skin.

"You're not playing fair," I mumble. He leans in and kisses me until my belly is on fire and my toes are curled.

"Sorry, can't help myself," he says, not sounding sorry at all. "Tell me about them," he urges softly, and it has the effect of a bucket of cold water poured over my head. I jerk away and sit up.

"Nothing to tell." I know I sound belligerent, but it's not something I like to talk about—to *anyone.*

"Where were you born? Where did you grow up? Have

you lived with many foster families? *Why* do you live in foster care?" He's counting on his fingers with each question. "That's a lot I don't know. Things about you that I'd like to know. Things that have made you who you are."

"Things I don't talk about," I tell him angrily. Immediately he's on the bed next to me, arm around my shoulder.

"Whoa, Jen, I don't mean to upset you. No pressure, honey. You don't have to tell me anything."

I lean into him, relaxing.

"Sorry, sensitive subject," I say. He just sits quietly with me, rubbing his hand up and down my back. I know Trevor; he might still be curious, but he won't bring it up again. He won't be angry or disappointed if I don't tell him. My sure knowledge of that is what makes up my mind.

"You heard what I told Mrs. Green," I begin, and he tenses for a brief second before resuming his rubbing. "My only memories of my father are shades of purple and black, lots of violence. I don't remember a lot of the specifics of life with him other than those impressions. Most of what I know comes from what I've read in the reports written about my life.

"I don't have any real feelings concerning him, you know? Other than fear. *That* is a feeling that I associate with him," I say. Trevor pulls me a little closer.

"He was killed by the cops when they were called to the house. One of the neighbors heard gunshots. He was shooting at me."

I don't tell Trevor, but that is a crystallized memory—always there, always clear. The fear of my father that I experienced that day and the utter hopelessness of knowing that there was no one to protect me were burned forever into my mind.

"The cops came," I continue, "and he wouldn't put his gun down, claiming he had the right to shoot me if he wanted to. He aimed at me, they fired at him, and he died."

I shudder with the memory of all of the blood on that day, and Trevor wraps both arms around me, reminding me of just how safe I am now.

"So they sent me to live with my mom. She hadn't wanted me originally, which is how I ended up living with my dad. She had . . ." I pause, looking for a word that can describe her life. "*Issues*, I guess," I finally settle on this all-encompassing description, inadequate as it is.

"By the time I went to live with her, she was living with her second husband, just another model of my father, another abusive lowlife. I wasn't really a welcome addition to the house, but she had to take me. There wasn't anyone else.

"I have to give her props," I say, shrugging. "She at least tried a little. I lived with her until I was twelve. It wasn't exactly like living here with the Grants, or what it was like for you growing up. It was better than it had been at my father's because her husband only beat me occasionally, and then only if I did something to draw his attention. But at least she didn't beat me. She actually tried to protect me a little. Not that she'd win any mother-of-the-year awards since she was so wrapped up in her own misery and ignored me as much as possible. And mostly *he* was unaware of me.

"But when I turned twelve I started to—" I stop abruptly, glancing up at Trevor, embarrassed. As usual, he's instinctively doing the right thing, which is to not be looking at me. I clear my throat and continue.

"I started to *change*." I emphasize the word, refusing to say that I began to develop, not looking like such a little girl anymore.

"And because he was a pig, he noticed *that*, and then it was hard to avoid him." I stop, hating to remember the next part, the part where he had come into my room and tried to force himself on me. I clearly remember the overpowering sickly-sweet smell of his sweat as he crushed me beneath his large, heavy body, the revolting smell of his breath on my face, his rough, probing, demanding hands. I shudder again at the memory, and Trevor pulls me over onto his lap, pulling my head down against his neck, arms firm around me, holding me together.

I breathe deeply of Trevor's clean smell, of his goodness and purity, and the memories I have of Trevor replace those of that horrible night. Trevor has often held me close, never with anything even slightly resembling demand or expectation. I wind my arms around him, holding him close, grateful for whichever fate has put him in my path.

I take a deep, bracing breath and continue.

"He didn't rape me," I say quietly, firmly. "He probably would have, but my mother came in then and saw him. I still don't know if she was angry that he was trying to hurt me or if she was jealous that he had turned his attention to someone other than her, but either way, she killed him. So now she's in prison."

I point at the box.

"That box, which you're so curious about," I growl at him, then kiss him on the jaw so that he knows I'm not really upset, "contains all of my worldly possessions. Not much to show for seventeen years."

I pull away from him but don't move off his lap. I lift the box over and hand it to him. He looks at me questioningly.

"Open it."

He flips the lid open with his thumb and peers in. My

birth certificate lies in the bottom. My mother's wedding ring from my father—a cheap, thin, gold band—is in there. There's a wrinkled Polaroid of my parents—my mother barely more than a girl—and myself when I was a baby. At first glance, it would seem they're happy, but if you look closely, you can see the strain and stress showing around their eyes and in the corners of their forced smiles. A key to a '69 Camaro from my almost-brother, who gave it to me as a going away gift and told me someday I could come back and he'd fit a car to the key for me. A few little odds and ends from my various foster families, nothing of any real value.

Mostly it's full of letters. Trevor flips through them, not really looking. Then he notices what they are, and he goes back to the top, looking at each one individually. When he realizes what they are, his eyes come up to meet mine, horrified.

"She sent all of your letters back?"

"Unopened," I say, turning one over to show him.

"Maybe you should go see her. Ask her why," he murmurs, making the comment that puts the thought into my head, one I never expected—or wanted—to have.

"No." My answer sounds firm, final. It's really anything but.

He tosses the letters back into the box, and his eyes go soft with sympathy.

"Don't feel sorry for me," I command, recognizing that look.

He only shakes his head.

"I can't help it. It kills me to think of how hard it's been for you."

"Don't, Trev. I can't take it. I don't want you to feel sorry for me," I repeat.

He gives me a wry grin, but even that is laden with his sorrow.

"I can't help it. It's how I'm built." His excuse is lame, but lame or not, I recognize that it's the absolute truth.

"You're such a geek, Trev," I sigh resignedly.

"I know." He reaches up to caress my cheek with his warm hand, his smile less sad now. "But that's why you love me."

"Yeah." I lean in and kiss him. "It is."

We sit silently for a few minutes.

"Hey, Trev?" I ask softly.

"Yeah?"

"Did you call me 'honey' before?"

He chuckles softly against my neck, and I can't help but grin. He is such an utter dork.

18

WILL THE REAL MOTHER PLEASE STAND UP?

SO I decide it's time to go and see her. The decision isn't made lightly. The Grants' desire to adopt me, as well as Trevor's comment and sorrow over the returned letters, has planted the seed—I can't keep it from growing.

I ask Pat to take me. It doesn't seem fair to ask the woman who wants to be my new mother to take me to see my old mother. I don't ask Trevor because he's been treating me like fragile glass since our conversation. I know he's told his parents because his mom is suddenly being really nice to me. His dad gave me a quick, hard hug, then ruffled my hair and challenged me to an arm wrestle.

Pat didn't even blink when I asked him to take me even though it's a two-hour drive—each way. He thinks it's a good idea, didn't even ask why suddenly I want to see her. I think he knows. He even takes the day off work, a gesture that means more to me than it probably even does to him.

Deciding what to wear takes me two full days.

I want to dress soft, with easy makeup and calm hair to show her that I'm a good girl, that I've turned out well, that she has had no negative impact on me.

I want to dress as harshly as I can, with the hardest,

most severe makeup I can manage, the shortest, tightest skirt, black lips, poofed hair, so that she can see just what her neglect has cost.

I finally decide to go just as I look these days—something of a compromise between the two extremes.

We go on a Wednesday. I have my iPod plugged into my ears, music blaring. It's rude, I know, something I wouldn't have cared about before Trevor the Polite got hold of me. I am a bundle of shaking nerves with tremors shimmering across my skin, and I don't have it in me to make small talk.

I close my eyes and pretend to be asleep just in case Pat tries to talk to me anyway, wishing I really could sleep. Thankfully, Pat leaves me alone, not even glancing my way, ignoring me as completely as I am him.

The two-hour drive seems to take forever, and yet all too soon we are pulling through the security gate at the penitentiary. My tremors step it up double time, my stomach clenching.

In order to be let in to the inner sanctum, you have to play a kind of game with the guards at different posts. Lots of suspicious looks at us, a walk through a metal detector, and a thorough frisking—me by a female guard who could probably kick my butt with her little finger, and Pat by a big, burly guy who I wouldn't want to tangle with. I suspect we're getting off fairly easy when Pat flashes his DEA badge.

Finally—too soon—there's only one iron door left between us and *her*. I feel dizzy, wondering if I might throw up on the clean white floor. Pat sidles over and gives me a one-armed squeeze.

"I'll be right out here," he says meaningfully. "Take as long as you need. I have plenty of reading material to choose from."

He gives me a lopsided smile as he indicates the three outdated magazines on the small table next to an uncomfortable-looking orange vinyl sofa. I try to smile back but fail miserably. He ruffles my hair and kisses me on the top of my head.

"You'll be okay," he murmurs. "She can't hurt you now. You're safe."

I nod tightly, then turn back toward the guard, who watches sympathetically. I'm probably not the first semi-orphan to grace this waiting room coming to see her wayward mother.

"Ready?" he asks, then without waiting for an answer—or maybe just not giving me a chance to chicken out—he twists a key from his overloaded key chain and the door swings open. He steps in and waits for me to follow, which I do quickly because chickening out is sounding really appealing right about now.

There are about a dozen tables scattered throughout the room. I'm surprised; I had been expecting glass partitions with a phone handset. This feels too intimate.

Three tables are occupied. At one table sits a large woman and a man with two small children, probably her family. I wonder briefly what took her away from them and whether she regrets the distance. Another table has an old woman who looks like a sweet grandma, though she's wearing the prison-issue white jumpsuit. She's being visited by another woman who could be either a daughter or a granddaughter.

The third table is taken by a skinny woman with long brown, lanky hair. She half stands as I enter but shifts her eyes behind me toward the guard and quickly resumes her seat. I also glance back toward the guard, and he nods me forward toward this stranger. I take a tentative step forward, then stop again.

"Sheila, you have a visitor," the guard calls harshly, retreating through the door and slamming it with a reverberating clang.

"Jennifer?" the skinny woman, who doesn't look familiar at all, asks.

Fear chokes me—not a fear that she might harm me physically, but a psychological fear that I can't even put a name to. I'm frozen, staring at this small person. My mother hadn't been small, had she? I remembered her as someone much bigger than me, much tougher. How can this woman, who is thin and shriveled and no taller than me, be the same woman?

She reaches up with one of her hands that had been resting on her lap beneath the table, and the chain connected to the cuff linked about her wrist drags loudly up the table. As if the action and sound is a switch, I feel myself unfreeze and my fear drains away. I nod and move to sit in the chair across from her.

She smiles hesitantly, turning her palm up in a helpless gesture.

"Hi—" I begin but stop short of calling her "mom."

She sighs as her shoulders droop a little.

"Jennifer, you've grown up so much."

"Well, that happens to the best of us," I say, using my sarcasm as a defense.

She shakes her head, eyes darting everywhere—my eyes, cheeks, lips, hair, neck, arms that are resting on the table— as if she's trying to take a thousand tiny photographs to store away.

"I—" She breaks off, then sighs again. "This is a little

awkward, huh?" she asks with a humorless laugh.

"I don't know you," I blurt. She jerks a little in response to my words. "I mean, I know *who* you are, of course, but you're a . . ."

"Stranger?" she asks when I fail to finish my sentence.

"Yeah." I nod, looking down at the scarred tabletop and tracing a carving with my finger. Apparently, JS hearts HM, if the table is to be believed.

She sighs and leans back in her chair. I relax fractionally when she's no longer leaning so intently toward me.

"Did I ever tell you how I met your dad?" she asks unexpectedly. For a brief moment, I'm confused—she knows Pat? With a wash of guilt and something deeper, I realize she isn't talking about Pat at all; she's talking about the man who tried to kill me when I was six.

"No, I don't think that particular story ever came up in one of our mother-daughter heart-to-hearts," I say, and she winces slightly at the cynicism. She doesn't comment, letting it go, leaning forward again and bringing both shackled wrists loudly up to rest on the table.

"It's a cautionary tale, to be sure. I was sixteen. I was a good girl, though you may find that hard to believe." She laughs sardonically, as if doubting it herself. "I had good parents, a good life. I didn't want for anything. But I was restless, you know?" She doesn't pause, not expecting an answer, but I could have answered yes. I know that feeling all too well. "Whatever I had, it was never enough. I always wanted something more, though I never knew quite what it was I wanted.

"I started hanging out with some kids who weren't the best influence, you know?" Again, no answer needed, but this tale is beginning to sound familiar. "It was *exciting*. We were always doing things to get the adrenaline pumping. And always at night, after I had gone to bed and snuck out my window. That added a higher element of exhilaration to whatever we did.

"We found someone who could get us some fake IDs." Here she glances at me for the first time, her eyes flickering up to gauge my reaction. How can I judge when I used to have one myself? When I don't seem overly shocked, she looks beyond me, lost in her memories again.

"We were always going to the bars. Back then they didn't worry as much about serving minors. They barely glanced at the IDs.

"Anyway, one night I met a man who was extremely handsome." She smiles in remembrance. "He was flirting heavily with me, dancing with me, buying me drinks. He made me feel very grown up, very desirable.

"I began meeting him regularly. Sometimes we would stay at the bar dancing, but mostly we would go back to his place to—" She breaks off, her cheeks turning pink, and I shift uncomfortably, not because she's letting me know they'd been having sex—that's no surprise—but at the way her embarrassment makes her look younger, a little more like the woman I remember.

"Well, anyway." She flutters her hands around, skipping what she thinks my ears are too innocent to hear. "I found out I was pregnant about a month later. My parents had no choice but to allow me to marry him even though he was quite a bit older than me. Also, looking back, I suspect they could see things about him that I couldn't. They never did like him." She shrugs, dismissing her parents' concern. "And I believe they were glad to be rid of me since I'd been so much trouble for so long.

"We moved away two weeks later when Kerry got a call from his friend Tom, who said he had a job here for him. I never talked to my family again, even when things got . . . *bad*. I didn't want them to know, didn't want them to see that they had been right.

"You were born not long after that." She clenches her fingers together and looks at me, shrugging again as if that story should answer all of my questions. Instead, there are a thousand new ones zooming around in my head.

"Touching," is the first acerbic word out of my mouth. She bristles, and her mouth tightens disapprovingly. "Doesn't really explain how you came to the decision to leave me with an abusive, homicidal maniac to be raised, does it?"

Her fingers whiten as she tightens her grip. Her shoulders jerk back. Anger flashes through her eyes.

"You have no idea what it was like, Jennifer." Her words are clipped.

"You're right, I don't. Why don't you explain it to me?"

"If I hadn't left him, he would have eventually killed me."

"Well, better your innocent, defenseless daughter than you, huh?"

"I had no way to take care of a baby, let alone myself. I had nowhere to live, no job, and no family. What was I supposed to do?"

"How about come and get me as soon as you did have those things. Or better yet, take me with you and figure it out like any normal mother. How long did you live with your next husband—Stan, was it?—before you had no choice but to take me in when my *father* was arrested for attempting to *murder* me? You know, after he'd spent all the rest of the time beating me to a bloody pulp almost daily." I clench my jaw, refusing to let the tears come.

Her jaw also tightens in response. Her eyes—disconcertingly like mine—brew with a storm. I can see a thousand words trying to make their way out, but she holds them back. In a sudden movement, her hands come up to cover her face, the movement startling me as the heavy chains drag noisily up the side of the table. Her shoulders relax to their former beaten position. When she drops her hands, I see tears and regret pooling in her eyes.

"I can't ever explain it to you because until you've lived it, you can't know. You're right, though. I had a responsibility to you. I shouldn't have left you there. No one knew as well as I did what he was capable of." She shrugs, but this time it's full of self-recrimination rather than nonchalance. "I began to hate you before you'd even been born because you were the thing that bound me to him, to the monster he turned out to be.

"I wanted out. That's what my life was about for too long—wanting out. And then you were born, and you cried and he beat me for that. You wanted to eat, and he beat me for that. You needed diapers and clothes, and he beat me for that. And every time I looked at you, all I could see was the beating that was going to come, and I blamed you, my beautiful, innocent baby girl. And I hated you for it more every day."

Her eyes hold mine, refusing to let me go while she spills the ugly truth. I can feel the tears on my cheeks, but I don't wipe them away. To do so would be to acknowledge them, and I can't do that.

"So I left. And then he died . . . was killed . . . and you were brought to me. At first, I didn't want you. But Stan made me keep you because we were able to get more welfare money for you." I look away, sick at heart. She wanted me because of *money*? How much could it possibly have been—fifty, maybe a hundred bucks a month?

She reaches forward as if to grab my hand, and I jerk backward. She looks over my head to where the guards watch through a window, then sighs and leans back, pulling her own hands back beneath the table.

"Of course you must hate me, even more now that you know the truth. But I swear to you, Jennifer, I came to love you, every bit as much as a mother should love her daughter. Even though things were bad with Stan, I was working hard and putting money away so that someday we could escape, you and me, and go far away to where no men could touch us. And then Stan . . . when he . . . when I walked in and saw . . ." She stumbles over the words, her eyes locked firmly on the tabletop.

"I remember clearly what you saw. I was there, remember?" I mean for my words to come out harsh, but they are whispered, tortured. She meets my gaze with her own anguish mirrored there.

"I had to kill him, Jennifer. If I hadn't, he wouldn't have stopped. He would have come at you again, and I wasn't always there, couldn't always be with you to guard you." Her eyes are pleading. I try to resist the look, but I can't because her words are the truth; I can feel it.

"So, here we are," I say, my voice resigned as I indicate the visitors' room.

"Here we are," she agrees sadly. "But I'm okay with that, Jennifer. I have to be. Because it got you away from him, put you in a safe place, and that's the important thing."

I think about telling her about just how "safe" my life has been, but I'm exhausted. There doesn't seem to be any point in hurting her.

"You sent all of my letters back, unopened," I accuse softly, thinking that had she opened them, she would have known that her sacrifice had been in vain.

"I wanted you to forget about me, to move forward with your new life." I want to ask her how she thinks I could have possibly forgotten the mother who had turned my life into such torment, but it's another unnecessary question that would only be hurtful.

"You live with a nice family?" she asks, sounding as if she really wants to know while also *not* wanting to know.

I shrug, looking into her eyes and holding them with my gaze as she had held mine.

"They want to adopt me," I say. Pain flashes across her face, but she covers it and smiles thinly.

"Do they? But aren't you almost eighteen? Why would they wait until now?" Then she gets an "ah-ha" look. "I guess the state funding runs out soon, huh?"

"It's not about money with *them*," I defend. Shame fills her eyes. "They *want* me."

"The father? He treats you well?"

I want to tell her that it's none of her business, but I want to be in her good graces because now more than at any moment before I want to become their daughter in truth, and I can't have that without her permission.

"He's great. He took the day off work to bring me here today."

"And the . . . mother?" she hesitates, reluctant for another to be named such.

"She's really nice." I pause, then decide to move on. I can't see the need to hurt her with details about the woman who wants to become what she should have been. "They have a son who's married and a daughter not much older than me.

I would have a brother and a sister. But they can't adopt me unless you sign a paper. Once I turn eighteen, I can make the decision myself. I really want it to happen before I turn eighteen. I want to belong to a real family." Even as I say the words, I feel myself getting lighter because it's the truth.

She looks away, her eyes filling with tears. I remain silent, waiting for her.

"It's probably for the best," she says, so quietly I almost don't hear. "It's the least I can give you." She looks back at me, and I can see the pain. "Send me the papers. I'll sign them." She pushes back and stands up. Immediately a guard appears in the room.

"One more thing," I say as she turns away, making a sudden decision, one I hope I won't learn to regret. She pauses as the guard places a hand around her upper arm.

"I'd like you to read the letters I send you and not return them unopened."

At my words, she turns back, amazement written on her features.

"*Send* me? You'll write to me?" Wonder lilts her voice.

"If that's okay," I say.

A brilliant smile breaks out, and she's transformed from the beaten, vaguely familiar stranger into the mother I had known for such a short period, and I remember that she *did* love me.

"That's definitely okay," she says as she's led from the room.

Another guard leads me out to where Pat waits. He pretends that he hasn't been waiting anxiously, but when he puts the magazine down, the edges stay crumpled from his tight grip. He doesn't say anything, but as I step forward, he opens his arms, and I collapse into them, letting the tears flow.

19

If All the Raindrops Were Lemon Drops and Gum Drops . . .

TODD HAS gotten a job at Talbot's wiping down the tables after customers are finished eating their burgers, and since it isn't too far from his house, Trevor and I volunteer to walk him there on the three days each week that he works. It's less than a mile each way, and any time I spend with Trevor alone is a good thing.

I know that his dorkiness has rubbed off on me when walking with him and holding his hand becomes something intensely pleasurable, something to look forward to.

Today we came back to Trevor's house because his parents are both gone for the day, so that means even more alone time. We're sitting on the trampoline (another geek activity that is becoming one of my favorite things to do), and Trevor keeps giving me that look, the one that says he wants to ask me something or tell me something that he thinks I won't like to hear—which means asking him what it is could be a big mistake.

"All right, out with it," I finally command when he keeps sighing.

"Out with what?" he asks too innocently, leaning back on one elbow.

"You know I can't stand the suspense. Just say whatever it is that you think I'm going to be mad about and get it over with."

"You can tell there's something I want to say?"

"Of course I can, Trev. You don't stop sighing."

"I sigh?" My observation disgruntles him.

"You sigh," I confirm. "So talk."

He sighs again, realizes he's doing it, and tries to stop mid sigh, which only causes him to start coughing. When he's done coughing and glaring at me—which may have something to do with my laughing at him—he finally clears his throat and takes a breath.

"Well . . . you haven't said anything . . . you know, about . . . about your . . ." He hesitates, searching for a word. "About your visit, I mean. And I was just wondering . . . not details, those are none of my business, of course . . . but just wondering how it went, how you're doing."

I knew that he would want to know how my visit with my mother went, but I also knew he'd wait until I brought it up. I guess for the last week his curiosity has gotten the better of him and he can't wait any longer. I want to tell him, but at the same time, I'm hesitant. So I shrug.

"The Grants are going ahead with the whole adoption thing," I say, striving to sound as if it doesn't matter either way, when the truth is that I want it more than almost anything. Trevor knows me almost as well as I know myself.

"That's great," he says, and he means it. "So will you change your last name?"

"Yeah, it'll be nice to have a real name, you know?"

"Jones isn't a real name?" He's being facetious, but there *is* an answer to his question.

"No, it's not. Jones is a name I picked out myself when I first went into the system. The last name that I'd had before was too infamous, what with all the press coverage, so it was thought that a different last name might help me to find placement faster."

"I didn't know that. That kind of sucks."

I laugh at his assessment of what had seemed so traumatic at the time.

"Yeah, well, life sucks and then you die, right?"

"How depressing. Do you really think that?" He looks at me, genuinely curious.

"It's been my mantra my whole life," I tell him. Then I grin at him. "But *lately* I've been changing my mind. *Someone* has been convincing me otherwise."

"Well, then good for that someone." He smiles at me, and I melt at the sight of the dimples coming out to play.

"*Raindrops keep falling on my head . . .*" I sing, softly.

"What's that?"

"You know, that old song. I heard it once and thought it had been written about my life because I feel like there are always raindrops falling on me, and just when I get them dried off, new ones hit."

"I guess it could be your song," he says thoughtfully, "because even though raindrops keep falling, the song is about getting back up, refusing to let it get you down."

"*That's* what it's about?"

"*Raindrops keep fallin' on my head,*" he begins singing, pitch perfect. "*That doesn't mean my eyes will soon be turnin' red/ Cryin's not for me/ 'Cause I'm never gonna stop the rain by complainin'/ Because I'm free/ Nothin's worrying me.*"

"Huh," is all I can really say because I don't know the words, only vaguely remembered the tune and the first line.

"Or something like that," he says. "I'm not sure those are the exact words, but they're close."

"I met He-Man and She-Ra," I blurt out.

"Okaaay, that's random. Are you trying to change the subject?"

"No, I'm serious."

He studies me, but I know my sci-fi geek as well as he knows me. I wait.

"All right, I'll bite. Where did you meet He-Man and She-Ra?" he asks, with one eyebrow cocked. The gesture is so cute, I smile and lean over to kiss it. Then I decide that's not enough, so I kiss his mouth. He kisses me back, sitting up taller. Then his arms are around me, and he flips me over onto my back, straddling my belly, and pinning my arms above my head.

"Trying to distract me?" he asks, grinning.

"Maybe," I say. Once, someone much larger than Trevor and with harmful intent held me down just like this. It shows the trust I have in both Trevor and myself that it doesn't bother me to be held so again. I'm proud of this. His hold on me is ultra light, and I know that if I move a fraction of an inch he will let me go. I close my eyes, and for a brief second, my mother's face flashes through my mind, and I imagine her being pinned down cruelly and repeatedly by first my father and later her second husband. With that comes a ping of sympathy.

I quickly open my eyes to let the pure sight of Trevor fill my vision and replace that of her.

"It would probably work if I weren't so strong, so immune to your charms," he says in a mock tough guy voice.

"Oh yeah?" I ask, giving him my best seductive look. "Kiss me, Trev."

Without any hesitation, he says, "Okay," and leans down to accommodate me. He backs up a few inches. "Now tell me about He-Man and She-Ra and whether or not you got me their autographs."

I laugh at him.

"Are you kidding? I was afraid of saying anything but 'yes, sir' and 'no, ma'am' to them. They're guards at the prison." My voice catches unexpectedly on the last word. Trevor pulls back, dragging me up with the gesture until I'm sitting cradled in his arms.

"Are you sure it was them? It could have been Hercules and Xena."

I smile, grateful as always for Trevor's instinct in pulling me away from dangerous emotional territory. I still can't figure out how he manages that, but I sure appreciate it.

"No way. I've watched their TV shows with you. They are both *beyond* gorgeous."

"You think Hercules is gorgeous?" he asks, looking down at me with mock jealousy in his eyes.

"Don't you?"

His face changes, and he shakes his head.

"I'm taking the fifth on that."

"Chicken," I accuse.

"Tell me about He-Man and She-Ra."

"Changing the subject?" I tease.

"Absolutely."

I give him a kiss on the jaw, then turn my attention to his hands, twisting my fingers through his. No eye contact for this conversation is what I need.

"Not much to say about them. They were huge and not a little scary."

When I remain silent for a minute, he gives my hand a little squeeze.

"And her?" I know exactly who he's talking about and decide not to play dumb.

"Much smaller than I remember, actually."

"Smaller?"

"I guess in my mind over time, she had grown to monstrous proportions. Of course, I wasn't all that old, so she probably was bigger than me then. I'm a little bit taller than she is now." I pause, remembering my first impression of her. "She looked like a stranger. I didn't recognize her at first."

"Were you scared?" he asks with his uncanny perception.

"Only to death," I tell him with a humorless laugh. "So she gives me this big sob story about her life and how rough it was for her, and why she had to leave me with my father and how much she hated me."

Trevor stiffens behind me.

"She told you she hates you?" He's righteously indignant on my behalf.

"Down, Chewbacca," I say, patting his arm. "She said she hated me then because I was the reason she was with him all along. When she left, she didn't want me." My voice breaks again at the pain of the words, the confirmation of what I had known all my life, that I was unwanted. I try to cover it with a sad excuse for a cough, but I'm not fooling him. He leans his forehead against my back.

"But then, she had to take me after he . . . well, you know. And she claims that she learned to love me."

"You don't believe her?" Trevor can hear the doubt in my words.

"I don't know. I guess I do, because at this point she has no reason to lie to me. But I've spent my whole life thinking I was worth less than nothing to her, so it's a little weird to try to change my thinking now."

"Are you okay with all of this?" He's worried about me, I can hear it.

"Yeah, I think I am. I can understand a little why she did the things she did. Not that it makes it okay," I clarify when I feel him stiffening again. "But I do understand a little. By the time she was my age, she was pregnant and living with a violent person far away from her home. I can't imagine that. I'd probably hate the baby for putting me in that situation also."

Trevor spins me around to face him, hands bracketing my face to be sure I'm looking directly into his earnest eyes.

"*You* are not the reason she was there. She made her own decisions. You were an innocent baby."

I nod, ignoring the tears that pool in the corners of my eyes.

"You're right, I was. And I've paid a heavy price for both the decisions she and my . . . father," I stumble over the word, "made. But she's paying the heaviest price of all. She killed to protect me, and now she'll be in prison until she dies. I'm free. I can change my life."

Trevor releases my face, hands moving up and down my arms as he smiles at me.

"You have changed, you know?"

"Yeah, I know," I groan. "I hardly recognize myself anymore."

Trevor smiles. "I'm not talking about your hair. I'm talking about *you*. You seem a lot happier now than when I first met you. You seemed a little, I don't know, *bitter* back then, I guess."

"Well, I'm surrounded by ultra-happy, sunshine-spouting people all the time now. Some of it had to rub off."

"Yeah, you've got a little geek going in you now as well."

I laugh. "That's my favorite new part of me."

"So, are you going to see her again?" he asks somberly.

I shrug. "I don't know. I told her I'd write her. She seemed happy about that."

"And you're okay?"

I smile at him. "I'm very okay. I have a real family now, one that *chose* me rather than one I was thrust upon, and I've got this really great guy I happen to be in . . . that I really like a lot." I say, shocked at the words I almost said.

"Where is he?" he demands, looking around the empty yard. "I'll kill him."

"You are *such* a—"

"Yeah, geek, I know."

"I was going to say great guy, but if you prefer *geek*, then . . ."

Trevor pokes my side, in the one spot that I'm most ticklish and that he knows so well, and I spasm away from him.

"Okay, uncle! Uncle! I give up," I laugh.

"You'd be horrible in a torture situation," he accuses.

"Remind me not to join the armed services, then."

"Oh, I will. With you in the service, our national security would be at serious risk."

He stands, pulling me up with him in one graceful motion, grace being something I don't think I could master if I spend a thousand years practicing. He starts jumping and holds my hands tightly since we have learned the hard way that I can't match my jumps exactly to his—being launched off the edge of the tramp once was enough for me.

"You *are* a pretty great guy, you know," I tell him.

He flushes, embarrassed.

"Yeah, whatever. Don't try to soften me up," he teases, but underneath that, I can see my words make him happy—which seems like a fair trade since he's constantly making me so happy.

20

THE THUNDER ROLLS

THE SOUTHERN sky is dusky blue, spattered with light gray clouds. To the north, however, there is a black wall, dark clouds nearly indiscernible in the roiling sky. Occasional flashes of lightning throw bleak illumination through the storm. *That's* the side of the sky that reflects my inner turmoil. I settle in Trevor's car and try to pretend that I can't feel the tension coming off him.

He hasn't said much, smiling and kissing me when he picked me up, but I can feel the difference anyway, no matter how hard he's trying. It's mostly silent in the car, the only sound my voice as I give him directions to Kyle's house. I know how much he hates these parties—and how much he dislikes Kyle—but Beth called and ran the guilt trip over me, which I in turn ran over Trevor. So here we are, because he will do almost anything to make me happy.

We pull up next to the curb even though there's still some room for parking in the large dirt front yard under the oversized willow tree. The house is a nice, two-story Cape Cod–style, which seems to take Trevor by surprise. I've been here before, so it's no biggie to me, but I try to see it through his eyes. I think about the last house we went to for a party and then this one and realize he probably expected run-down slum-type houses both times. I try not to be offended.

Trevor looks good tonight. He's wearing jeans and a long-sleeve weave Henley with the sleeves pushed up to his elbows, not quite fitting in with the crowd we'll be with tonight, but not looking like the geek he is either. It hasn't escaped my notice how differently he dresses now, many times wearing T-shirts or Henleys. Even when he wears his button-up shirts, he generally leaves the top three or four buttons open now, and, most importantly, doesn't tuck them in.

He opens my door and grabs my hand as I climb out, not letting go. The air is weirdly silent in the face of the oncoming storm, electric, not even a breeze to flutter the leaves. It feels ominous.

As we near the house, the silence is interrupted by the beat of the music coming through the door. There's no point in knocking so I push the door open, and we're assaulted by the blaring, pounding stereo and the smells of smoke and beer. To me it is the sound and smell of comfort and acceptance, but Trevor's shoulders tighten just the barest hint. I glance at him, and he smiles at me calmly. I can read the doubt in his tight eyes.

"Jen!" Kyle calls as he weaves down the stairs toward us. "And you brought my friend Trevor! How are ya, man?" he yells, pumping Trevor's hand. Kyle's eyes are glazed; it's pretty apparent that he's had more than one or two beers—and probably something more than just alcohol as well. But Trevor is nothing if not polite.

"I'm fine, thanks. How are you?"

Kyle laughs and smacks Trevor roughly on the back.

"You're priceless, my friend. Come on in and make yourself at home. You know the drill, sweetie," he says to me, dropping a sloppy kiss on my cheek. I wait until he's turned away before I wipe it off. I look up at Trevor, laughing at Kyle's ridiculousness, and see the flash of ire in Trevor's eyes.

"How did you say you know him?" he asks loudly, leaning down to be heard above the music and people talking.

I shrug. "I met him through Ella and Beth."

"He's not worried his parents will come home?"

I point into the den off to the right, where an older man is lounging on a leather couch, football game on the TV, earplugs in.

"His father?" Even with the noise I can hear the stunned disbelief in Trevor's voice.

"Only on the weekends," I say. Trevor processes this, never quite losing his look of incredulity. I'm not surprised. When you're raised in a house where happiness blooms all around, it's hard to imagine people living like this. This isn't so bad. There are worse ways to live. I should know.

"What if someone calls the cops?" he asks worriedly.

"Relax, Trev. Nothing bad is going to happen."

As if to belie my words, a sudden clap of thunder shakes the house.

"Come on," I pull on his hand. "Let's go downstairs."

Kyle's basement is a sort of makeshift dancing area since it's mostly unfinished, with cement floor and walls. Only a bathroom, laundry room, and small bedroom are completed. The latter is sparsely furnished—only a mattress sits in the middle of the floor. I'm well aware of its purpose, and that it had been finished by Kyle himself for nights such as this. I always steer clear of it—I might not be a paragon of virtue, but there are certain things that are mine alone that only I have the right to give away, and I have no desire to lose it to some sloppy drunk boy who wouldn't even remember me the next day. It's the very thing that was nearly stolen from me by my stepfather, which has only made it that much more precious to me

Trevor seems eased by the somewhat normal scene down here, seeming almost like a school dance. The music drops into a slow blaring ballad, and Trevor pulls me into his arms, relieved, I think, for something to do. Everyone around us is pressed closely together, and though Trevor now holds me *much* closer than he did for our first dance, it is still modest compared to the others here. I smile up at him. It's just another Trevor quirk that makes him completely unique.

After one song, the music moves back into a throbbing, upbeat tempo, and Trevor moves slightly away, keeping his hold on me. About half of the couples start bouncing with the new music while the other half continue to grip one another in oblivion. Trevor looks around at them, smiling wryly. We stay through a few more songs, dancing, then the heat becomes overbearing.

"Wanna go up and get something to drink?" I yell in his ear.

"What?" he yells back, but I only know what he's saying by reading his lips. I point toward the ceiling and imitate drinking. He nods, and we fight our way through the crowd, which has definitely thickened, to go back up the stairs. We squeeze our way into the kitchen, and Trevor pushes through until he reaches some cups. He grabs a nearly empty bottle of Diet Coke and fills two cups. I raise my eyebrows questioningly, but he just smiles and shrugs.

The pop is warm and not especially thirst quenching. My head begins to ache a little from the overbearing noise. Trevor snakes his arm around my waist, pulling me close and dragging me toward the back door.

We spill out into the backyard, which is nearly as crowded as it had been in the house, but at least the air is cooler now that the storm is near. A breeze lifts my hair off my neck, and it's somewhat quieter.

I look up at the black sky, where lightning silently shoots beams into the darkness. Thunder rolls slowly on the heels of the flashes. I normally love rainstorms, but I'm a little disappointed that it will force us back into the house when it breaks.

"Are you doing okay?" Trevor asks, watching me intently.

"Shouldn't I be asking you that? You forget—this is old hat for me."

"Oh. Yeah, right. You just seem a little . . ."

He trails off, and I look at him curiously.

"A little what?"

He shakes his head. "Nothing. Never mind. Do you want to go back in?"

"No, let's stay out here for a few minutes while we can."

Trevor's face reflects his relief at my words, though he turns to try to hide it from me.

"Jen! There you are, baby!" Kyle's too loud words come out the door as he stumbles through. Trevor's lips tighten at his endearment, and I wonder what he's thinking. Surely he's not jealous of *Kyle*?

"Hey, Trevor, my man, mind if I steal your chick for a minute? I have something I want to show her."

Trevor's face tightens at this, and I wonder if he'll say no. Instead, he looks at me, and I can read his face as if he spoke aloud. He's asking me if this is what I want. I kind of like this jealousness, so I smile.

"I'll be right back." I hand him my cup to hold for me. His eyes flash—or is it just the reflection of the lightning?—and so I give him a little break. I lean up and kiss him, making it clear to Kyle that we have progressed beyond mere friends. Trevor's eyes widen a little at this unexpectedness.

"Don't go away," I whisper, turning to follow Kyle, immediately regretting that I agreed to this when Kyle takes my hand and pulls me back into the hot, overcrowded house. His hand doesn't feel right in mine, too soft and sweaty. He pulls me into the den, which has been abandoned by his father, who is most likely upstairs in his room by now.

"What is it, Kyle?" I demand impatiently. The volume of the music and laughter drowns part of my sentence and takes the edge from my words.

"I've got something for you." He smiles in his impression of a villain and waggles his eyebrows. I feel the first stirring of discomfort.

"I should go back out—"

Kyle turns away from my words, pulling me further into the room. Suddenly Beth and Ella are there, throwing their arms around me in welcome. We try to have a shouted conversation, but the effort is too great.

Finally, Kyle walks over and closes the glass doors, muffling the music somewhat. Beth pulls me over to sit on the couch next to her.

"I was wondering if you had left your foster family and we hadn't heard," she accuses.

"I'm sorry, I should have called. I've just been—"

"I know, working on your project. What, did you decide to take a day off?" She looks around to see if she's missed him.

"Romeo is out back," Kyle interrupts, sliding down onto the coffee table directly in front of me.

"Romeo?" Ella questions with a laugh as she plops down

on my other side, sandwiching me between the twins.

"Either that, or Jen here is into making out with her friends." He laughs, but I can hear the question in his voice, wanting to know what's going on between us. I refuse to take the bait, but Beth jumps in.

"Part of the plan, right, Jen?"

I don't answer as they all laugh. I don't want to talk about Trevor to them.

"So, you said you have something for me?" I bring Kyle's lethargic attention back to me.

"Oh yeah, baby. Boy, do I ever. Rick!" he calls over my shoulder. A boy I don't know ambles over and hands something to Kyle. I stare at the elongated glass contraption, water in the bottom of the glass bowl, the small pipe jutting from the side already loaded. Kyle brings it to his lips and lowers his lighter, inhaling deeply. He hands it to me, and automatically I take it. I stare down at it, numb. It wasn't all that long ago that I would have taken this from Kyle or anyone gladly, figuring a hit or two never hurt anyone—and that actually sometimes it helped.

Now my mind is filled with other thoughts: the family I've nearly decided to stay with who will throw me out if they find out, Todd's trusting eyes, even Carol, eyes filled with knowing. Mostly though, the most important face pushes all the other thoughts aside, eyes filled with repulsion and hatred.

As if my thoughts conjure him, Beth and Ella gasp in unison, and I follow their eyes up to the glass doors to see Trevor standing there, watching me holding Kyle's surprise for me. There is no repulsion or hatred in his eyes; it is far worse. The disappointment and grief I see there cause my heart to stutter to a stop. I stand up quickly, thrusting it back at Kyle; my movements make me look guiltier. Trevor doesn't move, just watches as I hurry toward the door. I pull it open, then flee past his shocked face, ignoring the hand that reaches feebly for me.

I rush out the front door into the ripping wind and down the steps, thunder rolling across the sky in tandem with the lightning now. Fat raindrops spatter my face as I begin to run, away from what I am, from what I have always been, from what I will always be.

21

THE LIGHTNING STRIKES

MY SIDE aches, and my lungs scream in protest, but still I run. I'm drenched from the storm, which drives down furiously now. I barely notice. I run blindly, unaware of my surroundings, trying to find peace from my guilt, from my breaking heart. I'm not sure how long I've been running when I realize there's no escape.

As if my realization is the permission my body needs, it suddenly gives out. I stumble with legs gone rubber and collapse beneath a tree, landing on my knees and palms with a wretched howl that blends into the roll of thunder overhead. I drop to my side and curl up in a ball in the wet leaves, hating the tears and the pitiful sounds coming from me, but unable to stop them.

And then, like a miracle, he's there, pulling me up against him, breath heaving, his arms bands of steel that hold me together tight against his hard chest.

"I'm sorry, I'm sorry, I'm sorry," I gasp repeatedly as he rocks me. The fact that he's here, that his *kindness* runs so deep that he would follow me after what he saw, what he now knows, how much he must hate me . . . his compassion cuts me, amplifies my guilt.

He's talking as I keep gasping my apology, the words muffled with my head pressed against his chest, his hand smoothing my hair over and over. Eventually, what he's saying, what he himself is repeating over and over, begins to penetrate.

"It doesn't matter, Jen. It's okay. It doesn't matter."

My grief flashes into anger at his words, and I push away from him angrily.

"How can you *say* that?" I explode at him. "*Of course* it matters. *Of course* it's not okay! I'm a loser, Trev. You *have* to see that now. This is what I am. It's all I'm ever going to be! I'm not like you. I'm never going to *be* like you."

The sky lights up with a flash as a clap of thunder crashes across us. In the light I see his face clearly for just a second, and if I didn't know better I would swear he's smiling. Darkness descends again, and he becomes an indistinct outline. He reaches out, hand sliding down my sodden arm, and pulls my hand into both of his, not even caring that it's covered in mud and leaves.

"I don't remember ever asking you to be like me," he says, threading his fingers through mine.

"Trevor, I know you didn't. You *wouldn't*. You're too perfect." I'm sharp with him, but he doesn't pull away. "This wasn't supposed to be this way. When I started . . ." I trail off, knowing that now is the time, *now* is when I need to tell him the truth. I continue, "I never meant for this to be so . . ." A flash lights his face, and I see confusion. "You're all that is good, Trev, and I'm all that is . . . not."

He's silent for a moment, and I know he's coming to the realization that my words are true, that he's a fool to have wasted any time on me.

"Says who?" he finally asks quietly, and I almost don't hear him over the sound of the rain beating against the tree above us. I don't answer, and he gives my hand a little jerk.

"Who says that you're not good?" He sounds a little angry. "Who says that, Jen? Kyle? Beth? Ella? Your mother? *You*? Who gave any of you the right to decide who's good and who's not?"

"Oh, c'mon, Trev. Tell me that before you knew me you didn't think you were better than me, better than any of my friends?"

"Not better—*different*," he says, and I laugh scornfully, or rather I try to, but it gets tangled in my throat. He jerks my hand again, and the lightning reveals the intense anger on his face.

"No, I don't party; no, I don't dress in black leather and chains; that's not my style. That's how I was raised. I worry about getting good grades and I go to church and I watch sci-fi movies and I generally follow the rules. Most people would call me a geek or a nerd. *You've* called me that many times.

"But that isn't everything that defines me. I mean, look at me, sitting here in a rainstorm under a tree that's probably going to kill us when the lightning hits it, holding the hand of a pretty cool girl who really is the opposite of me, a girl that I happen to be in love with. A girl I couldn't have *imagined* would want to be with me. But here she is, letting me hold her hand, trying to tell me why *she* isn't good enough for *me*. That's crazy."

The rain is tapering off, slowing while Trevor is giving me this amazing speech, but I can't respond. My mind is stuck on one thing he said, the one thing that glares in the night brighter than any of the lightning that has come before. As if in answer, the lightning chooses that moment to streak across the sky, followed in quick succession by three more. It gives Trevor a clear view of my stunned expression.

"What?" he sounds defensive.

"Trev, what you just said . . ."

"Yeah?" Now he's wary.

"Did you say . . . in . . . *love* . . . with?"

His outline shrugs, and he shifts uncomfortably.

"Yeah, so what? Tell me you didn't know that."

The sky lights once more, the thunder rolling again, further away now.

"Wait, you *didn't* know?" he asks when my silence grows between us.

I shake my head, stunned by this revelation, especially after tonight's events.

"How could you not know?" he asks softly, squeezing my hand.

"I didn't think you . . ." I trail off, and Trevor leans toward me intently.

"It doesn't change anything, Jen. I've felt this way for a long time now. No pressure, I don't expect anything to cha—" His words cut off with a grunt as I launch myself against him, flattening him against the wet leaves beneath us, his arms instinctively coming tightly around me. I kiss him, not an easy task with the big grin on my face.

He reaches up and traces my face, pulling back when he feels the wetness there.

"You're crying?" he asks gently.

"I seem to be doing that a lot lately. Sorry."

"Did *I* make you cry?" He sounds horrified.

"Yup," I laugh. "Thank you." I kiss him again.

"Okaaay," he draws the word out. "I'm confused."

"Trev, I didn't mean to fall in love with you, I swear I didn't. But I couldn't help it. I've been so mad about that."

"*Mad?* . . . Really? Why would that make you mad? Because your friends wouldn't like it?"

I laugh again.

"I quit caring what *they* think a long time ago. I was mad because I figured there was no way you could ever love me, and that meant I had to bring you down to my level just so I could deserve you."

Trevor flips me over, and I find myself pinned down while he straddles me, my arms held above my head. He leans down so that his face is right above mine.

"You're an idiot, you know that?" His voice is softly menacing. I smile at him. A flash of lightning reveals he's also grinning down at me.

"We're *both* idiots, Trev."

He grunts in agreement.

"Maybe that's what makes us perfect for each other."

"Maybe so," he says just before planting a firm kiss on my mouth. He pulls up, drawing me with him. He scoots back against the tree trunk, pulling me against him and wrapping his arms around me against the chill air. I thread my fingers through his, pulling his arms tighter.

"Trev, I want you to know, I wasn't planning to smoke Kyle's—"

"It doesn't matter, Jen," he cuts me off. "I'm not asking you to change."

"It does matter. I want you to know. There was a time when I wouldn't have even thought twice about it. But since I've met you, I haven't wanted to do anything like that. I've watched you, I've hung out with your family and friends, and I don't want to do things that are self-destructive anymore. I don't want to be that person anymore. I want to be someone who your mom wouldn't be horrified to see show up on her doorstep for her son." A strangled sound comes from Trevor, but I put a finger on his mouth to stop his words.

"I want to be someone who my family would be *glad* to adopt. Mostly I want to be someone who deserves you. And I think that's a good thing, don't you?"

I can feel the tension in his shoulders, feel him wanting to argue. Finally he sighs.

"If you think it's good, Jen. But only if it's what *you* want. I don't want you to do it because you think it's what I want."

"Seriously, Trev, I think for the first time in my life I want to have a future, a *good* future, and I can't get there by living the way I have been."

He doesn't answer, just pulls me firmly against him. After a few silent minutes, he speaks.

"I'm glad you came into my life, Jen. I still don't know why you did, but I don't care. I'm just glad you did, glad you turned my world upside down, which is really right side up."

I swallow the lump of guilt in my throat. *Someday,* I think, *someday I'll tell him. Just not right now.*

"I am too, Trev. Who knew that you would be The One." I smile. "Which I guess makes me your Trinity."

"My Amidala."

"Your Zira."

"My Sylvia."

"Your . . ." I scour my brain, trying to remember some other great sci-fi love interest.

"My what?" he laughs.

"Ha! I'm your Saphira." I settle back smugly, only for Trevor to start laughing.

"What?" I demand.

"Saphira is a *dragon*."

"I know, but Eragon needed her, and she needed him."

"Okay, I'll concede that." I can hear the smile in his voice. "But I don't think she'd be much fun to kiss. I'd rather you were my Arya."

I turn into him, running my finger over his lips lightly.

"Maybe I'll just be your Jen," I tease.

"Sounds about right to me," he says, leaning down to show me how much better it is to kiss a human than to kiss a dragon.

22

ADOPTING A NEW LIFESTYLE ISN'T FOR THE WEAK OF HEART

THE ADOPTION is going pretty easily and quickly. I guess between my mother's willingness to sign me away yet again and the fact that the Grants were already state-approved to be my foster parents moved things along. I'm guessing my advanced age also has something to do with it. The Grants want to have a party on Saturday, the day it will be official, to celebrate. I'm pleased that they think it is something worth celebrating, because I definitely think it is.

Weird.

I'm also nervous about it because of my natural pessimism and sense of doom. Something will go wrong like it always seems to when my life is going too well.

I decide to call Beth and Ella and invite them over since they are my only real girl friends, and maybe this will be a way to make things right with them.

"So," I begin hesitantly when they pick up two separate phones on the same line at their house. "I was wondering if you both want to come by my house on Saturday, around five."

"Five? Isn't that kind of early for a party?" Beth asks.

"Not for this kind of a party. It's a family thing."

There is dead silence on the phone. Beth and Ella are really the only two real friends I've had since living in this area, but in their silence I realize that we've never *really* been friends, definitely not the kind of friends who go to one another's "family things." I clear my throat uncomfortably.

"Actually, it's a kind of celebration. I didn't want to tell you until it was done, you know, the whole didn't-want-to-jinx-it thing. But actually, the Grants want to adopt me. It'll be all signed and done on Saturday."

Another heavy silence, then Ella speaks.

"Soooo," she draws the word out, confusion lacing her voice, "you're saying that you're *not* planning a big blow-up? You're sticking around?"

"Well, yeah."

"So, when did all of this happen?" Beth sounds angry. "You haven't said anything to us."

"I know. I'm sorry about that. It's just been kind of wild, I guess." I feel like I have to defend myself. "It's all happened really fast. After I went to see my mother, I—"

"You went to see your mother?" Ella interrupts. "When was this?"

"Not that long ago, Ella. I just really didn't want to talk much about it."

"To us, you mean? You didn't want to talk about it to us? Who then? Who did you talk to about it, Jen? Your science project? Is he the one you confide in now?" Beth's voice is rising, and I feel myself flush with mortification. Then I hear her slam the phone down. There's only silence.

"Ella?" I ask, hesitant.

She sighs.

"Don't mind her, Jen. She's been fighting with her boyfriend, and she's got PMS all at once."

"Are you mad at me?" I ask.

"No, not really. I mean, I wish you would have told us sooner, but it doesn't really matter, I guess."

"I really wasn't trying to keep it from you. Things have just been weird for me, you know? No one has ever wanted to adopt me before."

"Yeah, but that was kinda your fault, right? I mean, you told us about some of the things you did to get yourself kicked out. You can't really blame any of them."

I flush again, embarrassed about both my past behavior and having thought it was funny to share the stories.

"I'm happy for you if you're happy, Jen. What time Saturday?"

Even as she asks me, I regret having issued the invitation. I suddenly don't want this pure event sullied by my past with them—too late now. The old Jen might have just told Ella to drop dead, but the new one who's been way too influenced by Trevor the Polite can't.

"Five o'clock," I hear myself telling her.

"Okay, we'll try to make it."

I hang up, hoping against hope that they won't.

***

Saturday morning is bright and clear. I hope it's a good omen. I ride in the car with Pat, Sue, and Tamara, who (I realize) will soon be my sister. That brings thoughts of Mrs. Green and her regret about never having had a sister. I glance at Tamara, who is texting at lightning speed as if trying to break the world record. Could be worse, I guess.

When we arrive at the courthouse—a place I've only ever had bad experiences with—I see that Jeff and Kari are waiting. Another jolt as I apprehend that he will be my brother and she my sister-in-law. The butterflies begin kicking around in my stomach.

The whole process is pretty un-dramatic after all. A conference-type room with a judge in plain clothes, a few papers signed by Pat and Sue, and just like that, I'm part of a family. Like an idiot I cry as my new mother pulls me into her arms with a cheerful hug.

I'm grateful for the party mainly because I need the steadying presence of Trevor. My new family is overjoyed, and I'm overwhelmed. I really need some time alone, but that won't be forthcoming until later. Trevor walks in, smiling with those killer dimples, giving me a big hug that comforts me. I feel both a part of and separate from the whole thing, and he strangely feels more familiar than my new family.

Pat barbecues hamburgers while people keep filing into the backyard, mostly neighbors and friends of the Grants. Some of Tamara's cheerleader-type friends come over, and apparently my new status as sister makes me acceptable rather than despicable because they all come over with smiles and hugs for me. This feels okay. I sit on the porch steps next to Trevor, who has one arm around my waist and his other hand tangled in mine while we talk to Tamara, her friends, and a few of Trev's geek friends who've come by.

This is just when Ella and Beth show up. I glance up to see the shocked expressions on their faces. I look around me and see how this looks to them. Me, in my white skirt, pink shirt, and easy makeup, hair dyed back to its natural dark brown, surrounded by the types of people I spent many hours making fun of with these two. I'm laughing and having fun while wrapped in the arms of the person who I'm supposed to be turning to win a bet. I stand quickly, guilty.

"Hey, Beth, Ella. Glad you guys came."

They look at each other, then back at me as if I've grown two heads.

"Are these your friends?" Sue comes over, happily greeting Beth and Ella.

"You girls grab a plate and makes yourselves at home," she says after introductions. They roll their eyes silently at each other, and my stomach turns with anger and shame. They are who I had been, and now it's *my family* they're bagging on. I can't stand it. Luckily, neither can they.

"We just came by to say . . . you know . . ." Ella trails off.

"But we can't stay." Beth is sharper. Trevor comes to stand next to me and takes my hand in his. Beth's eyes follow all of this, narrowing. "Seems like you've got all you need, huh?" she asks quietly, turning and yanking Ella with her as they leave.

"What was that all about?" Trevor asks, rubbing my arms as I shudder.

"Nothing," I say, forcing a smile. Trevor knows me, knows my smile is false, but he won't push it, not here.

"Let's go eat," I say, thanking him with my eyes for dropping it. I'm chilled now, and some of the light has gone out of the day that started so great. Because somewhere in Beth's eyes was a promise, and I don't think it was a promise of anything good.

23

BACK TO SCHOOL

THE FIRST day of school, senior year—which means this is my thirteenth year of having a first day of school, so I shouldn't be nervous, right? Especially when my changing schools almost yearly is taken into account. I'd always had the buffer of my toughness, my difference—until this year. Hence, the nerves.

Today I'm showing up to school like any other girl—jeans and T-shirt, non-descript hair and makeup. Plain. This terrifies me. Trevor had wanted to pick me up and drive me to school, but I knew that I needed to do this alone. So now here I am, kicking myself for being stupidly stubborn when I could have at least had *that* comfort.

"Jen! How're ya doin'?"

I turn around to see Brian waving at me. He seems a little unsure—I guess he's wondering if I want him to talk to me at school. It's one thing in Trev's basement when we're watching movies, but school is another thing. I nearly sag in relief at the familiar face.

"Hey, Brian," I say back, walking over to him.

"You look nice," he says, trying not to sound surprised but failing miserably.

"Yeah, nice," a familiar voice mocks from behind me. I turn to see Beth there, looking me up and down distastefully, like gum she wants to peel off the bottom of her shoe. "You almost look like . . ." Her eyes come up to mine and I can see the anger burning bright. "A cheerleader," she spits out. "See you around, *Jennifer*."

She walks away as my cheeks flame, and I turn back to Brian, whose eyes are round with alarm. I feel an overwhelming need to apologize to him on behalf of all of the people I have treated like that over the years. I open my mouth, but no sound comes out.

Suddenly arms snake around my waist from behind, and still on edge and defensive, I turn around and strike out.

"Ow!" Trevor grabs his chest where I slugged him.

"Oh, Trev, I'm so sorry." I lean into him, wrapping my arms around him. I feel like crying.

His arms come up to hold me tight, hands soothing my back.

"It's okay, Jen," he laughs. "It really didn't hurt. I was just joking." He pushes me back from him, sees the tears shining in my eyes. "Whoa, what's this all about? What's the matter?" He looks at Brian questioningly. Brian just shrugs, hurrying off before he has to try to explain the unexplainable.

"Did Brian say something to you?" He's disbelieving but willing to defend my honor all the same. The thought makes me laugh.

"Yeah, he told me I look nice."

"I'll kill him," he says sternly.

"Please don't. I don't want to have to visit *two* people in prison."

I have been back to see my biological mother. I wanted to thank her for not fighting the adoption so that I could have a name and a family before I turn eighteen, while I'm still young enough to *need* to belong to someone. In that visit and the letters we have exchanged, I've come to view her less as the mother who screwed up my life and more as just a woman who's lived a sad life, who could use a friend.

"Besides that, he's just being nice. I don't think I've ever looked so plain in my life."

"Plain?" Trevor scoffs. "I don't think plain is an adjective that could ever be used to describe you, Jen. You're the most beautiful—"

"Don't, Trev," I cut him off. "We're always honest with each other, right?" Even as I say the words, the familiar sting of guilt pierces me at the big thing—the big lie, if I'm being honest—I haven't yet told him.

"Exactly," he says, giving me a squeeze, "which is why I'm not lying when I tell you how beautiful you are. Best looking girl here."

I shake my head at him. I guess I can add blindness to his small—very small—list of faults. He looks around him dramatically, then leans down conspiratorially.

"I don't know if you realize this or not, but we still have our arms around each other. People are going to *see*."

I smile at his facetiousness and lean up to plant a serious kiss on his lips, which he returns enthusiastically.

"Guess that means the whole let's-keep-it-a-secret thing is over, huh?"

"Can't really remember why I wanted to keep it a secret, Trev."

"Good." He wraps his arm possessively around my shoulder. "Come on, let's go get our locker assignment."

"Locker? Singular?" I ask.

"Sure, why not? We can share one. I can teach you some organizational skills."

I grimace, and as we're walking away, I happen to glance over and see the mouse Mary Ellen glaring in our direction. Apparently she's witnessed the kiss, divined its meaning, and isn't happy about it. I heave a sigh. It seems that there aren't any new girl friends in my immediate future.

24

IF IT SEEMS TOO GOOD TO
BE TRUE ✦ ✦ ✦

I'VE HAD boyfriends before. None of them have ever
stuck for longer than a couple of weeks. The closest I've had
to anything of longevity was the year-long pseudo-flirtation
with Seth. So being someone's girlfriend is a new experience
in itself. Being *Trevor's* girlfriend is taking that experience to
a whole new level.

Over the summer, we hadn't really had to share each
other or our time with anyone other than our families and
the occasional movie with Trev's friends at his house—or the
few unfortunate parties with mine. But now, we don't share
a single class, only have lunch together every other day, and
still have family obligations, which make it hard to spend
much time together. Trevor comes to pick me up each morning, and in his usual style makes sure to hurry to walk me
to each of my classes, even though that leaves him to run for
his own classes to avoid the tardies that will mar his perfect
attendance record.

He ran for Student Body President, which soaked up even
more of his time, both when he was campaigning and even
more now that he's won. We spend as much time together as

possible in the evenings, doing homework—another first for me, caring about my grades—and on weekends.

On the days we have lunch together, we sit with his group of friends talking mostly about last weekend's sci-fi movie, whichever one we'd watched. On the opposite days, I sit with Brian, Jim—and Mary Ellen. Brian and Jim keep the conversation flowing, either oblivious to or ignoring the tension that exists between the mouse and me. I can't blame her for hating me—I would hate anyone who took Trevor from my attentions. Plus, she intimidates me a little, because I still know that she would be so much better for him than I am.

I've become a target for all of my old friends, Beth and Seth particularly. Ella seems a little embarrassed by their harassment, but she goes along with them anyway. That's something else I understand.

Even with the limited Trevor time and the less than stellar school experience, I've never been happier.

***

Trevor didn't pick me up this morning because he had to be to school early for an SBO meeting. Nothing unusual in that since he's been doing it twice a week for the last couple of months since the election. What is weird—no, not weird, *alarming*—is the fact that I come through the doors, automatically scanning for him as he always hurries to meet me, and instead of his waiting for me, I see him in conversation with Beth.

They stand with their heads close together, Trevor leaning down toward her as she is quite a bit shorter than him. Jealousy doesn't play a part in my alarm—I trust Trevor implicitly. It's not that I think I have some unbreakable hold over him, that he couldn't possibly stray from my immutable charms. It's more that I *know* Trevor, and one thing I know is that if he wanted to move on, he would do the right thing by telling me first before making a move in any other direction. His infallible politeness does have its benefits, dubious though they might be.

What worries me is that he's talking to Beth at all. Or rather, that Beth is talking to him. He knows some of how Beth has treated me since my "change" and because of his sense of honor toward me, he would feel like he was somehow betraying me by being friendly with her. And, okay, honestly I probably would also. Yet here he stands, deep in conversation, intent on whatever she's telling him. Somehow, I don't think she's telling him that she has seen the error of her ways and is now ready to join our little geekdom.

Trevor's cheeks begin a slow burn as I watch, and my own redden in response. As if sensing me watching, his eyes come up and unerringly land on me. In his eyes, I can see it; I can see exactly what it is that she has confessed to him. She also turns my way, and my eyes flick briefly her way to see the smugness in her own expression. I don't care about her, or her reasons. All that matters is Trevor.

My eyes meet his, and I can't hide it. He reads the truth, the confirmation of her words plainly on my face. My heart begins to pound as he walks my way. I want to turn and flee, stop him from what I know he is going to say. Of course he would come to me, ask me, want to hear the words from *my* lips. If I lie, I know he will believe me over Beth. I frantically try to form a lie in my head, imagine the words that will take that horrible expression from his face, make him smile and take my hand and walk me to my first class like any other day. I can see that it's too late—he already *knows*.

"Is it true?" he demands when he reaches me. In his eyes,

I can read the hurt, the disbelief. He waits while I swallow over the dry lump that clogs my throat.

"Trevor, I didn't . . ." I can barely get the words out. I didn't . . . what? Because actually, I did.

"What did you win?" he demands quietly.

You, I want to say, the best prize of all. I can see the pain in his eyes being replaced by something else, something I've always had in my own eyes—distrust. Anything I say now will mean nothing to him. I want to look away, to not witness all of the terrible emotions running across his face and through his eyes. I can't. I'm firsthand witness to my own destruction.

"I was a *bet*?" he bites the word. I can't speak, can't defend myself.

"I hope it was worth it," he murmurs quietly, the words laced with pain and resentment. The emotions in his eyes finally stop seething and settle on anger, even as I feel my heart breaking and my world tilt on its axis.

"See you 'round," he says coldly, turning away, *striding* away, as if he can't get out of my presence fast enough.

I make it into the girls' bathroom and into a stall before my legs give way. I sink to the floor. Silent anguish wracks my body in an ache so deep that tears seem pointless.

When I'm able, I push myself up. The bathroom is mercifully deserted. I see my pale, drawn image reflected in the mirror—a stranger. I can't stay here; I can't face anyone. I look ill. I feel dead. This observation drives me from the bathroom to the office, where the office secretary doesn't even question the authenticity of my "I'm sick" claim. In fact, she hurries to bring me the phone. I guess I look worse than I thought.

I call my mom—funny how quickly I've come to think

of Sue as that—who then comes to pick me up. She looks horrified as I climb into the car, and I'm forced to talk her out of driving me straight to the doctor's office. It's not easy, and some small part of my mind recognizes the love in her concern and is grateful of it.

We arrive home. I make it to the upstairs bathroom where I throw up this morning's breakfast. Even when my stomach is empty, it continues to clench and heave as if trying to expel my very soul. I am finally able to stop and crawl into my bedroom, pulling myself into the bed, blanket over my head.

My mom comes in with a cold, wet cloth, which she presses to my forehead. She's murmuring to me, but I can't make sense of her words; I don't want to make sense of her words. After an eternity, she leaves me alone in my dry-eyed misery. I'm numb, my mind reeling and refusing to accept that Trevor's gone.

A few hours later, Mom comes back into my room, quietly. When she sees I'm awake, staring at the wall, she sits and smooths her hand across my hair. I shudder in response to the touch. She says something, and the up-lilt at the end of her words suggest a question, but my mind refuses to open enough to comprehend her words. There's something about her words, something that nags . . .

Pregnant?

Comprehension pours over me as I finally hear her. *Is there any chance you might be pregnant?*

I think about Trevor, his innate decency and strong moral compass. That matched with my stubborn determination to hold onto my own virginity until *I* decide it's time to give it away, with how careful we have always been to make sure we didn't go too far, the unspoken understanding between us that *that* wasn't going to happen; and just like that, I'm laughing. Just a giggle at first, but it quickly escalates into a hysterical laugh. Mom's brows pull together in worry. For some reason, that makes me think of Trevor, his terrible face when he realized the truth, the finality of his words.

My hysterical laughter becomes hysterical crying as the pain crushes me. My new mother lies down in the bed beside me, curling herself protectively around me, just holding me and soothing me for the eternity it takes for my sobs to taper. I drop into a restless sleep, still in her arms, hoping to never wake up.

25

Life Goes On . . .
Until you Meet an
Angel, Anyway

A FEW WEEKENDS ago at Trevor's house, we watched a cheesy movie from the eighties about zombies—not strictly sci-fi, although there was a great debate afterward about that exact subject. I found the movie rather amusing, though Trevor and his friends spent a lot of time arguing the merits of whether zombies could really exist or not.

I can tell them now.

Zombies do exist. They don't exist to eat the flesh of those who are still living, or have rotting flesh hanging from their bones. They look just like everyone else. They get up in the morning, put on clothes, eat breakfast, and answer questions directed their way. They go to school, go to their classes, turn in their homework, then go home to have dinner with their families. The blissful relief of bedtime is when they no longer have to keep up appearances. It is also the time of nightmares—both waking and sleeping. In the morning, it all begins again. Zombies *are* the walking dead, only it isn't their bodies that have died but their hearts, their souls.

I know they exist because I have become one.

I guess there were some advantages to having never had

a serious boyfriend. I've never had to go through this misery, the misery I used to mock in others. I've known pain in my life—that's nothing new. That pain was always thrust upon me, circumstances beyond my control. This is different. This is of my own making.

I can see my family worrying about me, so I smile bigger, pull on those acting skills I've honed so well over the years. I'm not sure they're fooled.

***

"Hi."

I hear the voice and look up from the lunch table where I sit hunched over my chemistry book, which I'm pretending to study, to see where the voice is coming from, though I know it isn't for me—I'm pretty much a pariah now. As I look up I see a blonde girl looking directly at me. I glance behind me to see who she's talking to, but no one is behind me. She's looking at me and not someone else.

"Are you talking to me?"

She smiles and laughs a little, coming closer and setting her lunch tray across from my untouched one. She's small—both in height and width. She has blue eyes fringed with dark blonde lashes. Her features are small also, her face heart shaped, a slight cleft in her chin. Her smile reveals even, white teeth and dimples at the corners of her mouth. She kinda looks like what an angel might—if the angel were a teenage girl.

"Yeah, I am." She smiles.

I indicate my book, hoping she'll take the hint that she's interrupting me and go away.

"Studying?" she asks.

"Obviously," I say, sounding as unfriendly as I can.

"Does it help? Reading the book upside down, I mean."

I glance down and see that she's right. Embarrassed I slam the book closed, and she laughs. I know I should be offended that she's laughing at me, but somehow I'm not.

"I'm Jane." Her voice is lilting, and her hand thrusts out toward me. Hesitantly, I grab her hand and in spite of her petite size, her grip is strong and sure.

"Jen," I say. "I haven't seen you before."

"Yeah, I'm new here."

Ah, that explains it, I think.

"Explains what?" she asks, frowning, which does nothing to detract from her utter cuteness.

"Sorry, I didn't mean to say that out loud." When she continues to watch me, waiting, I hear myself explaining. "I'm not probably someone you want to be seen with."

"Oh yeah?" She cocks her head, studying me as if the answer is to be found stamped across my face.

"Why are you talking to me, anyway?"

She slides into the chair across from me, utterly graceful.

"Why not?" she asks curiously as she spreads her napkin across her lap, picks up her fork, and then stares distastefully at her lump of spaghetti.

"Shouldn't you be over there?" I ask, jerking my chin toward the table where all the cute, perky cheerleaders are sitting. She follows my glance, then grimaces at me.

"Please don't tell me you think I belong with them," she mutters, gamely stabbing her noodles and placing a cut-off bite in her mouth. "Besides," she says around her mouthful of pasta, "you look way more interesting than them."

I narrow my eyes at her, then start gathering my books together, letting my annoyance show.

"What did I say?" she asks after swallowing the lump of pasta with only a small shudder.

"I know your type," I mutter angrily.

"Oh yeah? Enlighten me," Jane challenges.

I lean toward her.

"You're a do-gooder," I throw at her.

"A do-whatter?" She laughs, twirling another lump of spaghetti on her fork—no easy task—and shoving it in her mouth.

"A do-gooder," I repeat. "You see me sitting here, all alone, and you think 'Oh, poor girl, so sad looking with no friends.' Right?"

She's staring at me as if I've sprouted horns.

"No," she says, finally finding her voice.

"I'm right. I know it. I mean, seriously, who else would sit and force that crap down their throats when it's so obviously disgusting?"

To my surprise, she laughs.

"It *is* disgusting, isn't it? I usually bring lunch from home. My mom is a *fabulous* cook, so I thought maybe I was being unfair to the . . ." She trails off as she stabs at the pasta again. This time when she picks up the fork, the whole glob comes along. She meets my eyes over the mess, and we both burst out laughing. I quickly swallow the nowadays-unfamiliar laughter, remembering that I'm mad at her for making me her charity case.

"Actually, Jen, I took one look at you and thought, now there's a girl who lives life a little left of center. You don't look like those girls over there," she thumbs toward the table I had pointed her to earlier, "and you don't look like anyone else either. I just thought you looked . . ."

"Interesting?" I ask facetiously.

She smiles. "Exactly."

"Well, I'm not. And I'm not who you want to be seen with if you want to have any kind of social life at this school."

"See, I knew you were interesting. Definitely a story there."

"No story, just—I used to be an outsider-type, I guess."
My face flushes at the lame explanation. "I mean, well, I was,
but then I started dating someone . . ." I trail off, shrugging.
I decide I better tell her the truth, since she'll hear it soon
enough anyway.

"See those guys over there?" I ask, pointing to where Ella,
Beth, and the others sit. She follows my finger and nods. "I
was one of them. Then I decided to make it a game to get one
of the school's . . . geeks . . ." I wince at how bad the word
sounds now, speaking of Trevor who is so much more than
that. "I made a bet to try to turn him bad. It didn't work,
since he's too good. So good, he rubbed off on me. He wasn't
very happy when he found out. Neither was anyone else,
since most people really like him."

"Fascinating," she says, leaning forward, chin on her fist.
"And interesting, definitely." She grins. "So do you plan on
trying to make me bad?"

I look at her angelic face and almost laugh at the
thought—except that laughter is no longer something I par-
ticipate in except as part of the acting gig, convincing others
of my faux happiness.

"No, definitely not."

"You have this same lunch every day?" Her sudden
change of topic leaves me spinning.

"Second, tomorrow." Second lunch, the same as Trevor,
where I have to try avoiding him, try to get through the
thirty minutes without falling apart.

"Me too," she sounds pleased. "Mind if I sit with you
again? You're the first person I've really met, and I would like
to hear more about how un-interesting you are."

I know I should tell her no, save her while I can. Honestly,
I could use the distraction, even if for just one day. I figure it

won't take much longer than that for her to have a crowd of her own friends with her sunny smile.

"Your funeral, I guess. I'll meet you by the door of the lunchroom."

"Awesome, I'll see you then. Thanks!" she calls as she walks away. Corny to thank someone for being willing to sit with you at lunch, but somehow, from her it just sounds right.

***

As it turns out, I don't need to meet Jane for lunch—we have chemistry together right before lunch. Jane is excited about sharing a class. I'll never admit it, but I'm also kinda glad because it's at least one person who hasn't learned to hate me—yet. We grab our lunches, this time Jane smartly choosing the salad. Since they're still moving in, her mom can't make her lunches yet. Jane leads the way to a table in the center of the cafeteria. *The center.* Argh.

"I moved here from Texas," Jane offers when the silence stretches.

"Hot there?" I ask inanely.

"Yeah, and humid too."

"Hmmm," is all I can think of to say. Silence reigns again.

"You don't have an accent," I tell her, probably something she already knows.

"We only lived there a couple of years. We were in Arizona before that."

"Oh." I think I can hear crickets chirping in the deafening silence.

"So, what did you mean I probably don't want to be friends with you?" she asks just about the time the quiet promises to become irretrievably awkward.

"Well, you know, the whole bet thing I told you about."

"*That's* why people aren't friends with you?" She looks around the lunchroom contemptuously—well, as contemptuously as one can look when one looks like an angel. "People here are really shallow."

I shrug. I hadn't given it that much consideration.

"I didn't exactly endear myself to any of them before I did that."

"But what about your other friends? Those ones?" She nods to where Ella and Seth sit, heads bent together.

"Yeah, they weren't really all that happy with me when it became clear I preferred Trevor and his friends over them."

"Wait—Trevor? That guy over there?" She points in Trevor's direction. My eyes go right to Trevor. I'm always aware of where he is. He doesn't notice since he's absorbed by his companion. He sits with the usual crowd, only now he always sits right next to Mary Ellen. She's beyond pleased at this change if the glow on her face these days is any indication. I cringe with jealousy and press Jane's hand back to the table.

"Yes. Him."

"I met him earlier. He *seemed* pretty nice, not the kind to hold a grudge." She's mostly right, but Trevor's never had anyone do something so horrible to him before, so for him it's a new thing. "Isn't he the Senior President, or something?"

"Student Body President," I correct automatically.

"How did a jerk like that get voted in?"

"He's not a jerk." My defense of Trevor is unyielding. Jane's blue eyes come to my taut face, and she smiles.

"You love him."

I cringe again.

"Crap. Am I that obvious?"

"I could tell yesterday when you were talking about him,

although I didn't know who you were talking about at the time. The question is, why?"

"It's a long story."

"I'll come over tonight and you can tell me then."

I groan at her utter cheerfulness. She isn't helping me with the melancholy, which I've maintained without any effort.

"I'll give you the short version," I tell her, hoping she'll drop it. "He's worth it."

She laughs at me, but again I'm not offended. It's hard to be offended when an angel is spilling her sunshine all over you.

"Not good enough. I want details. I need a friend, and I like you."

"You shouldn't. Listen, Jane, you're new here and it's not going to be long until you have plenty of friends what with all your happiness and joy." She laughs again at my cynical tone. "So don't waste your time with me. By tomorrow you won't need me."

"I don't need you now," she pronounces. "I *like* you. Even with all your doom and gloom," she adds. I decide to ignore her last comment.

"Besides that, don't you think it would be ridiculous for us to be friends?"

That stops her. She looks at me, a fringe of hurt in her eyes.

"I mean, seriously, Jane and Jen? That's so stupid."

Her eyes clear, and she grins as she punches me lightly in the arm. Right then I decide that I'm going to take advantage of her naiveté and be friends with her as long as I can. I smile at her—my first real smile since . . .

That train of thought sends my gaze back to Trevor, only to find him watching me, an unreadable expression on his face. I look away first, oddly ashamed of my smile that is now gone. I know I only imagined it, but I swear that there was a hint of a smile on his own face as he watched me.

26

OF NIGHTMARES AND HOPE

I STAND UNDER *the tree where Trevor found me once before, and though the rain pours, none of it touches me. Where before darkness prevailed, soft light, with an indiscernible source, now tempers its harshness. I don't really care to discover the source because it's illuminating Trevor, walking toward me.*

In his eyes, I can read forgiveness. He's smiling, and my heart soars. I hurry to him with urgency and relief as he holds his arms out to me, the way he used to.

I can't reach him. He still walks toward me but comes no closer. I strain with the effort of trying to touch him, my breath heaving. I know it's the most important thing in my life that I reach him before . . . before what?

Then I see her, the mouse Mary Ellen, as she steps up to him, leaning up to whisper something in his ear. Her face morphs into that of Beth.

Helplessly I watch his brows pull together, and his eyes fill with confusion as he looks at me. I want to scream a denial but my lips are sealed.

Beth morphs back into the mouse, giving me a knowing smirk as she tucks her arm through Trevor's and turns him away from me. He looks down at her, tenderness and love in his eyes as he smiles at her, his dimples becoming hers instead of mine. He looks back just once, and in that look I grasp the magnitude of his hatred, disgust, and disappointment that I have always known I deserve.

***

"Jen? Jen!"

I open my eyes and see a watery Jane leaning over me in the pre-dawn light. My chest is heaving as if I've been running, and my cheeks are wet with tears. For one second I'm confused, but then quickly I realize what's happening and sit up.

"Are you okay?" Jane's voice is laden with concern.

"I'm okay," I say, wiping my hands across my cheeks, embarrassed.

Jane has become my best friend. I was correct in my assumption of how quickly she would fill her life up with friends, but wrong that she would just as quickly drop me. I've never had a friend quite like her before, where I don't have to be a specific way to impress her or to retain her friendship. She has never wavered in her loyalty to me, no matter how misplaced. And she watches sci-fi movies with me, both the bad and the good.

Lunch has become an odd thing. I sit at a table filled with people, girls and boys who I never could have imagined as my friends. I guess they really aren't friends in the true sense of the word. They sort of *defer* to me in a manner because I am Jane's best friend. I'm okay with this because I no longer walk the halls in lonely misery. There's always someone there who's willing to walk with me, talking and keeping my mind occupied, which is a good thing.

It's a strange thing, this half-empty feeling I now have.

I drag it around all day, every day. If I keep busy and keep my mind occupied, I can keep it at a distance. It's when my world is quiet that the burden feels heavy. Nighttime is the worst, when I always have the same nightmare or some variation of it.

Jane gives me a hug, then struggles out of her sleeping bag. Whenever we sleep over at her house, we always "camp" in the living room. This is mainly because she shares a room with her nosy younger sister who doesn't know how to keep any of our conversations to herself. And since she's friends with a couple of Trevor's friends' sisters . . .

"Think you might ever stop moping about him?" she asks offhandedly as she stands up.

Jane knows all about Trevor. I told her everything, from my horrible bet and the reasons behind it—no matter how selfish those reasons sound now—to how much I had fallen in love with him.

"I *mope?*" I whine the question.

"You mope," she confirms. "I know he was a great guy, love of your life, yada-yada." She holds out her hands, and when I grab them, she pulls me forcefully to my feet. She's pretty strong for such a little thing. "But seriously, I see him around school. He doesn't look like *he's* moping. He's always with the mouse."

Usually when sweet Jane refers to Mary Ellen as the mouse, it lifts my spirits. Her words are too true, though, and reopen the dark, gaping hole where my heart used to be. I collapse back to the floor, stupid tears pooling in my eyes. Jane sinks back down in front of me.

"I'm sorry, Jen. I shouldn't have said that. I know how much he means to you."

I shrug and wave vaguely in her direction to forgive her.

"I think if you're this miserable without him, you should do something about it."

"Yeah, like what?" I moan.

"Fight for him. Make him want you again."

Her words freeze me. There was a time when I hadn't doubted for one second my ability to be able to make him want me without even having to work too hard. That was before, when there wasn't so much at stake. Now, the thought of fighting for him lodges in my head, in my chest.

"Fight for him how?" I hear the hope in my voice. So does Jane. She smiles.

"What is it that Superman said? Something like, 'Once you choose hope, anything's possible.'"

"I don't think that was Superman. I think it was Christopher Reeve himself who said that."

"Yeah, well, Christopher Reeve *is* Superman."

Sometimes I regret turning her onto my geek addiction because she's a much quicker learner than I am, and she's stubborn in her opinions about what she has picked up. She could even give Brian and Jim a run for their money in one of their great sci-fi debates.

Remembering those debates makes me lonely. I forever tried to escape them; now I'd give almost anything to be subjected to one again.

"I have some ideas," she says, "and they start with getting you looking decent again."

"I look decent," I argue defensively, though she's right. The longer time goes on without him, the less I care how I look to the point that I mostly go to school now within five minutes of rolling out of bed. "Besides that, Trevor isn't about things as superficial as looks."

"Yeah, I know. You've extolled his virtues to me until I

have them all perfectly memorized." She stands and pulls me up again. "He's deep and honest and funny and caring and kind and plays the piano like a virtuoso and sings like an angel and—"

"I'm that bad?" I interrupt her.

She shrugs. "No biggie. You love him. Someday I hope that I love someone so much that I drive all my friends crazy with talking about him like that. But I still think that superficial or not, not even the great Trevor is going to notice you walking around looking like a bag lady."

"I don't look—"

She cuts me off. "Come on, let's go get started on you."

"You act like there's a long way to go," I complain as she laughs, pulling me down the hallway into her bedroom. "You know, I thought you were an angel the first time I met you."

She looks at me and rolls her eyes. "I *thought* you were delusional when you kept telling me how perfect Trevor is, but now I *know* you're delusional."

"Yeah, I don't think that anymore," I grumble as she pushes me down in front of her vanity and begins gently pulling a brush through my matted hair. She laughs her angel laugh and negates my words just like that.

27

CHANGE DOESN'T ALWAYS MAKE SENSE

I STAND, STARING at myself in the mirror. Jane has been in my room many times, and she has seen my collage of photos (which I masochistically keep up even though they are only a reminder of what I have lost), and so she has seen the way I used to look compared to the way I have looked since she met me.

Somehow, she has managed to find that middle ground that I myself could never quite perfect, and she has transformed me.

I *thought* I had found that middle ground, a happy-medium, but I was wrong. I had become a pale shade of the old me with plain brown hair without much shape to it, and conservative clothes. Now, after a trip to her hairdresser and a shopping trip funded with filched money from my college account, I can see *me* again.

My hair is still dark brown—not quite black but almost—but with the lighter highlights it makes my eyes stand out. It's shorter than I've had it, well, probably ever. The shoulder-length A-line cut softens the highlights, wispy bangs pulled down to the side completing the look, making the dark hair feminine. Jane did my makeup, and it looks edgy and soft all at the same time.

Jeans with small holes shredded here and there, a long-sleeved black shirt with white cuffs and collar covered by one of my old red plaid vests, and black short boots with enough of a heel to be a little sexy but not too much completes Jane's makeover of me.

I feel good about this new look. The old me mixed with the new me. I smile at my image. I look good. I just might be able to make Trevor notice me once again.

***

When I walk into school, I can feel the change. I've been a ghost for the last few months, but not anymore. People are seeing me now. I smile.

Jane hurries over to me when she sees me, followed by her fan club

"You look great," she exclaims sincerely, a sentiment echoed by her gaggle of geese.

"Patting yourself on the back?" I smirk.

"How is that patting myself on the back?"

"Because you made me. I am your creation, Dr. Frankenstein."

"He wasn't a doctor, you know. Not in the book, anyway."

"Yeah, but he was in the movie that we watched, and that's what matters."

"Whatever, Igor," she laughs.

"Igor was the assistant, not the experiment. *I* am the experiment."

"Igor also wasn't in the book." This is a new voice, one I didn't expect to hear. My heart skips a beat as I turn to see Brian stepping toward me.

I swallow guiltily. I've pretty much ignored Brian and all

of Trevor's other geek friends since hooking up with Jane. I can't even try to claim that it's because they didn't want me around, not when they've gone out of their way to remain my friends in spite of what I've done to Trevor. Selfishly, it's because hanging out with them only keeps in the front of my mind what I now have to live without.

"He was in the movie though," I say thickly.

"Not if you're talking the 1931 version, where he was called Fritz," he argues lightly. I smile thinly, aware that everyone is staring at us as if we're talking Chinese—except for my new sci-fi pal Jane. She is looking at Brian with interest.

"You don't talk to me anymore," he accuses mildly.

"We'll see you later," Jane interjects when his statement draws the attention of all the geese. She gives me a hug, then hurries away, followed by the rest of the group. Brian waits expectantly.

"I know. I'm sorry. It just seems easier this way."

"Easier for who?" I'd almost forgotten just how honestly straightforward the geeks could be.

"Me," I admit. Brian's eyes widen at my own frank answer. He nods in acknowledgment.

"What you did to Trevor was . . . well, it wasn't very nice." I grunt at his mild assessment. "But it wasn't the worst thing you could have done. I mean, I think you really did like him, right?"

Like him? That doesn't even begin to cover it. It turns the thing that meant the world to me into something . . . I don't know . . . so middle school. But that's not a discussion I want to get into in the school hallway with Brian. So I simply nod.

"And I guess I thought maybe you really liked the rest of us also, or at least *most* of us." We're both thinking of Mary

Ellen. "You weren't, like, *using* us, were you?" He seems genuinely hurt by the idea.

"Of course not. I mean, let's be honest. At first, we were like oil and water. But I truly did come to think of you as friends."

He swings a hand vaguely in the direction that Jane has gone. "But now you don't need us because you have new friends?"

I shrug, looking away. "It's too hard, Brian. You're too close to him. There're too many memories of him associated with you. And I'm a coward."

"You still like him, huh?"

"I guess I always will."

"That's good. I wouldn't give up hope too quickly, Jen." My heart thuds at his words. Does he know something? "But then, no one's ever done anything like that to me, so I can't say for sure how long he might stay mad." And my heart drops. "But still, I wish you would at least talk to us a little."

I take a deep breath.

"You're right. I'm being selfish. So maybe on the days that . . . you know, that *he's* not at lunch I could still sit with you? Me and Jane?"

"You think she would sit at our table?" His eyes hold a little more than passing interest.

I shrug, messing with Brian, feeling lighter at this feeble link to Trevor being offered. "I don't know. I can try."

"Okay." He sounds slightly despondent. "It'll be good to talk to you again, anyway. See you around, Jen."

He walks off, and I can only stare after him. What an odd conversation. I have to admit, though, that I feel a little better now that he's said he still wants to be friends. I feel a *whole lot* better that he thinks Trevor might forgive me someday.

If there's one thing life has taught me, though, it's that hope can be a slippery slope.

***

I see Trevor for the first time since Jane's makeover of me later that day. He's walking with the mouse, of all people. I almost turn and head a different direction, losing courage, but he looks up and sees me before I can make the move. He stops when he sees me, and Mary Ellen, who'd been in the middle of jabbering something inane (I'm sure) stops also, consternation knitting her brow. She follows his gaze and sees me there. Her eyes clear, and anger tightens her mouth.

I ignore her because Trevor's *looking* at me. I'm reminded of the stunned expression he had the first time I turned my unexpected charms on him. This gives me confidence, and I offer him a half smile, lifting my hand a few inches in a small wave. Trevor's mouth begins to curve upward in response, but then he also seems to recall our first meeting, or maybe just the recent revelation made to him about me, and something in his expression changes. His mouth hardens and his eyes darken coldly.

She notices the change in him, and she grins triumphantly. She pushes her arm through his and turns him away from me. It's my nightmare, come true. I'm frozen in place, numb with hurt, and suddenly I feel foolish for having even tried. My clothes, my hair, my whole new look—ridiculous.

Tears blur my vision, and for the first time since I've known Trevor, I leave school, ditching my classes, not even caring about the consequences.

***

"You can't give up!"

Jane bounces on the edge of my bed while I lay curled in a ball, trying to resolutely ignore her. This is not an easy task.

"You probably misconstrued his expression, anyway. You have the lowest self-esteem I've ever seen in a person," Jane says, pushing against my stiff back.

I sigh. She's not going to let me ignore her, apparently. Though most times she's as sweet as any true angel could be, she can also be as stubborn and persistent as any demon. I roll toward her and sit up.

"I know Trevor pretty well," I explain, exasperated. "I know his expressions better than I know my own. He was really angry."

"Okay. But before he was angry?" she prompts. "Did he look?"

I guess my expression gives her the answer because she squeals triumphantly and gives me an exuberant hug.

"I knew it! I knew he would look."

"Well, he couldn't really help but look. I was right in front of him."

"But it is *how* he looked that matters."

"He looked delicious, as always," I say. She smacks me on the shoulder.

"That's not what I mean and you know it. Tell me everything, every little detail."

I do, trying not to let her contagious enthusiasm affect me. She's reading far more into this than I am. It's nice to have someone fuming along with me over the audacity of the little mouse—who would probably be one of Jane's close friends if I hadn't infected her with disdain for Mary Ellen before she had a chance to befriend her.

"He's remembering," she says.

"What?" Her words bring me up short.

"He's remembering how it was when he first saw you, when you first turned your attention on him."

I want to argue, tell her she's wrong, but I can't. She's right. I recognized it in his eyes, but I can't afford hope, can't afford the possibility that he will always hate me.

Suddenly my mind floods with the memory of the dance, the first time I had made myself known to him. I had honed in on him, stalked him—made sure he knew that I was completely available to him. He had looked at me then the way he had looked at me today. He had been angry then too. Angry because I had made him look, made him notice me. He'd told me that later.

Could that be why he had been angry today? Because once again I had made him look, made him notice me, whether he wanted to or not. Only this time it was with the knowledge of just how good things *could* be between us.

I look at Jane with a soft gasp. She sees the change on my face, the recognition of the truth, and a slow feline smile—one that definitely doesn't belong on her—widens her cherubic face.

"So, tomorrow we start again?" she practically purrs.

I smile, optimism filling me once again.

"Tomorrow we start again."

28

FRIENDS AND SISTERS—
SOMETIMES BOTH AT THE
SAME TIME

THE PICTURE collage hanging in my room—the origins of which still remain a mystery that no one has owned up to—is something of a torment to me. It's not the pictures of me and my new family; those make me happy. It's all of the ones of me and Trevor, or me and Todd—even the one of me with Trevor and his parents. *These* are the ones that torment me, make me cry.

Mom wanted to take them down when Trev and I first . . . I don't even know exactly what to call it. Broke up? Separated? World collapsed? But I threw a big enough fit that she finally relented and agreed to let me keep them as long as it was "healthy" for me. This means I have to be really careful not to let her see me when I stand in front of them, staring at them, pretending like nothing happened and we're still together.

A knock on my door sends me scurrying quickly to my bed, belly flop down, legs up and crossed at the ankles and the magazine that had been sitting there quickly pulled up to my face as if this were my previous endeavor before I call out to invite Mom in.

"A bet, huh?"

I flip over at the sound of Tamara's voice, surprised at how genuinely glad I am to see her. I grin at her, then quickly wipe it away.

"Well, look what the cat dragged in—a has-been cheerleader."

"But the *best-looking* has-been cheerleader on campus." She walks in, eyes roving over the picture collage that I had been staring at. She waves a hand at them. "Into self-torture, are we?"

"I already got the lecture from Mom. Don't need it from you also."

She plops down onto the bed next to me, pulling the magazine out of my hands. It happens to be open to an advertisement page about a fabulous new feminine hygiene product, which helps you to feel your very freshest.

"Does Mom fall for this I'm-just-fine-and-I'll-prove-it-by-reading-about-maxi-pads?"

I give her a dirty look, then stand up and walk away from her—but only to close my door. I turn back toward her, leaning back against the door with my hands tucked behind me.

"Of course she does. She really wants me to be happy."

"Huh," Tamara says, surprised.

"What?"

"There was no sarcasm in that sentence that I could detect."

"That's because there wasn't any. I *know* she truly wants me to be happy, and because she's taken me in and given me a home and family, I'm going to give her what she wants."

"You know," she says, closing the magazine and running her hand across its glossy surface, watching the movement, "when you first came here I resented you."

I laugh at this. "No kidding? I couldn't tell."

She smiles back at me, shrugging.

"I'm sorry I was so awful. But I didn't really like the idea of another daughter. I guess I kind of felt like I was being replaced. And for it to be someone who so obviously didn't want to be here . . ." She holds out a hand to me and pulls me to sit on the bed next to her when I take it. "But I am really happy that it *is* you. I like having you for my sister."

"Oh, great," I say in loud exasperation. "I finally get my emotions under control and here you come, blowing them all up again." I look at her and see tears in her eyes also. I lean my head down to her shoulder, letting the tears have their way, and she wraps an arm around me.

"I had a boyfriend once who broke up with me because he found someone he liked better. It hurt." She squeezes me. "But I didn't love him the way that you love Trevor, so I can't imagine what you must be going through."

"It's so horrible," I whisper. "I should have told him, as soon as I realized that I really liked him, when it changed from being a game to something more."

"Are you sorry?"

I think about this for a minute, wiping my nose with the tissue she hands to me. I sit up and look at her.

"No, I'm not." Her eyebrows shoot up in surprise. "It sounds bad, I guess. But I can't be sorry for the thing that put me and Trevor together. I'm only sorry that now he hates me."

"Hate is a pretty strong emotion. And one I don't think Trevor Hoffman is capable of."

"Strongly dislikes me, then."

"So what are you doing about it?"

"Have you been talking to Jane?" I accuse.

"Ah, the famous Jane. Mom *raves* about her every time I

call. So what does this mysterious, magical Jane have to say?"

"She did the Jen makeover."

"She did a good job. You look really good. Even with the runny mascara," she teases, wiping a finger beneath one eye.

"Thanks, but I'm still no cheerleader."

"Well, we can't all be perfect."

If only a few months ago anyone had told me I would be *joking* around with my *sister*, the *cheerleader*, I probably would have laughed—and not in the ha-ha, that's funny way but more like the yeah-right-that-isn't-happening-in-this-lifetime way. Guess you never can say never.

"She says I have to make him notice me again, make him want me back."

"Hmm, well, she's on the right path. But Jen, Trevor's about more than looks. I mean, he was with you when you looked like the queen of the living dead."

"Thanks," I mutter.

"~~couldn't even turn his head then. Proof he's not about~~ looks."

Tamara is being facetious, and I laugh at her. She's so not what I had thought her to be when I first came to this house.

"You need to remind him of the other reasons he wanted to be with you."

"But that's the thing. There really aren't any good reasons. *Why* was he with me?"

Tamara shakes her head.

"You have got to work on your self-esteem."

"You're the second one to tell me that."

"Then it must be true. Listen, Jen. You've spent your life being told you're worthless by a bunch of people whose opinions shouldn't matter. Time to stop listening to them and start listening to people who actually love you."

"Yeah, well, easier said than done, you know?"

"Don't keep acting like your life is over. It's pathetic and won't help you in your campaign. Be happy, show him that you're happy and you don't need him. Flirt with some other boys. Show him you're not just waiting around for him. *That'll* get his attention." She gives me another one-armed hug and stands up. "If Trevor is half as nice as I think he is, he'll forgive you. Then he'll be begging you to take him back."

"Thanks, Tamara. Who knew a cheerleader could be so helpful? I actually feel a little better now."

She smiles at me. "What're sisters for?"

***

It's the third Saturday. Senior center night. I missed the last one. I should miss this one.

I'm not going to, though. I miss all of the people there, Mrs. Green in particular. I think about her sitting there waiting for someone to come see her, and no one showing up. I can't be yet another person that lets her down.

That's the official excuse, and genuine as it is, there is of course another—the pull of Trevor, of being near him. So I hurry out the door before I can chicken out.

Mrs. Green is happy to see me. She doesn't remember a lot, but she remembers that I wasn't here last month. Before I can make up an excuse that at least *sounds* truthful, Trevor walks in. My heart stops as I watch him make his cheerful circuit. He hasn't seen me yet.

Eventually though, he makes his way around to where I am. He stops short when he sees me sitting there. He stares at me, disbelief and anger warring on his face.

Anger wins.

"What are you doing here?" he bites out tightly.

"She came to see me," Mrs. Green informs him sharply.

He looks at her, and immediately his features smooth out. Figures his innate politeness would extend to everyone but me.

"How are you today, Mrs. Green?" he asks kindly.

"Better now that Jen is here," she answers, patting me on the knee.

That reminds him, and he turns hard eyes back on me. Before he can chide me again, Joshua, the guy who's in charge of all the volunteers, hustles into the room.

"Hey, Trevor, you're here," he calls as he walks past us. "Glad to have you back, Jen. We missed you."

Trevor's jaw ticks twice before he turns abruptly away.

"I see why you weren't here last time," Mrs. Green mumbles. "That boy needs to learn some manners."

I choke out a laugh at that. If there is one thing Trevor definitely doesn't need, it's a manners lesson. He avoids me after that. He is *über* nice to everyone else, a contrast to the absolute silence he subjects me to.

When it comes time for his playing and singing, he does so with only slightly less enthusiasm than usual. His eyes keep flicking my way, and I'm very aware that my presence is an annoyance to him.

Maybe I won't come next time.

Maybe I will.

29

TWO DATES?

I'M STILL not sure how it came about, but somehow because of my every-other-day sitting with Brian and the others at lunch, and Brian's obvious infatuation with Jane, the in-between days soon find us all sitting at the same table.

This is incredibly awkward.

Trevor sits at one end of the table, and I sit at the other. My stomach churns the entire time, and while I studiously ignore him, I am constantly watching him. He is overly attentive to the mouse, and I am insanely jealous. She spends most of lunch shooting daggers at me. Who knew she had it in her?

Brian seems to be the go-between. Mark and Jim tend to stay at Trev's end, though Mark has been drifting a little more toward center. I dread these lunch days when I have to face Trevor, pasting a smile on my face and pretending his presence doesn't affect me.

I also look forward to them more than anything. Paint me a masochist.

***

"So, what do you want to do this weekend?"

Jane and I are standing near her locker, which I now

share. Using my own, the one I shared with Trevor, is too hard, so it sits empty since he also no longer uses it. *Probably shares with the mouse*, I think with a pang.

"You know me, I'm up for anything," I say, though we both know that's a lie.

"How about if I stay at your place on Friday after you get home from your family thing, then on Saturday—" She abruptly stops, her eyes moving past me to freeze on someone behind me. My stomach clenches. There aren't too many people who would have this effect on her, and only one pops into my mind. I slowly turn around, cheeks flushed.

It's not Trevor.

"Hey, Jen," Seth says, hesitantly. He shifts back and forth, unsure. "Can I talk to you for a minute?"

I look back at Jane, who's trying not to stare at Seth's multi-colored spiked hair, black lips, and many piercings.

"Sure," I tell him, seeing the surprised expression on Jane's face. "I'll be right back, Jane."

She shoots me a questioning look, and I almost laugh. It's much like the look my mom gives me when I'm doing something she doesn't approve of.

I follow Seth as he walks a few feet away. Jane stays planted in place; this does not go unnoticed by Seth.

"What's up?" I say casually, though I'm burning with curiosity—and suspicion. Why would Seth approach me now, after all this time?

"I know we haven't really been, you know, friendly for a while." I scoff lightly at this. "But I was wondering if you would ever consider, you know, going out with me sometime."

My suspicion ratchets up.

"Are Beth and Ella behind this?"

He looks surprised. "Of course not."

"Kyle?"

He shakes his head. "No one is behind this but me. You know I've liked you for a long time. Or at least, I thought you knew that."

I study him, trying to determine if he's being truthful. I can't see anything in his face that tells me he's being distrustful, but I still can't figure out his motivation.

"I did know that, at one time. But that was before . . ." I trail off. I *definitely* don't want to discuss Trevor with Seth. "Anyway, things are different now. *I'm* different now."

"I've noticed," he says, sounding hesitatingly accepting but at least not cynical.

"I don't party anymore."

"I figured as much."

"Then why?"

If he's taken aback by my directness, he doesn't show it.

"Because I've always liked you, and I thought it would be fun to hang out."

I stare at him, unsure of his intentions. There was a time when Seth was exactly my type. I can't really remember what attracted me to him. He's such the polar opposite of Trevor, who is now definitely more my type.

He shrugs under my silence. "Just a movie, maybe some dinner. You can even just meet me there if you want. Just a date, nothing else."

Hard to argue with that logic, right? So why does it feel so wrong?

"Okay." I say, making a snap decision I hope I don't live to regret.

His face brightens, and I swear he nearly smiles, which brings to mind the thought that I haven't ever really seen Seth smile—unless he was high.

"Friday night?" he asks.

I glance back at Jane, who is now standing with her arms crossed tightly, mouth grim and toe tapping impatiently as she watches us unhappily. I grin at her continued motherly presence.

"I have plans Friday." I'm surprised that he doesn't remember how sacred Friday nights are for my family. After all, we used to laugh about it. I'm not going to remind him because I now look forward to my Family Fridays. "How about Saturday? You can pick me up at my place."

"Okay." He seems a little stunned that I've agreed to go.

He leans down awkwardly and gives me an uncomfortable, one-armed hug, bathing me in the scent of smoke—both cigarette and otherwise—and I can't help but compare this to Trevor's clean smell. I push the thought away and hurry back to Mother Jane.

"*What* was that about?" she demands.

"I was being asked out on a date."

"With *him*!" Jane glances back to where Seth now disappears through the school doors. "Do you think that's safe?"

"Yes, *Mom*." I laugh. "He's an old friend. He was one of my first friends when I started coming to this school."

Jane knows my story, from my biological parents to the day she met me. I didn't really mention Seth as my almost-boyfriend to her because I figured that was an unimportant dead end of my history.

"You're not going to . . ." She looks genuinely worried. She brushes her hands forward, as if pushing her thoughts away. "No, never mind. It's none of my business."

"It's always your business, Jane. You're my best friend. I'm not going to do anything I shouldn't be doing." I smile and tuck my arm through hers. "I'll call you as soon as I get home and tell you everything that happened."

She cocks a brow at me curiously. "Why this sudden decision to go on a date?"

I shrug. "Because someone asked me. And because *he's* dating, so why shouldn't I?"

"Ah, so it's a revenge thing."

"No!" I immediately refute. "Well, okay, maybe a little. But what else can I do? Spend the rest of my life miserable because I screwed up and lost the guy I love?"

"You could get some cats, you know. Become that old lady who loves her cats more than people."

"I'd have to learn to knit. Make me some doilies to place on all of my furniture."

"And buy lots of cat food."

"And cat litter."

"No, if you're crazy enough, you can just let them poop all over the house. Then go on Oprah so she can tell you you're crazy, and she can get someone to clean up your house for you."

"Or maybe just stay crazy so I don't have to remember him."

Jane glances at me, face grim.

"Go on the date. Forget the cats," she says.

"I like cats, though. I like the idea of being crazy enough to forget."

"Well, I'm deathly allergic to cats, so you need to stay sane."

I sigh. "All right, I'll do it. For you."

"Glad I talked you into it," she says.

***

Homecoming is in two weeks. It seems to be all anyone can talk about. I'm trying to pretend it isn't happening at all.

Trevor and I had talked about going to it at the beginning

of the school year, before he learned to hate me. I know he's
still planning to go—he's pretty much required to as the student body president.

I also know he isn't taking me. I have a pretty good idea
about just who he might be taking.

Jane is going with a boy named Charlie. He asked her
quite a while ago, guessing (correctly as it turns out) that she
would have multiple invitations and he would need to beat
the rush. This is a crushing disappointment to Brian I know,
which might explain why he now looks at me expectantly,
waiting for my answer.

"What?" I ask, sure I couldn't have heard him right.

"I said do you want to go to Homecoming with me?"
he repeats. I'm beyond aware of the fact that everyone at
the table is either openly looking at us in expectation of my
answer or pretending to not be listening even though they
obviously are. There couldn't be a worse day for him to ask
me, I think, as my eyes go to the face of the only person at
this table whose opinion on this matters to me.

Trevor is staring right at me, his expression carefully blank.
Something flashes through his eyes, something that almost
hints at jealousy. He quickly looks away, turning his attention
back to the mouse, who had been watching Trevor watch me.

"Yes," I say, my mouth working before my brain has a
chance to catch up. As I say the word, I swear Trevor winces
a little. I drag my eyes away from Trevor, facing Brian, mind
firmly decided.

"Sure, Brian, why not?"

"Cool," is his only response, and I wonder if I'm not the
only one with an ulterior motive for wanting to go to this
dance—even if it isn't with the one either of us would have
had as first choice.

30

Date Disaster # 1

SETH PICKS me up fifteen minutes late. But at least his eyes are clear, so he's sober. My parents are polite, not even blinking at his appearance. Then again, they learned to love me when I looked similar, so I guess it's just part of their non-judgmentalism. Personally, I think they're just thrilled I'm going on a date.

I admit it—I dressed a little on the conservative side tonight as a sort of rebellion, I guess. I didn't want it to seem like I was sliding back into my old ways just to appease Seth. Though I'm willing to go out with him, my heart still belongs elsewhere, and I don't want him confused about that, or about any expectations he may have of me.

We go to a movie first. The car ride isn't bad because I can talk cars and haven't yet met a guy who's not willing to talk about his car. The movie is easy because it's dark and distracting, and thankfully Seth doesn't try to make a move on me.

Now we're at dinner. I realize just how thoroughly I really *didn't* know Seth before. We'd always hung out together with a group, but never alone. He's very fidgety, and I'm guessing he really wants to go out and have a cigarette but doesn't want to offend me. Or he's just really nervous. Or uncomfortable. Or sorry he asked me out. Or any combination of these.

It occurs to me that the awkward silence has stretched on for a while and that's why my mind is rambling so inanely.

"So, how is everyone doing these days, Seth?"

He looks surprised at my question.

"Everyone?" he asks.

"Well, yeah, like Kyle . . . or Dave . . ." I'm searching my brain, trying to remember the names of the people we hung out with only to realize I didn't really know any of them well enough to easily recall their names. "You know, people like that who don't go to our school."

"Uh, well, I guess they're about the same."

"Oh." I sit silently for a moment. "How about Beth and Ella? Are they doing okay?"

"They go to our school. You see them, like, every day."

"Well, they aren't exactly speaking to me, so . . ."

"They're about the same also, I guess," says the fountain of information.

Another dead silence ensues while I try to think of a subject that we might have in common.

"Any idea what you're gonna do after graduation?" I ask.

"Haven't even thought about it. That's still a ways off."

Well, I guess if you want to call six months a ways off, no point in making any hasty decisions. I can't help but mentally compare him to Trevor, who has already applied to colleges and has scholarships lined up. I shove that dangerous thinking away.

"No ideas? Dreams? Wishes?" I press.

"Oh yeah," he half-moans with a lopsided grin. "I dream of driving a 'Vette, partying with my friends, and having a hot babe by my side."

I can only stare. I don't know if he's serious or if he's joking and expects me to laugh at the lame joke. He's not laughing, only has a faint upturn of one side of his mouth, and though I'm appalled, I really think he means it. That's as far ahead as he can think, and it truly is his life ambition. I wonder cynically if I should high-five him.

Sadly, I probably would have in the not-so-distant past.

Seth's background isn't much shinier than mine, but at least he's had the stability of a family. That thought brings to mind a girl I had known of in middle school, one of those girls that everyone makes fun of and tortures just for fun. I was in a particularly bad home at that time, though that's by no means the reason I had joined in hurting her. I was a pretty tough cookie at that time, fighting a lot and usually winning because I had been taught how to fight dirty.

One day she came to school battered, and in one of my few moments of insight, I realized that it wasn't from any of the other kids at school—she received her bruises at home. I felt a sense of kinship with her and had managed to make it clear that she was to be left alone—at least as far as physical harm was concerned. And because I'd thrown my weight around enough, they generally followed my edict.

Of course, it wasn't long before I'd gotten myself thrown out of that home, though that time it was a particularly great blessing. I sometimes wonder what happened to that girl, if she got out of her situation.

The server brings our food, and I'm grateful that there is finally something to occupy us. I eat quickly, wishing this date could be over. Unfortunately the only thing the fast eating does is give me a stomachache and lots of empty silence while Seth slowly eats, and the server takes her sweet time wandering back with the bill.

Where's the ornery Italian restaurant waitress when you need her?

Finally, we finish, and Seth drives me home. Of course, he doesn't get out and walk me to the door. I'm grateful.

"Thanks, Seth." I say, knowing the polite thing would be to finish with something like *I had fun,* but I can't force myself to tell such a bald-faced lie. "Dinner was really good." There. That should satisfy all the polite geeks who would judge me. One in particular. I walk quickly toward my house.

"Hey!"

I look back. Seth has rolled down his window and is leaning out. For one horrified second I wonder if he expects me to run back and give him a kiss.

"Maybe we could go out again sometime. Maybe next weekend or something."

Is he *serious?* I mentally push my jaw shut, dismayed at the thought of another three-and-a-half uncomfortable hours with Seth.

"Uh, I can't next weekend." That's not a lie, I justify to myself. It's the truth because I really don't think I am capable of going out with him again. "Thanks, though. I'll see you at school on Monday." I wave and hurry through the front door before he can suggest another time. I slump back against the door as if I need to hold him out.

"That bad, huh?"

I smile wryly at my dad as he comes out of his office and nod.

"They can't all be Prince Charming," he says, squeezing my arm as he walks by, as usual seeing right to the heart of the matter. *No, they can't,* I think. Because there is definitely only one of him, and I had him, and I screwed up and lost him.

"I think I'll go to my room and cry," I tell the empty hallway. Instead of crying, I decide to call Jane and tell her just what I think of her talking me into this date—even if she really didn't.

31

DATE DISASTER #2 . . .
WITH A TWIST ENDING

ONCE THE cheerleader heard of my plan to go to Homecoming, she arranged to be home both the weekend before, for dress shopping, and the weekend of because she claimed her "older sister's right" to do my hair. She ignored my arguments that she isn't much older than me. I was grateful she was there.

She helped me find a dress that was feminine and pretty, not frilly whatsoever. She totally ignored my horrified protests when she pulled out multiple hair curling implements and insisted that I trust her. She wouldn't even let me watch in the mirror.

"You can wash it and start over when I'm finished if you hate it," she promised, which is the only reason I capitulated.

When she was finished, it looked . . . elegant. Not a word I'd ever thought would apply to me. *If only Carol could see me now,* I thought.

Now I'm standing in our living room next to Brian, who looks pretty cute in his tux, or at least a few degrees less nerdy, while my mom takes about a thousand pictures. I finally drag Brian out the door because I believe he would be content to stand here and pose all night to avoid being rude to my mom—and because Tamara is here. Cute college girl fawning over him? He'd stay.

We drive to the State Capitol building, which has been rented for the night for the occasion. I have to admit that the hulking, historical beast is not without its charms. Lit up the way it is now, it's a perfectly romantic backdrop for what I expect will be a completely romance-devoid night.

Jane and Charlie have already arrived and saved us a place at their table. I would have to be blind for it to escape my notice of how joyfully happy Brian is at this development. It's a large table, which means we won't be sitting alone, and my stomach churns at the thought of a particular someone who might join us.

I tell myself that I'm not looking for him, only admiring the beautiful building and the decorations as I look around. Why is it then, that as soon as my eyes land on him, they stop? As does my heart.

Trevor looks even better than I had imagined he would in his tux. And imagine it I had, from the moment Brian invited me. *That boy sure can clean up,* I think, pretending to be nonchalant. My heart, which had stuttered to a stop, begins pounding, and a flush spreads up my chest and across my cheeks, leaving a fiery trail across the icy surfaces. He hasn't seen me yet, or if he has, he's completely ignoring me. He stands with a group of the SBOs, laughing and sharing those great dimples with them. I'm insanely jealous of them.

I try to look away, aware that it's rude to stare at one's ex-boyfriend while on a date, but I can't force my head to move. Jane sees my dilemma and rescues me by standing up and walking in front of me, blocking my view.

"Charlie and I are going to go dance. You and Brian should come."

Because Brian is completely infatuated with her, he jumps up to follow her, nearly leaving me behind. She takes Charlie's arm, and he leads her away, forcing Brian to come back for me. Unfortunately, this clears my view of Trevor once again, and I'm glad I'm holding onto Brian.

Trevor looks up just as he's laughing at something someone said, and his gaze lands directly on me. The laughter immediately dies on his lips. His mouth snaps closed, and he swallows loudly. At least it *looks* loud since I'm too far away to truly hear it, and even if I were closer the blood rushing through my head would have drowned out the sound.

His eyes slowly travel over me, and I make a mental note to thank Tamara. As his gaze returns to my face, our eyes clash, and in that second I know that he isn't as immune to me as he sometimes seems. Reality crashes down in the form of Mary Ellen, who is definitely not at all mouse-looking tonight. She sidles up to Trevor, eyeing me suspiciously. She pushes her arm through his possessively and says something to him.

He drags his eyes away reluctantly, his jaw ticking in agitation. I've never wanted to claw anyone's eyes out so much in my life. Brian tugs lightly on my arm, and with a deep breath I blow my frustration out as best I can and follow him. I dance pretty unenthusiastically until I see Trevor and Mary Ellen are also on the dance floor, and Trevor is taking occasional glances at me. I see this because I'm totally watching him.

I pick up the pace and smile a lot. It feels completely false. I hope I'm fooling everyone else—or at least Trevor. Trevor and Mary Ellen do end up at our table, as do the rest of the lunch crowd and their various dates. This requires me to keep up the I'm-so-happy act until I'm nearly exhausted. I try to talk Brian into leaving, but he claims we can't go until the king and queen are crowned. I'm guessing he cares about that even less than I do, and I don't care at all. It's Jane sitting across from us that's holding him here.

Finally, the time comes to crown the unlucky suckers, and I breathe a sigh of relief. He won't have an excuse to stay after this. Our principal, Mr. Handlin, gets up to the podium. He's not such a bad guy. I can read him for the complete geek he was in high school, and since I have a thing now for geeks, I can't really dislike him.

"Okay, everyone," he wheezes into the microphone. "It's the time you've all been waiting for. Let's find out just who your Homecoming King and Queen are this year."

I glance over to where the cheerleaders and jocks huddle in anticipation, glancing suspiciously at one another to see which of them will take the crown. I roll my eyes.

"Your king is . . . Trevor Hoffman." This gets my attention like nothing else could have. I sit up straight from my slouched position. Trevor looks shocked, but I can't say I really am. I mean, he's dressing much less geekily this year, and he was voted Student Body President. Plus, with those dimples and amazing green eyes, he had to be a complete shoo-in.

Everyone at the table is congratulating him, Mary Ellen rising up to kiss him on the cheek. I burrow my fingernails into the palms of my hands and grit my teeth so hard I'm surprised they don't break. His eyes flick to mine when she does this, and I try to give him a smile that says I don't care. I can feel, though, that it's a tight grimace, and I have no doubt that my eyes are burning. He holds my gaze for a few seconds, then makes his way to the front of the crowd where he takes his place on the low stage.

I glance at the jock table and see that none of them seem disappointed at this. It says a lot for Trevor that those who expected to win are happy for his victory. A few of the cheerleaders look pleased at the prospect of joining Trevor for the traditional King & Queen Dance.

"And now, the queen," enthuses Mr. Handlin. I feel my stomach clench. I don't think I can stand to sit here and watch Trevor hold yet another girl in his arms because I'm more than positive that no one would have voted for the mouse. Not that it would be any better to see *her* in his arms, but dealing with *another* girl being held by Trevor is more than I can handle right now.

"I'll be back," I whisper to Brian as I stand. I figure I'll just go hang out outside for ten minutes or so. Brian nods, barely listening.

"The queen is . . ." I hurry faster.

"Jennifer Grant."

I close my eyes against the name. I don't know her, but I don't want to have to . . . My walking slows as the name sinks in. I turn around, stunned. That's *my* name. Some people are actually applauding (with the notable exception of the cheerleaders), and Jane is positively beaming, waving me toward the stage. There's no way . . . then I see the conspiratorial look that passes between Jane and Brian and realize they somehow rigged this. I just can't quite figure out how.

Anger suffuses me, and I consider turning around and continuing my exit—until I look up, and see Trevor standing there, crown on his head, happiness at winning gone out of his face.

I feel the pull of him, drawn toward the stage whether I want to go there or not. People are congratulating me, touching me as I walk past them, but I can only focus on him.

Too soon I'm on the stage next to him, having a cheap plastic crown placed on my head. I only have eyes for Trevor, though, who refuses to look at me.

Mr. Handlin comes between us, shaking both our hands.

"And now, I give you Trevor and Jennifer for the King and Queen Dance," he announces loudly, and my heart jolts. *The dance.* I had momentarily forgotten about that, but the dance means . . . me in Trevor's arms again.

The music begins, and for a long moment Trevor stands frozen. Mr. Handlin nudges him with a murmur, and he turns stiffly toward me. His inbred politeness won't allow him to leave me standing here alone like I know he wants to, and I am soaringly grateful for this.

He holds out a stiff hand, and as I place my hand in his, a molten blaze begins in my stomach.

He doesn't look at me, stiffly formal as he leads me down the steps to the dance floor. The lights are dim with a slightly brighter spotlight highlighting us. He forces a turn toward me and takes me into his arms. In that moment, I see it. His eyes are burning as scorchingly hot as my stomach.

He leads me into a dance, rigid and proper, holding me at a distance that would please the stoutest of Puritans. It's such a stark reminder of the first time I danced with him that I can't stop the smile that curves my mouth. Trevor stumbles a little at my smile, but in true courageous fashion, he holds my gaze, not turning away.

Soon other couples have joined us on the floor, but my focus has narrowed to the point that it seems we are alone. Once we are surrounded, it's as if something gives within Trevor. I can actually sense the capitulation flowing through him, and suddenly he pulls me close, never breaking eye contact, though in his I read something much different, something I haven't seen since *before*.

"Trev," I sigh, only meaning to think it, not say it aloud.

"Don't call me that," he murmurs. He lowers his head to mine, not demanding as he kisses me, lips gentle. My mind is a riot of emotions and questions, but I push them all aside, refusing to waste one precious second of this unbelievable moment on *thought*.

My world twists and tilts as he lets go of my hand and his arms come around my waist, pulling me even closer. I slide my arms up past his shoulders, twisting my hands in the nape of his hair as he deepens the kiss, becoming urgent.

Time passes slowly, and much too quickly. Almost in tandem, Trevor and I become aware of our surroundings, just where we are and what we're doing. His mouth abruptly hardens on mine, and he pulls away as if burned. Emotions shoot across his face while he tries to find one to settle on. I still have my hands tangled in his hair; he reaches up and gently pulls them down, disengaging himself from my embrace.

"I'm sorry, I shouldn't have . . ." he trails off, chaotic thoughts tying his tongue.

He turns quickly, striding away. He comes up short when he sees Mary Ellen standing at the edge of the dance floor. It's obvious she has watched the whole thing. Even I feel a little sorry at the hurt and betrayal I can see written on her face. I want to go after him but can't move.

Tremors begin in my hands, and I can feel a panic attack creeping up my throat as he disappears. Suddenly Brian is with me, wrapping his arm around me and pulling me close to his side as he hurries me from the dance floor and out the front door. I can hear the sounds of despair starting low in my throat, fighting for escape.

"Just hold on, Jen. We're almost there," he says urgently. Then he's shoving me into the front seat of his car. He jogs to the other side and climbs in. I look at Brian, sorry for the humiliation I must have caused him, grateful to him for coming to my rescue, but unable to form the words. I don't trust opening my mouth just now because I'm fighting the keening wails that are pushing at the back of my teeth. He seems to read all of this on my face, and he nods in acceptance.

A knock on his window startles him, and Jane peers anxiously in. He rolls his window down, and she leans in toward me, which puts her face directly in front of Brian's.

"Jen, are you okay? Do you need me to come with you?"

I can't answer; I can only shake my head. She looks to Brian for confirmation, like he's suddenly my caretaker. He shrugs helplessly, stunned by the nearness of her.

"Okay, I'll get Charlie to take me home so I can change, and then I'll go right to her house," she tells him, as if he had asked this of her. She gives Brian a little bicep squeeze in gratitude and then leaves to go find her date.

Brian watches her until she's out of sight, then looks back at me. His feelings are on his face as clearly as if he'd had them tattooed there.

"Well," he says, clearing his throat. "We're quite the pair, aren't we? Pathetic, both of us."

I can't agree more as I lean my head against the cool window and close my eyes against the painful brilliance of the retreating Capitol behind us.

32

ALL GOOD THINGS . . . WELL, YOU KNOW THE REST

TREVOR'S KISS centered me. I know it doesn't make any sense. I should be shattered. If I'm telling the truth, on the night of the ball, I did shatter—into a million tiny pieces. Jane and Brian kept me together, with a little help from Tamara, of all people. When I finally fell into an exhausted sleep—or maybe I should say when I finally passed out because I was completely spent—I came to a kind of peace with everything.

By Monday morning, I'm back together again, unlike Humpty Dumpty, who couldn't be put back together no matter how many horses and king's men tried. I can't really say why I feel so okay with everything now, but I have a theory.

I think that before the kiss I felt like there was no hope, that Trevor had finally seen the real me, and that meant there was no way to undo the damage. His kiss told me another story. Now I know that Trevor still loves me at least a little. I think this peace I feel is really a measure of hope. Genuine hope—not the hope I'd borrowed from everyone else, who kept trying to tell me how to get him back, not the hope I had tricked myself into believing. This hope is real.

Now I wait.

Trevor steadfastly ignores me—even more than before. I don't stress about it, don't hide from him. I feel a little bad because he doesn't look very happy. The one thing I notice most of all is that he and the mouse seem to be on the outs. Oddly enough, instead of this wrenching up her antagonism toward me, she has relaxed, and while she doesn't exactly treat me like a close friend, she doesn't glare at me anymore. She sits closer to my end of the lunch table, and she's even vaguely polite.

Hmm.

A couple of weeks pass in this strange manner until a Friday when my mom nervously approaches and tells me the Hoffmans have called and invited our family to go bowling with theirs. Our families doing things together is another casualty of Trevor and me—another thing for me to feel guilty about.

I think she's shocked when I smile calmly and tell her it sounds like a good idea, though she hides it well. I'm mostly calm about it if you don't take into account the butterflies that have decided to go into a frenzy in my belly.

It's only later as we're walking out the door that I realize I forgot to stress about my appearance. I'm wearing a plain white, long-sleeved T-shirt and jeans. I didn't even fix my hair or makeup. I don't really mind, though, because I know that these are only superficial things that mean nothing to Trevor. Guess it's about time they stop meaning so much to me as well.

Tamara has come home for the weekend—after a frantic call from me begging her to be here. Jeff and Kari meet us at the bowling alley. So when Trevor and his family walk in as we're all getting our shoes on, the sense of déjà-vu is strong.

Yet the differences are profound.

I'm no longer an unwilling outsider. I belong to this family fully, and I'm grateful for it. I have loved and lost someone who was nothing more than an experiment to me the first time around and who now means the world to me. I make sure my shoes are tied this time because somehow I don't think Trevor will catch me again if I fall.

"I miss you, Jen-Jen," Todd cries loudly, pulling me into his sweetly awkward bear hug. "Why don't you come see Todd no more?"

My throat tightens because I truly do miss Todd. Another casualty.

"I'm sorry, Todder," I tell him when he finally releases me and I can catch a breath. "I've been really busy."

"You come see me," he demands. "Jump with me."

I glance past him toward Trevor to see his response to this. He's tying his own shoes and is stalwartly ignoring the exchange, which I might buy except that I can see his jaw clenching.

"I don't know if I can, Todd," I tell him honestly. Todd doesn't forget promises, and I don't want to make one I can't keep.

"Why not?" He looks at Carol, who's treating me politely distant. "Mommy, why can't Jen-Jen come see Todd?" he whines.

Carol glares at me for a fraction of a second, as if I'm the one who brought the subject up. She walks over, rubbing her hand soothingly up and down Todd's arm.

"Well, Todd, I don't see why she couldn't," she grits out.

I glance past her, looking at Trevor meaningfully. She follows my look, reluctantly returning her gaze to me.

"Jen, we'd love to have you come by—sometime—to see

Todd." I know Todd can't hear the reluctance in her voice, but I can.

"I don't think—"

"Tomorrow!" Todd exults, cutting me off.

"Oh, well," Carol's hands flutter at her throat. "Um, maybe it would be better to come another day."

I'm beginning to feel a little angry at her because she attempts to make me the bad guy by telling Todd I can come, and then when I don't show up . . .

"How about Monday, right after school?" I ask. I happen to know that Trevor won't be there. He has SBO meetings then. Carol also knows this, so she nods reluctantly.

"Okay, that sounds good. How's that, Todd? She can come see you on Monday."

"Yay!" Todd calls, pumping his hands above his head. "Did you hear, Trevor? Jen-Jen is going to come and see me. Then she can see you too."

Trevor's eyes jump to mine and then away again. I'm relieved that there is no malice reflected in his expression or posture.

"I'm glad she's coming to see you, Todd," he tells his brother, no sarcasm or anger in his voice. "But I won't be there. I have to stay after school, remember?"

Todd's eyebrows knit together, then clear almost as quickly.

"That's okay, Trevor. I will give her a kiss for you."

Trevor and I both freeze at Todd's innocent words, while Jeff, Tamara, and Rob all guffaw out laughs that they quickly cover with coughs as they receive glares of warning from Carol and my mom.

"Uh, it's your turn to bowl, bud," Rob tells Todd, patting him on the shoulder.

"Okay." Todd happily skips forward, unaware of the

silence he leaves in his wake. He picks up his ball, walks up to the line, and swings his arm back and forth until he releases the ball. Once the ball hits the pins—knocking four of them down—he turns back to get his usual positive feedback from Trevor. Trevor sits silently, unaware of Todd for the first time since I've known him.

"Good job, Todd," I call, standing and high-fiving him on my way up to bowl, myself.

Todd grins at me, then high-fives everyone else—except Trevor, who's still silent. I throw my first ball—a strike, the result of my many nights of bowling with Trevor and Todd.

"Did you see that, Trevor? Jen-Jen hit them all!" Todd cries excitedly. "Give her a high five!"

Trevor, who is now standing, pulling on his bowling glove, looks at me, and in that glance, I see the torture. My heart contracts. If there is one thing I don't want, it's for Trevor to be in pain. So I smile, the same as I would if he were Jane or Brian, and hold my hand up. He leaves me hanging for a long second while he stares at me, trying to read me.

"Good job, me," I say wryly with a shrug.

He nods once, tightly, and finally lifts his own hand, slapping it lightly against mine. I pretend there isn't an electric tingle that flows down my arm from the point of contact.

One thing I learned from Trevor and Todd, if I learned nothing else, is that bowling is a game of cheering on your teammates—as well as the opposing team—and lots of hand slapping. Even though I can feel the tension coming from Trevor and to a lesser degree from his mother, I stick to the unwritten nerd rules and play the part. I'm having fun. I'm behaving—no tricks or games to try to pull Trevor in.

I'm sure it's my imagination that each time I high-five Trevor—and it's often because our turns come one right after the other—he holds my hand just a second longer than necessary, his fingers curving around the edges of my fingers, eyes intense for one private moment. This is only between us—no one else seems to notice—and is probably mostly my hopeful imagination. Because we're acting semi-normal, the others are able to relax and enjoy themselves.

Trevor walks to the snack bar and buys a couple of pitchers of soda. He returns with those and a stack of cups, asking each person what they want and playing host as he fills the cups and hands them out. The only person he doesn't ask is me. He simply fills a cup with diet and hands it to me. Only instead of it feeling like the first time when he simply *knew* what I wanted, it feels more like he just doesn't want to have to talk to me more than necessary.

"You're doing really well, Trevor," Tamara purrs, sitting next to him and patting his thigh with a big grin. He tenses and leans minutely away from her. Tamara has been flirting shamelessly with Trevor, to my delight and to his utter annoyance. I'm not worried about it because I know she isn't serious with it, but of course he has no idea. It sets him on edge, I can tell, and I almost call her off. Almost—until he glances at me to gauge my reaction. So I let her go.

"Hey, sis," Jeff says to me. He's taken to calling me that since the adoption became legal, and though I roll my eyes at him every time he does it, I am secretly pleased at his easy and full acceptance of me as his little sister. He treats me as if I have always been.

"I rented that movie you told me about. I have to tell you, I don't get it."

"Which one?" I ask. I actually gave him a list of movies that I told him to see.

"*Blade Runner.*"

"Ah," I answer. "That's one of my favorites. What did you think?"

"I liked it," he sounds surprised. "But it sure doesn't seem like the kind of movie you would like."

"Really?" I ask, tipping my head as I ask him. "What kind of movies do you think I would like?"

He shrugs. "You know, scary movies, vampire movies. Goth-type things."

I laugh. Jeff never misses a chance to goad me about how I looked when I first came to live with the Grants, no matter how many times my mom tells him to knock it off. I think she's still a little afraid he'll offend me. I'm not that soft though. I'm made of a lot tougher stuff than even I had thought.

"Well, I did like *A Nightmare Before Christmas.*"

"That sounds about right," he says as Kari elbows him in the ribs.

"If you liked *Blade Runner,* then next you need to rent *Minority Report.*"

"Another sci-fi movie?"

"I'm partial to the sci-fi stuff," I tell him.

"Oh yeah? Why is that?" he wonders. Suddenly I realize how this must sound to Trevor. I glance at him and see that he watches the whole exchange with a look in his eyes that I can't place. Would he think I set this up, having Jeff question me to show him that I'm still wrapped up in the activities that we did together? Honestly, though, while he did introduce me to them, I really have come to love all things sci-fi. A geek girl myself.

Jeff waits for an answer, so I give him a partial truth.

"I have friends who are into that, and they hooked me." I dare a glance back at Trevor and see that he no longer watches me, but his jaw ticks, lips clamped tightly together.

33

Na-nu, Na-nu

BECAUSE OF my new calm, my center of peace that at least keeps my heart from completely deflating, I decide that I have put off long enough something I should have done from the first day that Trevor found out about the bet. I kept telling myself that Trevor's anger would keep him from listening, that I needed to give him some time to calm down. And maybe that's true, but the bigger truth is that I'm a coward and haven't wanted to do it.

But here I go.

I watch him more closely now, waiting for the opportunity. I'm determined to see this through and not talk myself out of it.

I take a deep breath when I see Trevor standing alone for once, near a locker that's not ours but the one that he now shares with someone else. I shove away the thought of just who that someone might be, along with the feelings that accompany it, and walk toward him.

Another deep breath for courage.

"Hey, Trev . . . I mean, Trevor," I say nervously and pretend not to notice how he stiffens at the sound of my voice. He turns his shuttered gaze on me, and I nearly lose my courage. No time like the present, though, right?

"I know you don't want to talk to me, but I have something I want to say to you, if that's okay." I hate the wheedling tone coming out of me, but I'm helpless to stop it. He turns back to the locker, where he continues placing his books, neatly stacking them according to size. He might be dressing much cooler, but he's still Trevor to the core.

"All right," he murmurs so softly I almost don't hear him. He sounds resigned.

"I want to tell you I'm sorry for what I did." I take another breath and plunge on. "I *want* to say that, but it would be a lie. Because I'm not sorry."

He looks at me again at that, one brow raised curiously, lips tight with anger.

"I *am* sorry that I hurt you. I don't have the words to tell you how sorry I am about that." He turns away again, but his hands are still now, clenched at his sides, no longer stacking books. "I would do anything to take that part away. I would do anything to change the hurt I know I caused you. But I can't be sorry about making the bet with Ella and Beth because if I hadn't done that, I would never have gotten to know you."

Trevor lifts one hand into his locker, but instead of continuing with his book arranging, he leans it against the shelf, and I get the impression he's using it as support. His clenched jaw ticks, but I don't let his anger deter me. This might be my only chance to tell him what I need him to know.

"I know you have no reason to believe anything I say now, but I'm telling you the truth when I tell you that I wouldn't change one minute of the time I had with you. Well, maybe a few things, like taking you to those parties."

"Why *did* you do that?" His voice startles me, though his question is spoken quietly.

"Because I was trying to turn you bad, to make you be like me." He looks at me, surprised, then away again. "Stupid, I know. At the time it made sense to me. I had this fantasy that you would come with me, see how exciting and fun partying was, and turn into someone like me. But I'm glad it didn't work, that you stayed who you are."

He pushes off the shelf, closing his locker, and turns fully toward me for the first time. His gaze sweeps my mouth, and like a clichéd heroine from a romance novel, my pulse races and my breath stutters to a stop.

"You didn't get your lip pierced. Wasn't that the prize?" His voice is harsh and sarcastic. *Not* Trevor-like at all. I finger my lip self-consciously.

"I don't want that anymore."

"Why not?"

"Because I've changed. You had something to do with that. You had *a lot* to do with that. You made me want to be better, to be more like you. To be the kind of person you might *choose* to be with. But I guess I'll never be Mary Ellen."

"Mary Ellen?" He jerks in surprise at the mention of her name.

"It kills me to—" I stop short, clamping my lips together. I can't tell him what it does to me to see them together. It doesn't matter anymore. "What I mean is, I really do want you to be happy. With . . ." I swallow my jealousy. ". . . whoever."

Trevor crosses his arms, fists clenched, mouth pressed tight again. I think I've underestimated just how angry he still is with me.

"I just wanted to tell you that, you know, I'm sorry for hurting you but not for the rest. I know there's no hope for us to . . . well, you know. I just really hope that someday you might want to be my friend again. And I know it doesn't matter, and it will probably only make you more angry to hear this, but I still love you, and I guess I always will. For whatever that's worth."

Trevor nods tightly at my words, not relaxing his stance at all, and my heart crumbles beneath his uncompromising stare.

"Na-nu, na-nu," I say with a wry grimace, holding my hand up in a Mork salute. I turn away, determined to keep my head held high until I am out of his sight. Then I fall apart.

***

For the last three days I have been powerfully aware of Trevor, even more so than before. I made myself vulnerable to him—again—and was rejected. My center of peace has shifted just a little and my heart is bleeding again, but I'm dealing with it.

The thing I'm having a hard time dealing with is the looks I receive from Trevor, because he watches me more intensely than he has since Beth first blew my story. He alternates between staring at me angrily, fierce looks that would burn me where I stand if he had that power, and watching me curiously, as if I'm a puzzle he's trying to figure out. Those looks actually set me on edge more than the angry ones do.

I'm walking down the hallway, looking out for him and feeling jittery, not knowing what I might get from him, when the mouse materializes in front of me.

"Hey," she says softly. I jerk to a stop in surprise.

"Hey," I echo automatically.

"Can I talk to you for a sec?" She could have said King

Kong stood behind me, and I wouldn't be more startled than I am at her words.

Of course, there *are* plenty of kids at this school who sometimes act like primates, so maybe it wouldn't be that shocking.

"O . . . kay . . . ," I say slowly.

"I just want to say I'm sorry," she says sincerely.

Now I feel the need to sit down.

"You? Sorry? For *what?*"

"Because I haven't been very nice to you. I was really jealous of you and Trevor. I think that he liked me at one time. I mean, like a girlfriend, sort of."

I remember the first time I had honed in on Trevor, watched him posture for this girl at their lunch table, and I can't argue with her.

"Anyway, I liked him also," she continues, "but I was . . ." She trails off, embarrassed, then takes a breath and looks me in the eye, determined to give me the whole truth.

"I was playing hard to get." She stops, defiant, and I wonder if she's waiting for me to laugh at her. But how can I, queen of playing games that I am? When I only wait, she continues.

"I guess I shouldn't have done that. But then suddenly you were there, and I really didn't worry about you because I knew that he wouldn't fall for someone like you." She glances at me apologetically at her words. "But he did. And I was even more jealous because I thought you were just using him. And I was right." She glares at me defiantly again, waiting for me to deny her words.

"You're right—I was," I tell her. Now it's her turn to be surprised. "But only in the beginning. It didn't take long until I wasn't using him anymore. Until I genuinely started to like him and then to love . . ." I stop. I don't want to say this to *her* of all people.

"I know." She's nodding. "I could see that. And even though I didn't like you, didn't like the things you did, I knew you loved him. And I knew he loved you. But I was still jealous. And so I was mean to you. And I shouldn't have been. Even after . . . you guys broke up, I was still jealous because he still loves you."

My stomach flip-flops at her words, but however much I like hearing that, I know the truth now.

"Not anymore, he doesn't. And since we're apologizing, I need to tell you I'm sorry too. I haven't been exactly nice to you either. I've also been jealous of you because you have always been the one he should be with."

She smiles grimly at me, shaking her head.

"No, I'm not. Maybe at one time, but not anymore. Not that I haven't tried. But he's in love with you, and I'm not ever going to be able to change that. So now it's time for me to get over myself and to stop treating you so badly for something that I can't change."

"But he *doesn't* love me anymore, Mary Ellen. He's made that clear."

She smiles at me as if I'm dense.

"Then you haven't been paying attention. He's just mad. You haven't seen the way he looks at you."

With a shrug she walks away, leaving me standing there with my heart pounding, hope thrumming through my veins. Euphoria can be a good thing. Or devastating—you know, either way.

34

"You Spin Me Right 'Round, Baby, Right 'Round"

S O, JUST exactly how do you think I was voted Homecoming Queen?"

Jane gets an extremely innocent look on her face, which immediately makes me wary.

"I don't know," she says, shrugging.

"You don't find it odd that I go from freak girl to Homecoming Queen in a short period of time, especially considering the general feelings for me after what I did to Trevor?"

"No, not at all," she answers, voice full of a suspicious virtue.

I stare at her while she tries to maintain guiltless eye contact. Finally, she gives up, turning her hands up in supplication.

"I *may* have campaigned for you . . . but just a little, tiny bit." She emphasizes this by holding her thumb and first finger a hairbreadth apart.

"How much is a little, tiny bit?"

"Well, you know, I just told a few people about how bad you felt and that I thought it would really help you be happier. If they told other people the same thing, you can't blame me." She widens her eyes as she says this, and I don't know whether to laugh or cry. Instead of either, I just shake my head. I know without a doubt that she meant well. Jane is completely unaware of her charming powers, apparently.

Though the thought of someone campaigning for *me* to be Homecoming Queen six months ago would have been beyond laughable, I'm now grateful that someone loves me enough to care about doing such a thing on my behalf.

And, taking into account the kiss gifted to me as a result of her campaign, I decide I'm not all that angry or disappointed at all.

***

"Hey, Jen."

Simple words. Throwaway words. Words I hear a hundred times every day—okay, well maybe not quite a hundred, but *a lot* nonetheless. However, this time they freeze me in my tracks, where I might have stayed until the end of time if Mr. Hansen hadn't stepped out of his room and barked at me to get to my first class—which I'm now tardy for.

No, it isn't the words themselves. It is the *source* of the words. Because they come from Trevor as I pass him in the hallway. I didn't see him until the words were spoken because I had been digging through my backpack looking for my math book. By the time I unfreeze and turn to respond, I'm watching the back of his head disappear around the next bend in the hallway.

I make it to my math class, and I'm completely stressed. What does it mean, him saying "hey" like that, like we were . . . friends or something? Okay, maybe not friends—acquaintances.

In English, my mind is fogged in turmoil. Why now? It's

been over a week since I last talked to him, when I made my disaster of an apology. Has he decided to forgive me?

I'm off-balance and a little upset while I listen to my chemistry teacher ramble on about zinc and oxygen and other chemicals that I have a hard enough time figuring out when my mind is clear. I don't think he's forgiven me at all. *He's* messing *with me*, I think angrily.

By the time lunch rolls around, the anger is drained, and I'm just plain confused. I don't know what to think of the two little words he uttered to me this morning. Just about when I decide that I'm reading way too much into it and I need to chill and not worry about it, Brian turns my way.

"So, Jen, what do you think?"

Jane elbows me as Brian asks the question for what is apparently not the first time if the looks on the faces surrounding me are any indication.

"Uh . . . think of what?" I feel like I'm coming out of a trance. There are a few laughs from around the table.

"Saturday? My place? Movie marathon?" He repeats the highlights of the conversation I missed.

"Oh, well, um . . . who all is going to be there?" My eyes flick to Trevor, who listens to all of this. Brian knows exactly who I mean, and his eyes follow mine.

"Everyone," he says, shrugging.

"Oh." I don't know how to respond to this. I glance at Jane. "Well, Jane and I actually had plans on Saturday—"

"Only hanging out at my place," she interjects, and I can see by her smile at Brian that maybe there's a reason she's not backing me up. "So we go to Brian's and then we can sleep at my house as planned."

"Um, I don't know if that's such a good idea."

Brian, thankfully, understands my hesitation. He nods

in acceptance, though his shoulders droop in despondency. Next to me, Jane sighs—a little overdramatically, I think.

"Why not?"

For the second time in one day, two words are able to spin my world upside down. Once again, it isn't the words; it's who speaks them. My eyes dart to Trevor's face, but his expression is difficult for me to read. I have no answer for him. *He* should know better than anyone *why not*.

"You guys should come," he says, and then he *grins* at me. Not just any grin, but *my* grin, the one that brings out the killer dimples, the one given whenever he either wanted something or was genuinely happy about something having to do with me. The grin that knocks me to my knees. Good thing I'm already sitting down.

"We should?" I murmur inanely. He only smiles wider. Jane squeezes my arm beneath the table—I can take a hint, so I nod slightly.

"Cool!" Jane explodes next to me. "What time should we be there?"

Brian gives the details. I can only hope that Jane's listening because my mind is whirling. Trevor holds my gaze for a few seconds longer—a few seconds that feel like an eternity. Then he turns back to someone next to him, sending my mind spinning with all of this morning's confusion tripled.

So much for chilling out.

35

If Wishes Were Kisses

IT'S THE dreaded night of Brian's movie marathon—dreaded for me, anyway. Jane is overly excited about it, though she gamely tries to hide it because she can sense my mood, sense my desire to skip the whole thing. She even halfheartedly offers to skip out on it, to call Brian herself and tell him we can't come, but I hear in her voice how much she really wants to go.

"So . . . you and Brian, huh?" I tease her.

"Me and Brian what?" she asks innocently, then blows it by beaming a smile at me.

"Since when?" I ask.

"Well, not really at all—yet. But I've been picking up some very positive vibes from him for a while, since after the—" She stops dead, and I look at her questioningly. She isn't looking at me at all and is suddenly busy looking through her vanity drawer for just the right shade of red for her toes. Her face is flushed. Odd.

"After the what?" I ask slowly.

"Nothing, it doesn't matter," she mutters, still not looking at me. "What did I do with that Candy Apple Red polish?"

I walk over to her vanity and pick up the bottle, which

she had already pulled out five minutes earlier, and hand it to her. She stares at it blankly, then reluctantly meets my raised-eyebrow gaze. She sighs, pulling me down to sit on the bench next to her.

"All right," she surrenders dramatically. "Since the night of Homecoming, okay?"

I stare at her for a minute, then laugh. She frowns at me.

"Jane, I'm not so fragile that you can't say those words to me. It's not like I'm going to forget that night if we never speak of it."

"Really?" She eyes me skeptically.

"Really." I put my arm around her and squeeze her shoulder. "I know I was a mess that night, but I've been okay since then, haven't I?"

"Well, you *seem* okay, but we're just kind of waiting for the meltdown, I guess."

"*We?*"

Now she looks self-conscious.

"Brian and I."

"So you guys talk about me? Waiting for the next time I fall apart?"

"It's only because we care about you, and we're worried about you."

I watch her, seeing these very emotions flit through her eyes.

"Was I that bad?" I whisper.

She considers her answer, then decides to go with honesty.

"It was bad. I was really afraid for you."

I laugh again, mirthlessly.

"I talked to him the other day," I tell her. She's taken aback.

"You did?"

"I told him I was sorry for hurting him but not sorry about what I had done because I would have missed knowing him and loving him."

"What did he say?" she breathes.

"Nothing."

"Nothing?" She's angrily shocked.

"Yeah, but that's okay. I needed to say it. But now he's being . . . nice, I guess. Or maybe not nice, more like polite. I think maybe it's worse than when he was ignoring me."

"Maybe he's trying to, you know, let you know he wants you back."

"Hardly," I scoff. "He knows that as pathetic as I am, all he would have to do is say one word and I'd be back at his side in a flash. No, I think it's one of two things. Either he's just met the limit of the amount of rudeness he can dole out to one person no matter how much he hates them—because if Trevor is nothing else, he is the epitome of politeness and manners.

"The other theory—and the one I think is more likely—is that he's still so angry that he wants me to suffer more than ever, and the way to do that is to remind me of just what I have lost."

Jane pulls her eyebrows together.

"I don't think that's it. Trevor doesn't seem like he's that *mean.*"

I sigh. "Maybe you're right. I just don't know anymore. So it probably *is* the first theory, but the bad thing is, it's working on me in the second way."

Jane wraps her arm around me and grins wryly.

"You really are pathetic, aren't you?"

"I am," I agree. "So let's get this pathetic girl ready so I can go sit at Brian's house and be even more pathetic while I pine away and pretend I'm not."

***

I've been to Brian's house several times before, of course, but always with Trevor. This is my first time back since he started hating me. Brian's mom is one of those people who accepted me the first time I walked through her door—even though I looked scary—and has never treated me any different throughout my whole transformation.

Tonight is no different as she pulls me in for a hug, telling me how much she's missed me. When I introduce Jane, she winks at me with a grin, and I know Brian's been extolling Jane's many virtues to his mom.

When we walk in, almost everyone is already there since we had to wait for Jane's toes to dry before she could slip her sandals on. I think it's ridiculous, but then I see the look on Brian's face when he spies them and decide maybe she knows what she's doing. Not that she needs painted toes to capture his attention—his attention isn't anywhere else, which is highly unusual for Brian because he generally can't be distracted from the TV when there is a sci-fi movie running.

Of course, my eyes unerringly seek out Trevor first thing. This is a mistake because now my stomach is in knots. He stands at the fridge, handing out drinks. As if he can sense me there, he straightens and looks right at me. I freeze—but so does he. He only stares at me for a few seconds, then turns back to the fridge. I wince—guess the politeness is over.

But then he closes the fridge and walks right over to me, handing me a diet Coke. He doesn't say anything as I numbly take it from him, just offers me an unreadable look, turning away as soon as I have it in hand. Just like that, I'm off-center again.

I watch the movies blindly. My entire focus is on Trevor, who laughs and talks with his friends and who always seems to be near enough to me that I can't ignore him but far enough that it's clear we aren't together. He even talks to two of the other girls that Brian has invited, making my stomach roil.

He's definitely not ignoring me, though. Because I'm so focused on him, I see each time that his eyes flick my way. It's fairly frequently. If I was confused before by his behavior, it's nothing compared to how I feel now.

Finally, the eternal night ends, and people begin leaving to go home, except for us—Jane's trying to lengthen her time spent with Brian—and Trevor. Like there could be a more uncomfortable grouping.

"Hey, did you guys walk?" Brian asks Jane.

"Yeah," she tells him. Brian only lives a few blocks from Jane, and neither of us has a car, so how else would we get here? Fly?

"Want me to walk you home?" he offers gallantly. I would have said no, but Jane glows at the suggestion, so I just shrug.

"I'll come with you," Trevor suddenly offers, and my heart flip-flops. Why would he even want to?

"Okay, let's go then," Brian pipes in before I can say anything.

We walk through the house so Brian can let his mom know where he's going, then out the front door. The sidewalk is not wide enough for three across but not narrow enough for only one, which means that Brian and Jane go ahead, holding hands, leaving me and Trevor side by side. I figure it goes beyond Trevor's ability to be so rude as to walk in front of or behind me when it would be so obvious, which explains why he falls into step beside me. Our arms swinging by our sides accidentally brush—we both flinch. Trevor immediately shoves his hands into his pockets; I fold my arms across my belly.

Brian and Jane are in their own world, walking close, heads together as they talk quietly. Their intimacy makes for an uncomfortable silence between us.

"So . . . how's Tamara liking school?" Trevor finally asks. I guess he's as uncomfortable in the silence as I am. Odd question, though, since he's seen her recently.

"Good. She's doing all the typical Tamara stuff—sorority, clubs, that kind of stuff. She'd be a cheerleader if she had the time, I'm sure." I smile.

"Yeah, that sounds like her. Seems like you guys get along a lot better these days. I remember when you used to call her 'cheerleader' like it was a bad thing."

I'm stunned that he's bringing up anything from our time before. I take a breath to calm my heart.

"There were a lot of things I thought were bad back then." I shrug nonchalantly, though I'm feeling anything but. "Tamara's not so bad. I like having her for my sister."

"That's good," he replies. Silence descends between us again.

"I think you—"

"I wanted to say—"

We look at each other and smile uncomfortably at having both spoken at the same time.

"Go ahead," I say.

He clears his throat.

"I just wanted to say thanks—you know, for coming over to see Todd. It means a lot to him. He doesn't talk about anything else for two days after you've come."

I think about the precious time I've spent with Todd— and seeing the trampoline in the backyard, bleak and empty. Kinda like me.

"Oh." I don't quite know how to respond. "That's okay. I like Todd."

"He's easy to like. Still, you don't have to do that."

It occurs to me that maybe he's trying to tell me *not* to come to his house anymore.

"If you don't want me to . . ."

"No—no, that's not what I'm saying. It's . . . it's fine. It's a good thing. It's . . . Todd likes having you there."

I take a deep breath again. My heart aches for the days when it was easy between us, when I could reach out into that small space between us, take his hand, and have him glad of it. Not this strained awkward politeness. I look away and quickly wipe the tear that spills.

"It's, um, it's nice of you to come to the senior center too."

My stomach clenches at his words. I know he isn't happy about my continued appearance there.

"If that makes it bad for you, having me there, I could maybe come a different time or something."

He's quiet for so long that I begin to regret my words. While I would come a different day rather than not at all to see my friends there, it's also one of the few times I get to see Trevor still acting like the old Trevor.

"No, it's okay. We need all the help we can get."

Not exactly the enthusiastic response I might have hoped for, I think. But also not the harsh rejection it could have been—only a mild one. We arrive at Jane's house, and I'm both relieved and disappointed. From the sound of Trevor's sigh, he's only relieved. I try to ignore the cracking of my heart at the sound.

Trevor reaches out and grabs my elbow, and I stop cold. He releases me almost as soon as he touches me, pulling his hand back as if burned. He looks embarrassed but nods toward the porch where Brian and Jane stand close together.

"Uh, maybe we should give them a sec."

We stand in the taut silence. Trevor is standing close to me, and I can't help but think about the dance and the kiss—and all of the kisses that came before that. I'm torturing myself with these thoughts when I glance up at him and see him staring at me intently. He's remembering as well.

The air around us is charged. Trevor leans in a hairsbreadth. I match him.

"Trev," I breathe—like an *idiot* because that breaks the spell. He takes a step backward. "Trevor, I—"

"What was that?" he interrupts. "Before, what was it that you were going to say?"

I blink a couple of times, trying to clear my head, wondering how I almost had him kissing me again and now he's stepping away.

"Oh, um, I was just going to say . . . I think you're doing a really good job as the student body president."

He looks at me oddly.

"Really? That's what you were going to say?"

I shrug. "I didn't know what else to talk about."

Sensing dangerous territory again, he takes another step backward.

"Okay, well, thanks, I guess. Hey, Brian!" he calls. Brian turns toward us. "You ready?"

"Yeah," he calls back, reluctant. He gives Jane's hand a squeeze, then bounds down the stairs toward where we stand.

"Bye, Trevor," Jane says.

He waves at her, then turns and begins walking back down the sidewalk. I stare after him, hurting. Brian gives me an odd look as he hustles to catch up with Trevor.

"See ya, Jen."

"Bye, Brian," I say.

"Bye, Trev," I whisper.

36

Playbills and Pianos

THREE MISERABLE weeks later, I'm standing in front of my lonely, messy locker, trying to locate a paper that I know I put in here yesterday, or thought I did anyway—kinda hard to know for sure without any organization to speak of going on in here.

"There you are," I grumble as I catch sight of the paper. I pull it out from beneath the stack—which then goes tumbling to the floor. I growl as the rest of the papers hit the floor and scatter around my feet. I'm still scowling at them, as if that would cause them enough fear to quickly jump up, reassemble themselves, and fly back onto the shelf in my locker when I hear laughter behind me—laughter I know better than my own.

I slowly turn around and see Trevor standing a few lockers down, leaning against one of them casually, hands in his pockets.

"Think that's funny?" I mean it to come out sounding sarcastic, but it sounds pathetically whiney instead.

"Yeah, I do."

He grins as he straightens and walks toward me, the grin that brings out the dimples and nearly takes my knees out.

I'm *such* a marshmallow. He stops right in front of me, stooping to gather the papers into a quick, tidy pile. He hands them back to me, still smiling while I'm trying to play catch-up with this new development. Then he pulls a paper out of his nicely organized backpack and sets it on top of the stack in my hand. I give it a cursory glance, but none of the writing registers. I'm much more interested in looking at him.

"I'm playing at the Theater Group's show this Saturday."

At the what? He reads my silent confusion and taps the paper that he has given me. I look back down and see that it's a flyer, the same as all the others that are hanging around the school. I know about the Theater Group, of course, and am dimly aware that they have some kind of event coming up. Beyond that I haven't really paid attention.

"You're playing in the show?" I repeat inanely.

"Yeah." He smiles at me again, scattering logical thought.

"Oh, cool," I mumble.

At least, I think that's what I say.

"Will you come?"

"Come?" I echo. "Where?"

He rolls his eyes, grinning.

"To the show."

"To . . . the . . . ?" A flicker of intelligence lights in my brain, and I glance back down at the paper. "Come to the Theater Group's show?"

For the first time, he looks a little uncomfortable.

"To see me play," he says with a wry grin, shrugging.

"Oh. Yeah. Okay. Sure. I'd . . . I'd like that."

"You don't have to—"

"No!" My interruption is a little sharp. "I mean, no, I know I don't have to. I *want* to."

"Good. I'll see you there." His grin is back as he glances

past me into my wreck of a locker. "You should clean that out," he laughs as he walks away.

I watch him go, my mouth hanging open. I begin chiding myself for my lack of clever conversation while I had the chance, then suddenly it sinks in. Trevor just invited *me* to come see him play this weekend. A slow smile crosses my face as I turn to shove the papers back into my locker. It stays even when I realize that the paper I had been hunting for is now buried somewhere back in the stack.

***

Typically, I begin to doubt Trevor's intentions for inviting me. It has to be something bad, right? Some new way to torture me, make me suffer. So in the end, I don't tell anyone—not even Jane. My lame excuse for being unable to hang out with her on Saturday night as I usually do barely registers with her as she enthusiastically assures me that it's okay. Brian has asked her if she wants to do something with him that night.

I change my clothes six times until I finally decide downplaying is the way to go: plain, fitted gray T-shirt and jeans. I'm still insecure about his reasons for inviting me, so I don't want to make it seem like I'm expecting anything. That I happen to know he really likes the gray T-shirt on me doesn't mean anything.

I arrive just a few minutes late. I don't know where he's at in the program, so I don't want to miss it; I also don't want to run into anyone I know and try to explain my sudden interest in the school's Theater Group. I pay for my ticket and sneak into the darkened auditorium. It's only full about two-thirds of the way back, so I'm able to sit alone in the back, unnoticed.

The program they handed me as I walked in tells me that Trevor will be about halfway into the program. The program is mostly a mishmash of dancing, singing, and acted-out play scenes. It's actually pretty good, but because it's all a bunch of gooey romance, I feel like closing my eyes and plugging my ears. Romantic-type things don't sit too well with me these days.

Then Trevor walks out on stage, not in a geek tuxedo as I had expected, but dressed simply in a long-sleeved black Henley and jeans. He looks incredibly sexy. He sits at the piano, sideways to the audience. As if these things weren't enough to take my breath away, he begins playing. Recognition shoots like a lightning bolt into my belly.

My song. He's playing my song. A couple drifts out on stage and begin moving to the music. I don't know what to think, how to feel. What is it he's trying to tell me?

Trevor begins singing. I knew that he could sing, of course—he sings every time we're at the senior center. I've never heard him sing like *this.* I listen breathlessly, my heart thrumming with his music, his words of love and forgiveness flowing down my spine right to my toes.

The song trails off, and the couple on stage embrace as the spotlight fades. The audience bursts into applause and whistling, but I can't move. I watch Trevor stand, but instead of bowing, accepting his accolades, he's heading down the steps from the stage to the auditorium floor. Then he's striding up the aisle toward me as the next act begins on stage.

I panic just a little, wondering if I should stand so that he can see me, so that he knows I'm here, that I heard. Turns out to be unnecessary because he already knows where I am.

He stops right in front of me and reaches a hand out. Stunned, I place my hand in his, and he pulls me to my feet.

Even in the dimness, I can read the intensity in his eyes. He brings his hands up, cupping the sides of my face, wiping my tears away with his thumbs.

"Thank you," I whisper.

"I love you," he answers, and all the shattered pieces of my heart knit themselves back together.

"I'm so sorry, Trevor," I whisper urgently, knowing this might be the only chance I have to tell him. "I'm sorry I wasn't a better person, that I did everything wrong. But I'm happy—*so* happy that I got the chance to love you. I swear, though, I never meant to hurt—"

He stops my words effectively with a kiss. My toes curl, and the tears begin flowing again, which is funny since I can't stop smiling. When he pulls back, he's grinning at me, dimples out for me.

"I love you, Trevor."

"Call me Trev," he says, leaning down again.

"Trev," I sigh as he presses his mouth to mine again, letting me know just how complete his forgiveness is. *Geek*, I think fondly, glad that this particular one is mine.

37

WHOLE AGAIN

YOU HAVE *no* idea how good it feels to have your arms around me."

Trevor squeezes me from behind. I feel it to the center of my bones, even through all the thick layers of our coats, scarves, and gloves. Last night wasn't the first snowstorm of the season, but it was the first one that stuck. Trevor had to grab a broom and push all the snow off the tramp before we got on. We now sit, with him wrapped around me from behind, keeping me warm.

"You have no idea how good it feels to have you in my arms again," he murmurs in my ear, sending shivers down my spine that have nothing to do with the cold. I turn sideways so that I can see him.

"Trev, I wish I could tell you how sorry—"

His mouth on mine effectively shuts me up.

"No more apologies," he says. "We're both sorry for being idiots, but it doesn't matter anymore. We're here now, that's all that matters."

While it's not the easiest thing to do in the world—kissing while smiling—I'm finding these days that I'm getting better and better at it, because I can't seem to *stop* smiling, especially when he's kissing me.

"Wait a minute," I say, pushing back—but not too far back. "What do you mean we were *both* idiots? Exactly when were you an idiot?"

"From the second Beth told me. It shouldn't have mattered *why* you originally came to me—only that you did." I look at him doubtfully, and he continues. "I was miserable without you. Every second of every day I wanted to come to you, apologize for acting like a jerk, and ask you to forgive me."

"Forgive *you?*"

He ducks his head, kissing me on the nose.

"I guess I still haven't asked for that, have I?"

"You don't need to, Trev. There's nothing to forgive." He's already shaking his head.

"Do you know why I was so angry?"

"Because I did a really horrible thing that hurt you."

He looks ready to argue, then reconsiders.

"Okay, that's true—to a degree. It wasn't the worst thing you could have done. I always knew there was *some* reason for you to decide you liked me out of the blue like that. After a while, it didn't matter anymore. Most of all, it hurt my pride when she told me, but I didn't want to admit that to myself." He grins deprecatingly. "I didn't know I had it in me to be so prideful."

I roll my eyes. That's such a geek reaction to pride.

"And I wondered if it had all been a lie. That hurt my pride too, that you could have fooled me for so long and so thoroughly. It took me a while to realize that I didn't really care if it had been a lie because I wouldn't have traded any of my time with you. Plus, I could see that you were genuinely unhappy when we were apart. That about killed me, seeing that."

He swallows over a lump in his throat, his eyes coming to mine, filled with remembered misery. "By the time the dance rolled around, I knew I couldn't be without you much longer. Every time I tried to come to you, my stupid pride got in the way. After that kiss . . ." He trails off and leans down, kissing me again as if talking about it reminds him that it has been longer than five minutes since he last did so. That's one of the best things about being back with him—he's making up for lost time, and I'm reaping all the benefits.

"I was going to come to you then, especially after Brian told me how messed up you were that night."

"Brian told you?" I ask angrily. He grins at me, and my anger drains away.

"Don't be mad at him. He was worried about you. And he was pretty upset with me for causing you to be that way." He winces at the memory of Brian's description. Wow, I must have been worse than I thought.

"So why didn't you come to me then?"

His cheeks flush, and he looks away, ashamed.

"Because when you came to school on Monday you didn't look upset or messed up at all." His eyes come back to mine, shadows in his. "You actually looked calm and happier than I had seen you look in a long time." He shrugs and gives me a quick kiss. "That dang pride came flooding back. I wasn't happy that the kiss had obviously affected me worse than it had affected you."

"Are you kidding?" I ask, stunned. "It flipped my world upside down. But it also gave me something that I hadn't had since all of this started."

"What's that?" He frowns in confusion.

"Hope."

He thinks about this for a few seconds, then his face clears.

"Ahhh, so *that's* what it was. Then I'm an even bigger idiot than I thought."

I punch him lightly in the shoulder.

"Quit talking about my boyfriend like that." He grins at my words, pressing his mouth to mine again.

"Is that what I am?" he teases. "Your boyfriend?"

"Actually, that word seems a little lame when talking about you. You're so much more than that to me."

My reward is another kiss, one that has me curling my toes.

"So, what was with your suddenly being nice to me, then?" I ask curiously.

He shrugs again, looking embarrassed now.

"What?" I press, more intrigued than ever.

"Keep in mind the whole pride thing . . ." he begins, smiling. "I was trying to play your game."

"My game?" Now I'm just confused.

"Trying to, um . . . trying to get you to *want* me, I guess."

I laugh. "Trev, all you had to do was breathe to make me want you."

"No, not like that. I mean, I was trying to make *you* come to *me*. Like you did with me in the beginning." He hugs me tighter. "I'm just nowhere near as good at it as you are."

"It was working, though." Now it's his turn to look perplexed. "The first day you said 'hi' to me, I was completely off-balance for the rest of the day. *Especially* when you told me and Jane to come to Brian's party." I laugh again. "I guess now I understand how . . . *bewildered* you were when I first started coming on to you."

"Hey, kids," Carol calls, stepping out of the house. I'm pressed pretty closely against Trevor, so I shift to move to a

Carol-respectable distance. Trevor's arms are like bands of steel, however. He keeps me held tightly against him.

"I brought you some hot chocolate," she says, waiting while I pull off my gloves to take it—Trevor pulling only one of his off—before handing them to us. This requires Trevor to release me with one arm, but he keeps the other firmly bound around me. Carol smiles at me, and in her smile is an apology.

"It's nice to see you back here, Jen. It's good to see Trevor smiling again."

I stare at her, unable to respond. She turns to trudge back into the house. I gape at Trevor.

"She knows she treated you badly," he tells me. "It was the whole mother bear thing."

"Well, I guess honestly she's handled everything pretty well. From me showing up here on her doorstep for the first time looking like I did, to hurting you like I did. I don't know if I would have been any different than she has been. I would probably be worse." I take a drink of the chocolate, warmth flowing through my belly.

"So, you weren't smiling much, huh?" I tease. He sighs.

"No, I was pretty miserable to live with."

"I'm sor—" His mouth cuts my words off yet again. I smile at him.

"If you keep doing that, I'm going to keep apologizing all day long."

"You don't have to apologize to get me to kiss you." He laughs, then throws my words back at me. "You just have to breathe."

I turn to face him fully, tugging on the hideously lop-sided scarf that I crocheted with Mrs. Green. He'd refused to let me throw it away, but I did make him promise that he would never wear it in public.

"So, I'm sorry about everything. You're sorry about everything. No more apologies. Can I just tell you the one good thing that came out of this?"

"You realized that Seth would never be right for you?" he teases, but there's an edge to his voice.

"You know about that?" I ask, awestruck.

"Okay, since we're doing the whole tell-all, this is one last confession." He takes a breath. "I followed you on your date with him."

I lean slightly away from him, mouth hanging open.

"I heard you were going to go out with him, and I *burned* with jealousy. No, burning isn't the right word. I was more like an *inferno*. So I followed you. I sat in the movie theater in the back and watched you. I really couldn't follow you into the restaurant and be inconspicuous, so I went to your house and hid, waiting for you to come home. When you were walking up to your door, I wanted to come out, sweep you up, and give you a kiss that would make it clear to Seth that he couldn't have you."

His words sink in, and I can't help it. I start laughing.

"You're as pathetic as I am," I gasp out.

"Worse," he qualifies. "I'm a pathetic geek."

I snuggle back into him. "Yeah, well, so am I."

He holds me tightly against him until I finish chuckling.

"So what did you learn? Besides the fact that you have a penchant for pathetic geeks?"

I sit up again, wanting to look at him while I tell him.

"Well, besides *that*, I learned that I'm a lot tougher than I thought. In my life, I've always been taught that I shouldn't expect happiness because it's not for me." He opens his mouth to argue, but I press my icy fingers to his lips. "So when I finally found happiness, it didn't really surprise me to have it taken away. I mean, everything was going so well for me, I knew it couldn't last.

"But what I learned was that I could be *devastated* and survive. That just because one good thing goes away, it doesn't necessarily mean *all* the good things have to go away, even if the one good thing that did is the best thing. Does this make any sense?"

He captures my hand, pressing it more firmly against his lips. He nods in response.

"So ten years from now, when we're married and maybe have a family or whatever, if something bad happens, I'll know I can handle it. That it won't kill me, because if I can survive losing you, even for a little while, I can survive anything. I'm stronger than I thought. The legacy I thought my parents left me is null and void."

Suddenly he's smiling at me again, cradling my face in his own icy fingers.

"What?" I ask, taken aback by his joyous smile.

"Just happy that you're still planning to be around me ten years from now."

"Yeah, you're not getting rid of me so easy next time."

"Next time?"

I run my finger across my eyebrow.

"I was thinking I could use a piercing here . . ."

He laughs, tackling me down on the trampoline.

"Then I'll get you one. I'll pierce your entire face—no, your entire body if you want. Just don't torture me anymore."

I roll him over onto his back and straddle his belly, pinning his arms above him—something I wouldn't be able to do if he really tried to stop me.

"I don't want any piercings, my Lincoln Six Echo. I only want you."

Trevor flips me over so that I'm lying beside him.

"I only wish we were Highlanders so we could live together forever."

"But then I'd have to spend my life worrying about someone beheading you. I'd rather just live a boring, peaceful life."

"Are you calling me boring?" he teases, leaning over to kiss me and show me just how *un*-boring he is.

And so my life of being a geek girl who loves her geek boy begins.

ACKNOWLEDGMENTS

TO LINDSAY and Lexcie, for your unfailing support and enthusiasm, and without whom I would not be where I am today. To Kelly, who could give a lesson or two on how to make a girl feel loved.

To Jeffery Moore and Camelia Miron Skiba, friends, cohorts, and authors extraordinaire in their own rights, without both of whom *Geek Girl* would never have been anywhere near what it is. I count on your discerning eyes more than you can know. You are invaluable to me.

To all the wonderful people of Cedar Fort: Angie Workman, who first took a chance on me; Laura Jorgensen, who has been willing to support my ideas, no matter how strange they must sometimes seem, and who always answers my rambling, repetitive emails; Melissa Caldwell, who took the rough stone that was *Geek Girl* and polished it, making it so much better. And of course to everyone else at Cedar Fort who have and who will help me along this wondrous journey.

Last, but by no means least, to all of my amazing readers. Writing would be nothing but a fun pastime to me without every one of you. You have no idea how much I appreciate your emails, Tweets, FB messages . . . and every other form of communication you find to let me know you liked my words. You are golden, one and all!

DISCUSSION QUESTIONS

1. *Geek Girl* begins with Jen making the bet with her friends. What do you think her motivations were for the bet? Do you think she had specific motivations in choosing Trevor over another of his friends?

2. Beth, Ella, and Seth, Jen's Goth friends, were all minor characters, and yet they were pivotal to the story. Why do you think it was important to include them to understand Jen's story better? Do you think the story could have been told just as well without them? Do you think Jane was important to the story? What about Todd and Tamara?

3. Jen's personal morality seems in contrast to the way she lives her life. Why do you think she is this way?

4. Do you think Jen was right in her decision to go visit her mother in prison after all those years? Do you think it helped her resolve some issues and feelings from her past?

5. Do you think Trevor overreacted when he found out about the bet? What do you think his reasons were for being so angry at Jen for it?

6. What was your initial reaction at Trevor's forgiveness of Jen? Did it feel realistic? Do you think he should have forgiven her sooner? Why do you think he waited so long to tell her that he had forgiven her?

About the Author

CINDY C Bennett was born and raised in beautiful Salt Lake City, growing up in the shadows of the majestic Rocky Mountains. She and her husband raised two daughters, two sons, and a plethora of pets.

In addition to writing YA fiction, she volunteers her time working with teen girls between the ages of twelve and eighteen, all of whom she finds to be beautiful, fascinating people who constantly inspire her stories. She developed a love of writing in high school English when a teacher introduced her to the joys of escaping reality for ten minutes each day in writing.

When she's not writing, reading, or answering emails (notice there is no mention of cleaning, cooking, or anything vaguely domestic), she can often times be found riding her Harley through the beautiful canyons near her home. (Yes, she rides a Harley.) Learn more at www.cindycbennett.com or www.cindybennett.blogspot.com.